DEAL
WITH THE
DEVIL

ASTORIA ROYALS
BOOK 4

GARLAND
AWARD WINNING AUTHOR

Edits by:
Julie K. Cohen
Suzanne McKenna Link

Model Cover Designed by Bookin' It Designs
Photographer: Wander Aguiar/ Model: Clever
Discreet Cover Designed by The Author Buddy

Published by Deborah A. Garland
www.deborahgarlandauthor.com

ASTORIA ROYALS

War is on the horizon.

Power is the name of the game so the O'Rourkes shore up alliances by marriage, even if it means walking down the aisle with an enemy.

In this gripping and deliciously sexy new Arranged Marriage Mafia Romance series, the O'Rourke Family takes no prisoners to protect the women they've strategically married, even if love wasn't part of the plan.

With the stakes as high as ever, the charismatic, breathtaking, and sometimes ruthless O'Rourke brothers intend to not just survive this war the Russians are threatening, but to win it.

At all costs.

Read the entire Astoria Royals Irish Mafia Series. All arranged marriage romances can be read as a standalone, but are best when devoured in order:

Sinful Vows

Savage King

Sleeping with the Enemy

Deal with the Devil

Ring of Truth

Reckless Obsession

Shattered Veil

ALL BOOKS BY DEBORAH GARLAND

Houston After Dark (Romantic Suspense Series)

Off Limits Lover ~ Rough Lover ~ Hard Lover

~ Untamed Lover

Wild Texas Hearts (Cowboy Series)

The Cowboy's Forbidden Crush ~ The Cowboy's Last Song
The Cowboy's Accidental Wife ~ The Cowboy's Rebel Heart
The Cowboy's Christmas Bride ~

The Cowboy's Wedding Planner

The Billionaire Harts (Billionaire Standalones)

The Good Billionaire ~ Daring the Billionaire ~ Bossy
Billionaire ~ Rebel Billionaire

Undeniably Yours (Billionaire Standalones)

Accidental ~ Unexpected ~ Convenient

Forever Mine- (Millionaire/Small Town)

Wait for Me ~ All for Me ~ Live for Me ~
His Christmas Surprise

FROM THE AUTHOR:

The setting of Astoria, New York, is a real sprawling waterfront incorporated village in Queens County. It is named for John Jacob Astor, the richest man in America at the time, who was considered royalty.

The Astoria Royals romances are based on fictional characters, and, in some cases, locations are made up for storytelling enjoyment and drama.

About this story...

This romance contains subject matter that may be sensitive for some readers, including explicit sexual situations, graphic violence, and sensitive subject matters such as church sex scandals, school shootings, terminal illnesses, the loss of a parent, and a brief mention of child trafficking. If these themes bother you, please skip this one, or read with caution.

An important message:

It has come to my attention that a secondary character in the Astoria Royals series has the same exact name (and spelling) as a character referenced in another mafia series by another author. Alexei Koslov, my bratva pakhan's name was created by me (using Google search for Russian names) without knowing the same name and position of said character was already used by another author. My use of the name was not intentionally copied and there is no implied overlap with the other author's copyrighted material. The use of the same name is purely coincidental.

TWO YEARS AND THREE MONTHS EARLIER

CHAPTER ONE

LACHLAN

"You cannot go in there!" A low-level Russian *bratok* jumps in front of me and pushes on my chest. His eyes widen, figuring out I'm a wall of pure muscle, tattoos, and a boatload of scars.

Stepping onto Alexei Koslov's estate, I give this piece of shite the benefit of home court respect for exactly two seconds. "Touch me again, and you'll end up in Astoria Harbor tied to a block of cement."

"Dima, stand down." Sergei, the one Bratva security boss who maintains a modicum of my respect, strolls down the grassy knoll.

"He just walk right past mine," Dima whines in his broken English.

"Go back to the booth and keep the damn gate closed," Sergei snaps.

"I'd just climb the gate if it was closed," I sneer for effect.

With Dima gone, Sergei shoves his veiny tattooed hands, just like mine, into his trouser pockets. The move stretches open his suit jacket, exposing the heat on his waist. That impressive 19mm Parabellum military import is most likely untraceable. "What do you want, Lachlan?"

"Maksim. Get him, or I keep walking, and you'll have

1

to shoot me." Which I know he won't.

There's a code among the Irish Mob, the Bratva, and the Italian Mafia. You can't kill high-level bosses without a meeting. And since no leader would ever give permission for one of their senior commanders to be murdered, as my brother's enforcer, I'm pretty much untouchable.

And I'm rumored to be insane. I love testing these motherfuckers, forcing them to guess how far I'll go. My wrecked cheek from a knife attack not only adds to my menacing appearance, it jacks up the fear in lesser men.

Sergei rubs his forehead. And with exhaustion in his deep voice, he mutters in his thick Russian accent, "What did Maksim do now?"

I don't envy anyone who serves under the Russin Enforcer. He owns more real estate in crazy town than me. I have discipline. Maksim doesn't.

"I just came from the hospital. Liam Reilly is in intensive care with a drug overdose."

"And that has to do with Maksim, how?" Sergei shakes his head, unimpressed with the mention of Jack Reilly's son, and that disappoints me.

These Bratva brothers aren't doing their homework like they used to. Jack Reilly is one of our most staunchest and *ruthless* allies.

"It was laced with that shite Maksim is having cooked up somewhere. I saw the tox report. It's the same formula the ME noted in an autopsy for that dead couple fished out of the East River a month ago. It's fucking deadly."

"How did you see an ME report?" Sergei dips a bushy eyebrow at me. "And how did you get that kid's tox records?"

I tilt my head, feeling sorry for the bastard. "Do you really need to ask me that?"

"Balor?"

"Aye. His hacking skills are getting better every day. Not worse."

"That is a crime."

I grab Sergei by the shirt collar. "I like you. I respect you. Get Maksim here, or I'll act like I don't."

"I get you. But not here, not now." He shoves me off and glances over his shoulder at the crowd milling around on the pakhan's compound—a palatial estate with tall white columns and manicured gardens. "It's Anastasia's birthday. Koslov will kill anyone who disturbs her party."

In the distance, tables with flickering candles and centerpieces made up of mini bonsai trees and white lights sit under a party tent. Golden numbered balloons tied to the entrance billow in the wind.

The Bratva princess is twenty-one. Ripe for a marriage deal.

"Get your pound of flesh from Maksim tomorrow." Sergei gives me a once-over. "Did you come here alone?"

I bark a laugh. "That's how good my men are. You're surrounded, and you don't even know it."

Sergei exhales. "Do it for Stasia, okay? It is her birthday. The girl did not do anything."

Alexei's daughter is a wildcat, but she deserves a special night without bloodshed.

"I'll leave, but remember this one, Sergei." I hold out my hand to him.

Reluctantly, he shakes it. "I doubt you will let me forget."

My oldest brother, Kieran, Gabe Parisi Jr., and Alexei Koslov work *around* each other, not against. A provincial city outside Manhattan, Astoria is rich in opportunity. But it's small and can't survive a war between two powerful crime houses. Three would level the place.

My da, who retired and passed the crown to Kieran, worked his arse off to carve out a lucrative business model for us. I can't fuck it all up in one night.

I turn to leave when the moonlight shines down on a gazebo in the distance. The silhouette of a lithe female glows against the reflection on the harbor.

Sergei's radio crackles, and since I'm halfway between the guards' booth by the gate and the main house with a party in full swing, when Sergei leaves, I'm out of visual range from both ends.

Something pulls me toward the woman. I say *something* because I was programmed not to be distracted. I spent a year in Dunbar Valley, a camp where my da sent me to be 'trained' after I nearly upended his hold on power.

Trouble clings to me no matter what I do.

My size sixteen shoes crunch the grass blades, stiff from the falling temperature. I brace against the brisk March wind as I stroll toward the gazebo. I'm transfixed on the sight of this female and want to take her in without being noticed.

Women's bodies get me off. They mean nothing to me. I mean nothing to them, except a thrill for those who actually know who they lured into their bed. It's always *their bed* because no one knows where I live.

I'm the O'Rourke Enforcer for the Irish Mob. The elusive square on a bingo card that will make someone famous if they take me out. Only, it would have to be anonymous, or they'd be gunned down in the street within an hour. My men are that loyal. That's how *I* trained them.

All the crime families—the Irish, the Italians, and the Russians—have businesses to protect. No one wants a war.

These thoughts sit in the back of my head as I approach the woman.

Wearing an opaque dress that shows off a thin frame, she stops in the center of the gazebo and lifts her arms. She bends one of her legs and spins elegantly.

She's dancing. In the cold.

My throat tightens.

Katya...

Alexei's daughter. His *illegitimate* daughter. The ballet dancer.

She's a star at East Side Performing Arts in Manhattan. Balor keeps meticulous tabs on everyone in power *and* their family. He tracks the strengths and weaknesses of each house.

With both feet on the gazebo's icy wooden floor, one arm raises, and the other lowers into a seductive side bend like her spine is made of rubber. Fucking impressive.

Katya straightens, and the line of her slender figure takes my breath away. A closer look reveals hard nipples from the cold, tender buds I want to taste and bite. A spark flickers in my chest, startling me. Not the way my heart rate shoots up when I end a man's life. This kind of adrenaline surges differently through my veins, leaving a sweet taste on my tongue.

When you know, you know.

That ridiculous love proverb whispers through my brain, and I squash it. Love isn't in the cards for me. I have no use for women other than to satisfy my body. I won't gift my family with any offspring because my father took from me the *only* thing I ever wanted.

I should have been my family's ticket to heaven. Now, I'm going straight to hell.

My gut twisting in confusion, I step back. But I keep my eyes on Katya Koslov gently spinning until she stops and hugs one of the carved posts.

The light shines on her face, and I track her gaze to the

guests in her father's garden, all whooping it up for her sister. Her half-sister, Stasia, basks in Alexei's limelight.

It hits me how Katya is always in the shadows, like now. Like me.

I wonder if she knows how lucky she is not to be on her father's pedestal. Anastasia is Alexei's weapon, and he'll use her mercilessly to make a lucrative deal. That's how our world works.

I turn away when a sweet voice sails over my shoulder. "Don't go."

As if I'm zapped with 200 volts of electricity, my feet can't move. I take a breath, and it doesn't burn. What is this? I turn around, and Katya stares at me.

"Did you mean me, little one?" I ask.

"Who else would I mean?" She frowns. "Were you watching me?"

"Aye." I never lie. Don't have to.

"Why?"

A cool calmness spreads through me, and the rage sitting on the surface of my skin slowly fades. Underneath is the blessed peace I stopped feeling at eighteen. The kind of serenity I got serving the church. That joy was stolen, replaced with darkness.

"Because I do whatever I want. I saw you and wanted to keep looking." My feet move toward her before I tell them to. "You dance beautifully."

"Thank you. It's the one thing I have that's all mine."

Mine…

Adrenaline powers through me with the urge to claim this delicate whisper of grace.

Getting closer, I see she's more lovely than I remembered. Perhaps my eyesight is failing me, or I didn't want to admit that such delicate beauty exists in the ugly world of her father's ruthless brotherhood.

"Why are you here?" she asks me.

I doubt she's interested in the gritty details behind my pursuit of vengeance for a family ally, but her fearlessness in asking intrigues me. "Business, little one."

A smile lifts the corner of her upper lip. "That doesn't interest me."

Fuck, she's sassy on top of being bloody adorable. Why do I sense she doesn't show it to anyone? A chaos of crazy ideas sizzle in my head, one telling me to grab her, steal her, and bring her home.

No... A missing Russian princess will tear Astoria apart. I escaped one scandal. I can't ignite another one.

"It's cold out here. You should get inside." I harden myself to turn away from her lovely face. "And forget you ever saw me, little one."

CHAPTER TWO

KATYA

Shouting and a door slamming across the hall breaks my concentration, and I tumble forward from a holding position. After rustling and banging keep me puzzled, I tiptoe out of my bedroom and cross the hall. Through a narrow sliver, I peek in on my sister to make sure she's all right, but there's a flurry of chaotic movement.

"What are you doing?" I ask, my brain not processing what's happening.

"I'm leaving," Stasia cries out, shoving clothes into a suitcase. "I hate him."

"Who? Who do you hate?" I stand in the doorway.

She turns her back to me and her shoulders come up around her ears, like she's choosing her words carefully. "Papa."

"What did he do?" My gaze drifts to the yard where my father's henchmen are finally breaking down her lavish 21st birthday party tent from a week ago. A lingering reminder of the grand event.

If she's mad about the royal treatment she gets, I should leave first. Papa has never, nor will he ever, worship me like Stasia.

I slip into her bedroom, a palace compared to mine. But she's been living here longer than me. I was brought here seven years ago, when I was twelve. My bedroom is nice enough. Papa let me have whatever I wanted for it, but it was Yulia, the live-in housekeeper, who did all the work.

Stasia turns around with mascara running down her face and answers me. "He's making me get married."

I should look surprised, but I've learned a lot about this world in seven years. Our father leads the Bratva here in Astoria. Stasia is his only legitimate daughter. Of course, he'd arrange her marriage. The only true surprise is that she's not already wedded to one of Papa's allies with a few kids.

I gulp down a ball of fear in my throat. In two years, Papa might arrange my marriage. I snort to myself, dismissing that. He's been telling lies about me since the day I got here. That my mother was his whore.

Nothing was further from the truth. *Maman* was his girlfriend on the side, not his whore.

It surprised me to find out Yulia knew all about *Maman* and me. At night, when I got older, after tucking me in, she whispered more gossip. How Papa was forced to marry his father's business partner's daughter when they were eighteen. He never loved her from what I heard, and his wife didn't love him either. But she gave him two sons, my half-brothers, and my sister, Anastasia. I never met Alexovich and Sasha. They tragically died in an ambush many years ago.

Yulia said Stasia's mama was never the same after her sons were murdered. She died in her sleep shortly after. It was rumored she took pills and killed herself. That left Stasia with no brothers and no mother. *Maman* brought me here because Madam Koslov was dead. I wasn't sure that day if she planned to stay with me or leave me here, but I never saw my mother again after that day.

When month after month went by and no letter came explaining why she left me, I lied to myself that she was busy. Or maybe she was scared, given how Papa ran her off the property.

I wised up to who my father was and assumed he had her killed. I could never ask, so I had to keep the worry all to myself. I only cried to Yulia, who felt like my mother after a while. She would whisper comfortingly to me, stressing that I am Papa's blood, and he will never hurt me.

Maman was not his blood.

Still, to everyone in Papa's brotherhood, I am illegitimate. Which I am. Technically. When I finish college, I hope to get a job dancing for a traveling ballet company. I'll be out of Papa's life, and he can forget about me.

But Stasia, the only one in this family that I have grown to care for, is packing to leave.

No. No. No.

I close her bedroom door. "Who does he want you to marry?"

"A monster," Stasia says with dread in her voice. She mumbles something else in Russian, she's so upset. She speaks Papa's precious mother tongue, but doesn't have an accent.

I immediately think of Lachlan O'Rourke and his thick Irish brogue. The memory of him from last week fills my head, and I shiver. The Irish Enforcer has quite the ruthless reputation in Astoria. Dark hair, dark eyes, ridiculously tall, and hulking, he's a predator in the shadows, stalking prey. Even with all that brooding and anger simmering off him, the man is utterly breathtaking. And I oddly find the scar across his left cheek sexy.

A monster…

The idea of Stasia marrying Lachlan sends a fit of furious rage through me. Anger I've never felt before.

"In English, Stasia. I'm trying to help you." I don't speak with my French accent anymore. Papa yelled at me when I slipped. At night, I dream of *Maman* talking to me in French.

"Luka Gideon, the pakhan in Boston." My sister sniffs.

11

"Papa wants to form an alliance in exchange for more *bratoks* so he can crush the Irish and the Italians."

"Oh..." I say, but don't like the idea of anyone crushing the O'Rourkes for some reason.

"Oh?" Stasia puts her hands on her hips. "The man is twice my age!"

"Forty-two isn't that old." I wonder how old Lachlan is. Thirties at least.

"The blood under his fingernails is older than me."

"Papa kills people, too."

"Yeah, so?" She wipes her rosy, tear-stained cheeks. "He'll never murder me."

"I doubt your husband would murder you."

"No. But he can hurt me if I don't...give myself to him." Stasia sits on the edge of her bed and sniffs. "How can Papa do this to me?"

An idea tickles my brain. "Perhaps you can ask someone for help instead of leaving."

She scoffs. "Like who?"

"The Irish. Their enforcer, Lachlan, seemed—"

Stasia's jaw drops. "You stay away from him, Katya. He killed *a priest.*"

"What?" I go breathless, his handsome face flashing in front of my eyes. There must be some mistake. "If he killed a priest, why isn't he in jail?"

Stasia lifts red, swollen eyes. "Did you just get here yesterday? No one in the brotherhood, the mafia, or the Irish *mob* goes to jail around here."

"Maybe he had a good reason to kill the priest." Although, I hear the Irish are very religious.

"Anyone who would risk the damnation of his soul won't sympathize with a Bratva princess."

"I guess you're right," I say softly, thinking she has a point.

Stasia shakes her head and zips up her suitcase. "I'd

marry *Lachlan O'Rourke*, before that Boston monster Papa is selling me to. I'm out of here."

Hearing how she'd rather marry Lachlan sends waves of irrational jealousy through me.

"Where are you going?" I slowly grow alarmed.

Stasia brings me to her bed. Fingering my long, blonde braid, she says, "I can't tell you, but believe me, it's safer if you don't know. I don't want that information in your head. Papa's people have a way of knowing if someone is lying and getting information out of them. Especially women." She kisses my forehead, and I throw my arms around her. The reality washes over me. I will be alone in this house with Papa.

At least I have Yulia.

"How can you leave? Do you have money?" I ask, wondering which guard she sweet-talked.

Stasia studies me. "I have some money. Enough. Papa doesn't hide his extra cash very well. There's so much of it, he doesn't even realize it's gone. I have enough to live on for a while. I'll figure out how to get more when I'm settled somewhere."

"Take me with you, please?" I grab her wrist. I can't imagine waking up in this house without her.

"Katya, I can't take you with me. Yulia will look after you." She pries my fingers from her hand and stands up. "You just made the Dean's List at East Side Performing Arts, for crying out loud. Papa didn't let me go to college. I'm so proud of you. Keep dancing, *mladshaya sestra*."

After being here for seven years, I know that means *little sister*. I never learned to speak Russian, and Papa forbids me to speak French. He didn't blink when I asked to attend college. It's why I figured he'd let me have a life outside the brotherhood and not Stasia, because he had no plans to arrange my future, just hers.

"I will keep dancing." I hug her. "Will you write me?"

"I can't." She shakes her head. "Papa checks the mail."

I remember my welcome packet from East Side, then lift off the bed. "Wait here." Running as fast I can, I even leap into a full *èlancer*, stretching my spread legs to dive across the hall and land in my room. Something I've done for years as a game, pretending that ugly carpet was filled with scorpions.

At my desk, I rifle through the paperwork I got at orientation. Thumbing through the papers, I find the details just for me. I scribble the one I need on a piece of paper and dive back into Stasia's room, startled to see she's got one leg out the window.

"Are you crazy?" I tug her back inside. "You're leaving in the middle of the day?"

"Papa is across town at a meeting, and the guards are watching the main road for an ambush." Her words send my spine tingling. "It's supposed to snow tonight, and I can't take a chance on being stuck in a blizzard. I'll be fine."

"Wait. Don't bring your suitcase. Papa will think you left on your own. In fact..." I look around. "We have to make it look like someone took you."

Stasia goes still. "You want him to think someone kidnapped me?"

I shrug. "This way, if he finds you, he won't punish you."

She grabs me in a massive hug. "Oh my God, that's brilliant." My sister opens her suitcase, and puts her clothes away while I trash her palace of a room, releasing years of jealously.

"Here, take this. Students have mailboxes on campus. This is mine. You can write to me there. Papa doesn't know about it. No one does." I have a driver who brings me back and forth to school. I don't consider him a guard. No one cares about hurting me. My father told everyone he only took me in because I'm his blood. Stasia is his jewel. I'm the daughter of his whore. "Send me your address, and I'll try to mail you some of your clothes."

How, I have no idea. But I'll figure out a way.

Stasia takes the paper with my school address without looking at it and shoves it inside the pocket of her thick, white cashmere coat. "Okay."

"Please write me and tell me where you are when you get there."

"I'll try." She kisses me on the forehead again, and her eyes trail over my shoulder.

"I turned off the camera in my room." She checks her watch. "Get out of here and do something in your bedroom to make it seem like you've been there the whole time. Do your stretching with that classical music you love." She winks at me. "I'll miss you, *mladshaya sestra*."

"I'll miss you, too." It hurts my heart already.

In a flash, she's out the window, and with no guards manning the gate, she slips away.

I watch the first snowflake fall. And from Stasia's open window, I stick out my tongue to taste it, closing my eyes to remember my sister.

Please, please don't let that be the last time I see her.

*

"*Who took my diamond?*" Papa screams at the staff later that night when Stasia doesn't come down for dinner.

As his guards furiously search the estate, guilt strikes me. I didn't realize suggesting she fake her kidnapping would make Papa turn against everyone in the house.

Yulia yells at him in Russian while holding me against her chest. Angry words I don't understand and lots of spittle fly between them. She lifts her spine and waves her arms, presumably to say *I've* been dancing all day.

Papa drags her away, and a door to the basement slams shut while she screams.

Shaking, I lower myself to the floor with my head down. When I hear a gunshot, I know Papa killed her. She was home when Stasia left, and it's her responsibility to keep an eye on us, even though we're technically adults.

Papa comes back from the basement and marches to the security booth near the gate by the street. He drags each guard on duty that afternoon from the booth. One-by-one, they're thrown down by Maksim and shot, execution style. I flinch and turn away, covering my ears, so I don't hear the shots, but still, I feel the pulse of each round of gunfire. How unfair! They were following orders to wait at the base of the driveway to make sure Papa doesn't get ambushed.

What have I done? My father has gone mad!

Am I next?

Dressed in a soft wool sweater dress and suede boots, I look up from a corner in the dining room. My father stands over me, covered in blood, a massive gun in his hand, the tip smoking. Vomit crawls up my throat, but a wave of bravery comes over me as I claw at the wall to stand up.

"I didn't ask to be brought here. I have been a good daughter. Given you *no* trouble."

He waves the gun. "You were home. Your bedroom is right across the hall."

I consider the cameras and try to undo my mess. "I heard nothing, Papa. Maybe... Maybe she left on her own."

"She would not leave me. *She* knows her duty." He tracks an angry gaze over me. "But if you hear from her, you are to tell me. Do you understand?"

"Yes, Papa." He won't kill me if he thinks I need to be alive to get a message from her. "I will. I promise."

He leaves, and I stare out the dining room window as food on the table sits uneaten. The snow Stasia mentioned blankets the entire estate. I take my dinner to my room, but I can't eat.

I watch the snow fill the sky and stare at the gate, hoping Stasia changed her mind. Only to swallow my emptiness at all the fresh powder with no footprints.

I bury myself completely under the covers, but don't really feel like I've slept. I just shake the whole night. I have one last class in the morning before Spring Break. Not that I'll be going anywhere.

Ever again.

In the morning sun, amidst a sea of white, I'm exhausted, but classes aren't canceled. I ask my driver to stop at the diner to get a coffee. Yulia used to make a carafe just for me since Stasia and Papa drink tea. The smell of fresh roasted beans greeted me every morning. Today, only the smell of bleach wafted through the entire first floor.

At the diner counter, I order a large, dark roast coffee. My eyes wander further inside while I wait. My heart stops. Lachlan O'Rourke struts to a booth. He's dressed all in black again. In fact, he looks the same as he did last week. But his wide shoulders and height look more dangerous from far away. He wears the same expression I always see. A wicked smile. Word around town is he's insane. Is that why he killed a priest?

I get my coffee and think about our conversation by the gazebo all the way to school. The sound of his voice with that accent gave me butterflies.

When I get to school, I ace my exam faster than any other student. I don't want to go home, so I duck into the library's computer lab, figuring I have thirty minutes before the driver comes looking for me. I use an outdated desktop in the lab because I don't want what I'm about to look up in my phone's browser history.

I easily find news articles about a catholic priest who was found shot dead in his bed. It isn't hard to locate since priests don't get killed every day. In fact, I only see this one incident, and I assume it's what Stasia was talking about.

There's no mention of Lachlan. Stasia reminded me that the Russians, the Italians, and the Irish rarely face justice. Fergus O'Rourke, Lachlan's father, must have had it 'taken care of.' That's how powerful the former Irish King was. He made that kind of heinous crime go away.

Reading on, I see the priest's name.

Father Eamon Gallagher.

At the time of his death, he was an assistant pastor in a different parish and wasn't living in Astoria.

There were no arrests.

The article goes on to say:

Sources, who wish not to be named, said Father Eamon had been accused of 'hurting' altar boys. Another source mentioned the incident where Charles Foster, the father of an altar boy, had directly confronted Father Eamon a year before the priest's death. That confrontation had ended with Mr. Foster falling in the sacristy during a scuffle and hitting his head on a fireplace hearth. There were rumors a third person was involved in the dust-up between Father Eamon and Mr. Foster, but no one has come forward. Without an eyewitness, and considering Father Eamon had suffered significant stab wounds to one arm, and the knife found at the scene belonged to Mr. Foster, his death was deemed self-defense. The Astoria priest wasn't charged.

I stiffen. Was Lachlan that third person?

Did he kill that priest a year later because of these allegations?

So much has come out concerning church scandals. I hadn't heard anything about St. Agatha's in Astoria. Maybe this Father Eamon was the only one. But he's dead.

And Lachlan killed him — according to Stasia.

I can't ask him. There is no reason for him and me to ever speak again. Either way, the priest's death is not something to bring up in casual conversation.

God, how my body tingles every time I see Lachlan. It doesn't respond like that to anyone else.

Weeks go by, and Papa barely speaks to me. I've never felt more alone. Another woman named Maya works in the house now. She's friendly, but I miss Yulia.

And I miss my sister. I check my school mailbox every day. Nothing. I worry I'll never hear from Anastasia again.

PRESENT DAY

CHAPTER THREE

LACHLAN

"Bless me, Father, for I have sinned." I sit in the darkened confession booth and make the sign of the cross.

"Good heavens, Lachlan, who did you kill now?" Father Patrick drawls to me in the Irish lilt I trust. He and I have a special relationship. He listens to my confessions and forgives me.

"Two eejits who stole from us."

"Stealing is not a capital offense."

"It's in the bible. Thou shall not steal. The crime of theft was punished by losing a hand. Back then, *that* was a death sentence. No antibiotics to treat infections, or reasonable means to stop bleeding."

Father Patrick turns his head to me. "That's a stretch, Lachlan."

I shrug. "Look it up."

I know the bible cover to cover. Both books. I wanted to serve God, but it got ripped away from me in the blink of an eye.

"Anything else, Lachlan?"

I clear my throat. "No. But I'll be back tomorrow. I'm collecting money later this afternoon, and I'm guessing someone's gonna end up hurt."

I don't kill people who owe us money. Not right

away.

Death is an ambiguous deterrent to others. Seeing someone beat to shit, or on crutches, head wrapped up in gauze from dozens of stitches sends more of an effective message.

"Jesus Christ," Father Patrick mutters. "Lord, forgive me." He crosses himself, spouts the usual blessing I need to say, and shuts the window.

Confessing what I do for my family is how I sleep at night. Not that I get much sleep. A few hours each night when exhaustion drains me is all I need.

When Father Patrick's feet walk past below my door, I wait a minute and get out. The smell of the candles triggers me, considering what happened here years ago. What I did. What I suffered for it. I finger the scar on my left cheek and choke back the bittersweet perfume.

I may not have meant to kill Charles Foster, but murdering Father Eamon was premeditated and a long time coming. My first real cold-blooded kill. The evidence against him was damning, but church lawyers swooped in and got him off. Paid off the judges. He'd been hurting kids for years — all while I'd stood behind him on the altar, listening to his lies about decency. I worshipped him and wanted to be just like him. I felt so betrayed.

Da dragged me here to St. Agatha's and made me confess to the pastor himself. Confessions are inadmissible. Not that anyone at St. Agatha's would turn me in, not with how much money my family gives to the church. Or what my da would have done to anyone who hurt me.

My punishment? I couldn't go to seminary school. Da wouldn't support me being a priest.

"Do you know what I did to get you out of trouble? You owe me. You're good with a gun all of a sudden? Taking a man's

life without permission, dispensing justice without fearing the repercussions of the police, God, or me? This is your calling and your penance, Lachlan, my boy. You'll work for me. You'll get those hands bloody for our family. And you will follow orders. My orders."

Then he sent me off to Dunbar Valley. I was failing at Fordham anyway.

After listening to my gory confession about killing the eejits, Father Patrick is no doubt hitting the bottle in the rectory. I smile, having the entire church to myself. Sitting in the back, I enjoy the quiet after a night of blood-curdling adult male screams ringing in my ears.

I take out the antique rosary I purchased in a silent auction. Spent almost one mil for it. I have more money than I know what to do with. My brother, Kieran, is the head of our family now. With Riordan his underboss, Eoghan the consigliere, and Balor our hacker, we share profits equally. Then give cuts back to our parents, and our sister, who lives in East Hampton.

Eoghan sends allowances to my twin brothers, who live in Seattle. They're doctors and don't want to work in the family business. But they are still O'Rourkes and entitled to a cut of my family's money.

I run through my prayers, fingering each bead on the rosary. The Hail Mary murmurs off my lips as I pray for my family. Particularly, my new sisters, Isabella and Priscilla. Kieran's wife is heavily pregnant with twins, and Riordan treated us to a case of the world's most expensive scotch, announcing his wife is pregnant as well.

After the rosary, I start my daily Irish novena of fifteen prayers directed toward my ma, who's battling MS.

Hail and blessed be the hour and moment in which the Son of God was born of the most pure Virgin Mary, at midnight, in Bethlehem, in the piercing cold. In that hour vouchsafe, I beseech Thee, O my God, to hear my prayer and grant all my desires for Ma through the merits of Our Saviour Jesus Christ, and of His blessed Mother.

Amen.

When I finish the third prayer, I feel someone watching me. I open my eyes and reach for the gun inside my jacket, the one I promised Father Patrick I wouldn't bring to confession.

My heart stops when I see a woman lingering outside the candle room. A whisper of a woman with blonde hair in a long braid captures my attention.

"Katya," I mutter, uncocking my gun. I'd not spoken to her since the night of her sister's 21st birthday party.

Stasia disappeared a week later.

Katya's eyes widen when our gazes lock right before she hurries out the side entrance near the altar.

Not so fast...

It was over two years ago, but like the ink indelibly etched into my skin, I've not been able to erase Katya Koslov from my mind, the way she danced and the sound of her sweet voice. I've kept her on my radar, keenly watching from the shadows. Her father makes an appearance with her here and there. Even though she walks several beats behind the ruthless pakhan, like she means nothing to him, she's been the star *and* tormentor of my dreams.

Shoving the rosary into my pocket like it means nothing, I push off the pew kneeler. The dark green cushion top sighs in relief from my massive weight of over three hundred pounds.

I hike up the side aisle, and not the center one out of respect. As the stinging smell of frankincense from the candle room fades, another scent grabs me by the throat. Floral perfume lingers in the doorway where Katya watched me.

Why was she watching me?

Seeing her always unravels me. Which is why I kept my distance after she enthralled me that night. When I'm too wound up to sleep, and no amount of coming in the shower exhausts me, her face in all the photos I've snapped calms me.

I've been struggling to understand why. Although, knowing every verse of the bible, I'm a believer of not questioning the unanswerable. Like the emerald beads in my pocket, Katya's become a source of serenity for me.

A pleasure with absolutely no guilt, unlike my other activities, murdering and beating people to a pulp. I had no choice to be who and what I am. My humor is a defense mechanism to fight the darkness in my soul. Choice... When was the last time my decisions were my own, really my own? I kill for my family. I fuck for my body. What have I done for my soul?

I halt in the small vestibule, breathing in her scent, realizing I can't remember the last time I got laid. Damn, it was *before* that night of Stasia's party. Katya has infected my brain to the point I haven't even wanted to fuck someone else.

Wait, do I *want* her? That way? The way I roughly fuck women who are brave enough to invite me into their beds?

Hell, no.

I have to get out of here before I need extra time praying tonight for jerking off in a church.

The strong July sun blinds me when I push the door open. The rays seep into my body even more ferociously thanks to my black jacket.

I cover my eyes, but nothing can keep my brain from finding Katya. Like a heat-seeking missile, my gaze tracks her down.

She sits on a bench at the entrance to the modest cemetery beyond the grounds of St. Agatha's. I'm thrust back to the night, seeing her alone in the gazebo. The memory of her voice, and how she looked at me, washes over me like a drowning wave.

Fury soon ignites my rage, seeing she's alone. Why is the Bratva princess outside, unprotected?

Suffocating emotions I've pushed out of my mind, fire back, and I'm not in control of myself. My pace quickens along the paving stones my family paid for. I don't need to jog, my long legs get me wherever I need to go in a hurry. Plus, when I run, I'm told I look like a freight train. I always wonder if smoke comes out of my ears.

It takes *a lot* for me to run. Nothing is that important for me to look like a maniac and draw unnecessary attention to myself.

I halt when Katya turns around and springs from the bench.

"Oh!" she cries out, her sweet voice hitting me in the chest.

With no one around, she looks achingly forbidden. That's why I can't shake this craving I have for her. It's right in the fucking Book of Genesis! I breathe easier, realizing what's captured me.

Just because I figured out why the fuck I'm so fascinated with her doesn't mean it's not eating me alive. Knowledge is supposed to be power. Basking in her eyes, I'm the most powerless I've ever felt in my life.

Sign... It's a sign.

What makes you weak should be avoided.

"Where is your guard?" I bark.

She clasps her fingers in front of her narrow, trim torso. "I don't have a guard. Just a driver. He's probably getting gas. I came outside, and he was gone."

Seriously? She doesn't have a fucking guard?

"Does he do that a lot? Leave you alone?" My harsh voice makes her blink.

"Um, sometimes. Why? What's the problem?" She rocks back and forth on her heels.

I dial my shit back. Up close, the difference in my size compared to hers alarms me even more. "You're a Bratva princess. You shouldn't ever be alone in public."

She bellows a laugh that can bring me to my knees. "Princess. That's a good one." Staring at me under her lashes, she adds, "What are you doing out here?"

"I saw you in the church," I say, keeping my voice even. "You shouldn't spy on a man like me."

"I was lighting a candle for my *maman*." Her delicate shoulders slump. "I wasn't spying on you."

I stalk toward her, testing her. To my surprise, she doesn't run away. "Good thing. I don't like people watching me."

"I'm not afraid of you." Katya smiles, and my axis shifts. "I'm sorry if I interrupted your prayers." She folds her arms softly, no sign of tension in her body.

"Why are you praying at St. Agatha's? Aren't you Russian Orthodox?" I recall seeing her with her father at the church where he begs for atonement.

"No." She snorts, and it sends jolts of lust through me. "I'm Catholic, like you. French, actually. Well, half. My mother was French."

"Is that so?" I heard her mother was Koslov's whore, but I won't disrespect her by bringing that up.

Christ, this girl is young. At thirty-eight, everyone seems younger these days. And shorter compared to my six-six height.

"Yulia, Papa's housekeeper, used to bring me here." She lowers her head and discreetly crosses herself. "Before she…died."

I heard Koslov shot his housekeeper after Stasia

disappeared. For someone who murders for a living, even I despised *that* move. The handful of guards he executed? That's the cost and filthy side of this life. I had to kill a guard once and beat the ever-loving shit out of another one. It's not fun.

"I don't come to masses." I find myself wanting to talk to Katya and keep listening to that angelic voice. "Not anymore. I don't need to hear sermons and songs. And I don't subscribe to talking to Jesus through saints. I come here to talk directly to him."

"Jesus or God?" she asks, with a sweet curiosity.

I shove my rosary deeper into my pocket. Getting back to my novena will have to wait. "Jesus. He's God's messenger."

"Hmmm. I got the feeling in my studies that they're one."

"The trinity, aye." I nod, enjoying the conversation.

None of my brothers want to talk about God or Jesus. Like if we say their name, they'll notice we're murderers and punish us.

Katya's eyes light up, and it's clear she doesn't know about my past. "Aye. What is that? You say it a lot."

"Aye? It's Irish slang. It means yes."

"Aye," she chirps.

Where did this girl get her courage? No one fucking talks to me. This is the second time, and she's got me gooey all over again.

But why? Why *her*? She's pretty. Very pretty. I don't dwell on the importance of beauty the way my brothers do. Yet, something deep down in my gut has been off since I saw her dance in that gazebo.

This siren calling of hers sucks me in again. The tingling down my spine and the tightness in my throat knock me sideways.

No...

I don't want to feel like this for someone, let alone someone I can't have. Her father would never give her to me. Moot point, though, because I refuse to take a wife.

Proving she's not afraid of me, Katya ambles right up under my nose, not an ounce of hesitation in her steps. Exhaling a long breath, she says, "Actually, I'm glad I ran into you."

"Why? Talk, little one."

Warm brown eyes lock with mine again. Her sun-kissed skin hints of warm blood in her veins from a culture that doesn't thrive on death like her father's. Curiosity burns me where she got those sculpted cheekbones and a long, slender nose.

She may be invisible, as far as being illegitimate, but she's three dimensional to me. Goodness shines from every angle. She's the polar opposite of me, and what I stand for. Yet, her aura reminds me there's a heart beating in my chest.

"I have to talk to someone." Her trusting gaze destroys me. "You're smart. You...know things. How to...fix things."

Sensing her panic, I pull her against me. If she runs, I'll chase her. Catch her. But I'm so fired up from the mixture of emotions, I might hurt her. The feel of her body fires raw electricity through my veins. Aw, fuck. This shit isn't supposed to happen to me.

"What, little one? Has someone hurt you?" Murderous rage fills me. It would hardly be a romantic gesture or suspicious for me to kill someone for her. It's what I do for a living.

"No. I know we haven't spoken since that night. But after that, I've always felt I can...trust you." She keeps her gaze right on me.

With deep brown eyes like chocolate, I wonder if she tastes just as sweet.

I stop at the bakery most mornings after nights of sinning. At home, I make a pot of black coffee and down an entire box of pastries. Then I get some sleep and meet Riordan for a real breakfast at the diner. Wait... Not anymore. Now Riordan wakes up next to his wife.

So does Kieran.

Have I been lonely?

What the hell is happening? Perhaps I feel alone because I'm not as close to my brothers anymore. Kieran, Riordan, and I were Irish triplets, even though we were born two years apart. Da let Ma have a year with each kid. They had an arranged marriage, but all I saw was love.

It was just never for me. I wanted love from God and the church. I ruined that when I lost control of the rage that swims in the blood of every O'Rourke.

"Aye, you can trust me." I pull Katya closer, and her mouth tips open, revealing an adorable little pink tongue. "What's wrong, little one?"

Her mouth is sexy as fuck with luscious lips coated in shiny clear gloss. She's the picture of natural beauty. "It's my sister."

I stiffen. "What about your sister?"

"I did something terrible."

My body sears with heat. "Did you kill her?"

She snorts that damn adorable laugh again, and this time it hardens my cock to steel.

"*What?* I could never..."

Her throat clearing finishes her sentence: *She could never murder someone.* Like me.

"What did you do that was terrible, little one?"

"Papa tried to marry her to the Boston pakhan. She didn't want to get married, so she packed up to run away."

Aw, fuck my life. I'm standing here, and a clue about

the biggest mystery to hit Astoria just got dumped right into my unsuspecting lap.

After Stasia went missing, we assumed she was abducted. But months later, no ransom or demands from a rival Bratva or any other crime family came in. Stasia was a tough bird. Had someone taken her, I bet she fought like a demon. Enough to get killed. That had been my theory all these years. What in the world do I do with this new information?

"But..." Katya adds.

"*But...* Go on."

"I messed up her room, so it would look like she was abducted."

A war has been simmering for over two years now because of it. Because of Katya. The look of stress on her face kills me.

"It's not your fault, little one." I caress her cheek, my fingers tingling at her smooth skin. "Your sister made her own choice to leave."

"I thought if she came back, Papa wouldn't punish her for running away."

"You're very smart. He would have. Have you heard from her?"

"I got some postcards."

My heart races, thinking I can solve this. "From where?"

"That's just it. All over. California. Oregon. Texas. But... It's not her handwriting." She swallows hard. "Now, I'm worried, someone actually did kidnap her. Why wouldn't she call me after all this time?"

Someone is sending Katya postcards, but not asking Alexei for money. This makes no sense. "Do you have the postcards with you?" I peer down at her, thinking Balor can examine them for more answers.

"No. They're in my mailbox at school. I don't trust my

father. He's more crazed than ever. He sleeps on a couch in his war room. There are top security investigators from Moscow living at our house." She yanks on that golden braid, visibly shaken.

Yet, she's looking at me like I'm a source of strength. Fuck, I want to be that for her.

She sees through my harsh lines and doesn't flinch that I'm cursed with a fucked-up face thanks to a scar from mistakenly protecting a monster.

"That's smart, Katya." Saying her name out loud pulls me into a dream, suggesting when my nocturnal ejaculations soak my bedsheets, her name hisses from my sleeping mouth.

"Katriane," she whispers with a rough drawl on her r — very French.

Fuck, that's sexy.

Those ballet moves that captivated me that night, warmed my frozen heart with her beauty and grace. Since then, I've been watching her from the shadows. I fantasize she's an assassin coming to kill me. The more I watch, the more I want to watch. I find myself taking photos of her to study her habits. I never had feelings for a woman, and brushed it off as a harmless fascination. Now, with her right here in front of me, she feels real and genuine. But I don't know what to do with these emotions of being so drawn to her. It's confusing as hell.

My eyes shoot to the carved marble Jesus nailed to the cross, hanging above the church's set of double wooden doors. *Is this some kind of fucking test?*

Or a gift.

"I'm so worried, it's destroying me." Katya presses her face against my chest and sobs. I throw my arms around her, a feeling so foreign, yet so perfect. Like I've been here before. "I worry, I'll never hear from her again because..." She gasps for a breath.

Did she feel it, too? That undercurrent grounding us? Pulling us under?

"Because?"

"I'm leaving." She staggers away, the look in her eyes sad.

My breath seizes in my lungs. "What do you mean, you're leaving?"

"I'm auditioning for a spot at the London Conservatory of Dance for my senior year. With no way to contact Stasia, if she actually writes to me again, I'll never know."

London...

Katya is moving to another country? "Your father is letting you move to London?"

She rolls her eyes. "He doesn't care about me."

Glancing around the empty parking lot where a piece-of-shite driver dropped her off, Alexei has been masterful at sending that message. I'm gonna take this crap up with Maksim. She needs a fucking guard. Guards report to him, the way mine report to me.

As far as her moving away, there's nothing I can do about that. I breathe easier, thinking with her away, this gut-twisting obsession I've been drowning under will finally ebb, and I can refocus on death and sex with strangers.

Going back to my old sexual habits has vomit creeping into my throat, and next, I'm coughing back stinging bile.

"Are you okay?" Katya squeezes my arm.

"I'm always okay." Anger seeps under my skin, seeing a dark blue BMW lumber into the parking lot. Shooting across white lines, it races this way.

Playing with fire, I pull her toward me and put a knife to her throat. She gasps, and I say, "Trust me, little one. This is for the best."

I'm the fucking Irish Enforcer. Alexei's pathetic driver let his charge wander unattended into my web. He deserves the scare, and it gets me off.

With tires screeching, and the stench of burning rubber choking me, I chuckle darkly as the tool opens his car door, gun drawn. This fucker is TSTL!

"Drop knife! Let girl leave!" The man struggles with basic fucking English. "Katya, get in car! It is much all right!"

"What's your name?" I snarl to keep my reputation intact.

"No mind my name, enforcer." At least he's smart enough to know who I am.

I lower the knife and glance down at Katya. "What's his name?"

She purses her lips. "Are you going to kill him?"

"Just beat him senseless."

"Then how will I get home?" The humor in her voice is refreshing.

I consider if I want her to see me tear a human's arms and legs off. It strikes me who I really am and what I'm capable of. I'm wicked and cruel. The filth of my sins is no match for this angel. Hating myself, I release Katya.

Her eyes lock on to mine and weaken my damn knees. This *isn't* good.

"Go home, little one." I steer her to the Beamer, anger getting the better of me. I don't understand these emotions and can't do anything about them.

"Forget I came here, okay? And what we talked about," she says, fear changing the shape of her face. She looks shaken and so unhappy, it guts me.

Growling, I watch the car drive off, her last words ringing in my ears: *Forget what we talked about.* She made Stasia's disappearance look like a kidnapping. Her father will kill her if he finds out. Fuck! I grip the knife, not realizing I'm squeezing the sharp edge. The pain doesn't register until I see blood drip onto the pale pink pavers.

I'd rather bleed for Katya on this sacred ground instead of someone else who lied to me.

CHAPTER FOUR

KATYA

The entire ride home from the church, I can't stop shaking. Lachlan and I were getting along. I don't know what I did to turn him off and make him angry.

Maybe it was wrong for me to be so forward and talk to him. He never spoke to me before the night of Stasia's party, just nodded politely. Looking back, any time I saw him, he never spoke to anyone other than his brothers.

After that night, I only saw him as the monster Stasia later coined for killing a priest. A weird obsession about Lachlan O'Rourke developed since then.

That feels like a lifetime ago.

The driver drops me off at Papa's estate, and the house is buzzing as usual. Maya runs around filling coffee mugs, filling plates with food, and clearing trays.

"Ah, you're here. Can you help me ice the strudel?" She figured out my place here in House Koslov a long time ago, and never hesitates to put me to work.

But I love baking. I love sweets.

"Where have you been?" Papa's voice makes me jump.

My driver may have told him I was at St. Agatha's. But I doubt he'll tell Papa Lachlan held a knife to my throat and admit he left me alone.

"I stopped at the church." I pick up the bag of icing and move to the bread tins steaming with cinnamon-smelling goodness.

Papa narrows his eyes at me. "For what?"

"To say a prayer for Stasia." I lie, since I'm not allowed to mention *Maman*.

His glare of suspicion unglues me until he stares down at the icing bag in my hand. "What are you doing?"

"I'm helping Maya with the strudel."

He hisses at our housekeeper, and she backs away.

"Sir." She curtsies. "I am overwhelmed with so many of your men here all hours of the day and night. I can use some help. My sister is here from Costa Rica and —"

"She can start tomorrow," Papa growls at her. "You do *not* make my daughter work for you."

"She doesn't make me, Papa." I step in front of Maya, guilt crawling through me for not protecting Yulia. "It's July, and I don't have classes. When I'm not rehearsing for my audition, I have nothing else to do."

"Audition?"

"The London conservatory, Papa." I wonder if he even remembers where I go to school. His accountant calls me every August and asks for the tuition bill. "They have one spot open for next fall. It's for seniors only. I'm old enough to live there on my own."

"Da, you *are* old enough," he says, looking awful in his dingy white dress shirt and wrinkled charcoal pants.

All these years later and he's still obsessed with finding Stasia. Spending vast sums, losing sleep, and losing his mind while his brotherhood falls apart. His underboss fled to Russia, and he hasn't replaced him.

Maksim, his enforcer, is vying to be underboss. He's here all the time. The man makes me sick. Sure, Lachlan kills the same as Maksim, but I've been watching the Irish Enforcer for a couple of years. Despite what he does for the mob, Lachlan is devoted to the church. He may have been praying for forgiveness for his killings, but his atonement felt genuine. He seemed more relaxed there than any other time I'd seen him.

I move toward Papa with a stiff spine. It hits me. I am the woman of this house and taking care of him is my responsibility. Something I've neglected.

"Papa, you look terrible. Let's get you cleaned up with fresh clothes." A sense of pride to tend to him fills me with a rare touch of happiness toward my father. The powerful pakhan can't look disheveled.

You're a Bratva princess...

Lachlan's words send a shudder down my spine. I never felt like a princess until he looked at me.

"Come with me." Papa grabs me by the arm   , his fingers digging into my skin. "Sit," he says, pointing to a chair in his office, then barks something in Russian leaning into the hallway.

Moments later, a man dressed in a navy suit comes in. He looks to be about fifty, with harsh facial features and deep lines around an ugly mouth.

"This is Rahil Nikitin. You are going to marry him."

I freeze as if I've been dunk into water. "What?"

"You are *going* to marry him."

My breath leaves my lungs. "No!"

"You let a child talk back to you, Alexei?" The man sneers, his beady eyes fixed on me. "I need a wife. I am running for mayor."

"Here in Astoria?"

"Moscow."

I stumble back. "Moscow? I don't even speak Russian. I don't want to live in Russia."

"Hush! You will do as I tell you." Papa's anger sends chilling goosebumps across my skin. Everything is sharper because he's crazed over Stasia.

I consider telling him about the postcards from her, but if Papa knows I've had a private mailbox all these years and never told him, I can't imagine what he'll do to me.

Just like Stasia, who learned of her fate to marry

against her will and then left, I already know I must do the same. Perhaps Lachlan will help me. Ask his hacker brother to trace the postcards somehow to help me figure out where my sister is. Then lend me the money to go be with her.

I glance at Papa and then at the ugly man. He doesn't look too eager to marry me, either. I pray he'll go back to Moscow to make the preparations, giving me time to escape.

"Yes, Papa," I say and run to my bedroom.

CHAPTER FIVE

KATYA

All my assumptions are devastatingly wrong.

Since I learned of my forced engagement seven days ago, I quickly became a prisoner in the house. Papa took away my phone and my computer. He learned a harsh lesson from Stasia leaving and put a male guard at my door. There's a rotation of female guards who watch my every move, even when I shower and pee.

Rahil didn't go back to Russia. And I'm to wed him tomorrow. My head is spinning, and I feel like I'm caught in a nightmare I can't wake up from.

A dressmaker showed up with wedding gowns a few days ago. When I refused to choose, Papa picked the most expensive one, but it's also the ugliest.

With a female guard standing in the corner of my room, I stare out the window. All morning, strangers have been milling over the property, setting up for the engagement party tonight and the wedding tomorrow. It's the same tent used for Stasia's party, but doesn't look as pretty. They dressed the tables with flowers and silk-wrapped chairs. Red roses everywhere make me think of blood.

To men like Papa, everything is a show to send messages. Flaunt his wealth and power. The mayor of Moscow is incredibly powerful, and Papa just aligned with him.

I can't believe this is happening. Every second of every day I looked for an opening to escape, to run away. But unlike Stasia, I had no opportunity. Papa wasn't going to make the same mistake twice. He's got me locked down. For the first time in my life, I want violence. Papa carries a knife on him. I'm quick and light on my feet. I can grab that knife, hold it to his throat. Only, Papa is a giant, and I'm small and not very strong.

A gun. I must get my hands on a gun. I shake my head, knowing I could never pull the trigger to kill anyone. Papa says I look like a Koslov, but I've only ever felt *Maman's* kindness in my veins.

I've been a good girl all my life. Did what everyone told me to do. Lachlan fills my mind again, and I amble over to my bed to pray. If a man who has all the power in the world prays, there must be some magic that happens from prayers that he sees and feels.

His unique rosary of emeralds and what looked like diamonds comes to mind. I glance at the guard who keeps an even face, not even looking at me.

I don't have a rosary, but I have my necklace with a gold cross. The only gift I got from Papa for my eighteenth birthday. I hold it and whisper the only prayer I know.

I'm barely one Hail Mary in when the door to my bedroom flies open. The guard pushes forward, but upon seeing Papa, she goes back to being a statue.

"You're not dressed?" he says to me and stomps into my closet.

"Dressed for what? The party isn't until tonight."

"Rahil will be here any minute." He comes out and tosses a pale lavender dress at me. "Put this on."

"It would help to know the schedule you've created for me." I stand up to him. "I'm almost twenty-one years old."

"You've grown some courage, I see." For the first time, he looks at me with respect.

"I have." I square my shoulders, and consider this is a moment to beg him to tell Rahil to go back to Russia and find a wife there. I also consider telling him about the postcards, but he can accuse me of keeping that information from him.

"You will have a nice life in Russia. Live in a palace. Have maids and guards. You'll be royalty there." He grips my chin. "I expect you to be grateful I have chosen a man for you who will give you a privileged life."

For a moment, I see it from that angle. I don't suppose the mayor of Russia can keep a wife a prisoner or hurt her. Perhaps I can cultivate a relationship with a guard, who... Who, what?

No, I don't want this. I must figure a way out. Russia is very isolated and so far away. Not that I have real friends here. Stasia was my best friend. Who wants to be friends with a Bratva princess? I choke, thinking of Lachlan calling me that. I guess I am. Only, not in a good way. My so-called *value* got me forcibly engaged to a disgusting old man.

"Yes, Papa." I lower my head.

"Get dressed. The party starts at five p.m."

"Then why is Rahil coming over now?"

"You must sign the contracts with him."

I wonder how much I'm being sold for, but I don't dare ask.

The next few hours pass in a blur. It's a hot, sweltering night, and I'm standing on the patio overlooking at least one hundred people slogging around, drinking, and eating. No one talks to me. Not even Rahil, who didn't even look at me when we signed the marriage contract.

His complete disinterest in me is my only comfort in this horrible situation.

A woman in a bronze satin dress watches me from a table near the garages. While everyone sips champagne, she drinks what looks like water from a cut crystal glass. My eyes trail down her body and the shiny fabric hugs what looks like a baby bump.

Why is she looking at me?

I take a few steps to the right and snag a glass of champagne for myself, even though I'm not twenty-one. Sipping it, I glide further down the patio and duck behind one of the two tall hydrangeas. The white pompoms have bloomed, but I can see through the sparse branches.

The woman gets up and mingles through the crowd. With nothing else to do, I watch her. She strolls right up to Rahil, who puts his arm around her waist while talking to men in suits. A few seconds later, the woman steps away, and Rahil follows her.

I finish the champagne. At the end of the patio, I dash down the steps but bump right into Rahil. His eyes burn with hatred toward me.

I feel ya, mister.

"Hello," I address him with a bow.

"What do you want?"

"We've not even spoken," I say.

"There's no need for us to speak."

"Then you won't mind if I continue my ballet lessons and education."

"Ballet? I need you with me on the campaign. You belong to me."

I shudder, feeling sick. "I see." Boy, do I see. My eyes trail to the woman in bronze, who hovers a few feet away. "And you are?"

"She is my mistress," Rahil sneers.

I glance down at the woman's hands, holding her stomach. "Congratulations."

"You don't talk to her." Rahil grabs me, tearing my dress.

Rage bubbles up, and I step on his foot with my heel, enjoying how he cries out. Until he pushes me. Hard.

"Take your hands off me," I yell. "Who the hell do you

think you are?"

I smile but make the mistake of turning my back on him. He pulls me by the hair and drags me into the walkway between the house and the garages. The pain is excruciating, my legs kicking from being hauled practically off my feet.

"Rahil, stop!" the woman cries out.

"Quiet!" He pushes me against the side of the garage.

Panic fills me. All I can think to do is fight back, so I kick him in the shins.

"Fuck," he growls and slaps me in the face.

It stings, but I eye him defiantly. "Is that all you got, asshole?"

"No." He lifts a closed fist.

There's sharp crack of pain and everything goes dark.

*

My brain snaps awake, and I scream, but I'm held down by a woman on my bed.

I notice the bronze dress and kick wildly. "Get off me!"

"Calm down, Katya," the woman says. "I sent your guard away."

My face throbs, and I taste blood in my mouth. I push her away and run into my bathroom to look in the mirror. My entire face is swollen, my right cheek already purple. I slowly open my mouth, expecting to see missing front teeth. My teeth are fine, but there's so much blood, I vomit into the sink from the stress.

Who the hell is that horrible man?

"Let me help you." The woman stands in the doorway. "We're in this together."

"Who are you?" I turn murderous eyes on her.

"My name is Nadia. I am Rahil's personal assistant." She touches her neck. "I am also his mistress, like he said."

"You can have him." I push away from her. "*You*

marry him."

"I cannot. I am already married. My husband is in a work colony. It is a prison, and he will not divorce me." She sits me down and hands me a washcloth soaked in cold water. "I will sneak to kitchen and get ice in a moment."

"Whose baby are you carrying?"

"Rahil's. But he must marry you. He is powerful man in Russia. He is what you Americans call a Tech Billionaire. He sent a team of his best people to help your father find your sister."

"And I'm the payment?"

"Your father's money is financing his campaign. But he also needs wife." She holds her stomach. "I am liability. A nosy reporter found out about us. Rahil needs a young, beautiful American wife with Russian blood to detract from our relationship. I can help you when we get home."

I pull away from her. "I don't want your help. Get out of my bedroom. *Papa!*" I yell, certain when he finds out what Rahil really is, he will call this off.

There are other ways to find my sister.

"Your father ended the party and left with Rahil. We need to get the swelling down by tomorrow." She sounds panicked, like she didn't expect him to be violent. "We need your makeup to cover the bruises. We have a flight tomorrow night to Moscow at ten p.m."

Over my dead body. And if that's the way out, so be it.

CHAPTER SIX

LACHLAN

"When you said you needed to blow off steam, I thought we were driving upstate to ambush that theft ring." Griffin Quinlan gapes at me while we idle in front of a high-end strip club.

A place I haven't been to in…damn…more than two years. Griffin is aware of my extended bout of celibacy. Just not why.

"I need this more right now," I grumble, checking my wallet for twenties. *Fuck, only hundreds.*

"Okay." Griffin looks for a place to park. "I won't lie. I prefer coming here without you. You either scare the fuck out of women, or they're drawn to you like bees to honey."

Or flies to shit, which is why I want to rid myself of this obsession with Katya. If Griffin knows I've given up pleasures of the flesh, others do, too. After two years off the map, it's time to restore my brutal reputation—and not quietly.

"Maybe you should stop coming here. Settle down like Ewan."

Griffin nods with a smile. "Being an uncle is more fun. You'll find out when Kieran's twins are born."

"Aye. Priscilla is pregnant, too."

"She is? And I'm sending her out on shakedowns?" Griffin looks horrified.

"Riordan's wife is a badass."

"Crazy how all that went down, aye?" Griffin slaps my arm. "Marriage and kids aren't for me. Not yet, anyway."

"Aye," I repeat. "Never."

"Never? You don't *ever* want to get married?"

"No." I'm happy being alone. Secure. Nothing can hurt me. No one can be taken away from me if I don't open my heart.

My throat tightens painfully when Katya comes to mind. I don't want to think of her. Although, since she grabbed me, I still feel her touch on my skin. Finding out she's leaving Astoria to pursue a dance education in London gives me peace to move on with my life. Forget about her.

"Is that Alexei Koslov?" Griffin tosses his blunt out the car window and looks around. "What in fuck's sake is the *pakhan* doing at a strip club?"

I sit up and excitement pricks my nerve endings seeing a dozen *bratoks* in suits surrounding him. "Let's go find out."

With Griffin on my six, I strut over to a huddle of Russians who don't make eye contact with me. I'm feared and well respected. Sergei, my old *comrade*, gives me a slight nod, not afraid to meet my eyes. Time to call in that favor from years ago when I agreed not to pummel Maksim in front of Alexei's rich friends.

"What is your king doing here?" I ask Sergei.

"Bachelor party," he says and hands me a lit cigarette.

I don't need a drag to choke. "*Alexei* is getting married?"

"No." He points. "The guy putting his suit jacket back on is. He's from Moscow."

The guy looks drunk and disheveled, with his pants unbuckled and hanging off his hips. Fucking pieces of shite cheating on their fiancées with strippers makes me sick.

"How many strippers did he bang?"

"All of them."

I feel dirty just looking at him. My brothers, Kieran and Riordan, had their share of women before they got married, but they're *not* cheating dogs. Eoghan and I are never without female company. Well, before I gave it up. I have no clue what Balor is up to. He's either a virgin or a Dom with twenty subs.

"Why is Alexei hosting a bachelor party?" I ask Sergei to get thoughts of my nerdy little brother with a whip out of my head.

"We're asking ourselves that same question." Sergei smashes his blunt under a polished shoe. "Especially since the scumbag is marrying his daughter."

"Who's marrying whose daughter?"

"Mr. Popular over there is marrying Alexei's daughter."

My brain is ready to explode. *Stasia's been found?* And Alexei arranged for her to marry someone already? I'm gonna hold Balor's head under water for not telling us. Yeah, he must be getting laid all the time.

"When did he find Stasia?" I ask.

Sergei turns toward me. "Stasia? We have no idea where she is. That creep is marrying Katya."

A fiery rage like I've never felt before explodes behind my eyes, and I grab Sergei. *"What?"*

Guns click all around me as Griffin yanks a loaded Smith and Wesson from his waistband. "Lach, what the fuck are you doing, mate?"

This gets Alexei's attention before he dives into an old-style Town Car.

The man who's drunk, the old slob who just nailed every stripper, who's marrying Katya, *my Katya,* hurls by the dumpster.

"What is this?" Alexei barks.

Out of respect, I let go of Sergei. "My mistake, pakhan. A misunderstanding."

Alexei eyes Sergei, who's gone pale.

"Da. A misunderstanding, pakhan." Sergei backs me up.

Alexei looks worn out and tired. He says something in Russian, and his men fall in line behind him.

"Big day tomorrow." Sergei, whose color returned, gives me a friendly pat on the arm.

"Tomorrow?"

"Da. Wedding at St. Agatha's, 11 a.m. There's a lavish reception at the compound, then they're flying to Moscow tomorrow night."

"Over my dead body," I mutter, watching the Russian entourage drive away.

"What the hell is going on?" Griffin pulls me back to his Escalade.

"Alexei is marrying Katya off to that lowlife who banged all the strippers."

"Shite," Griffin mutters and then grins. "Maybe you should stop the wedding and marry her yourself. I'm betting she's a virgin, and you can get your groove back, showing her the ropes." He smacks my arm and gets in the driver's seat. "Come on, if that scum banged all the strippers tonight, I wouldn't stick my dick in them with ten condoms on."

His suggestion rings in my ears like a hail of gunshots knocked out my hearing. When he grabs the gear shift, I close my hand around his and squeeze.

Griffin wails in pain. "Jesus, fuck, what are you doing?"

"I'm gonna need fifty men. Heavily armed, lots of rounds, sharp shooters on every fucking roof." I bang out a text to Riordan:

Me: I need the helicopter tomorrow.

"What the hell is going on?"

"For tomorrow, to stop the wedding, like you said."

48

Griffin's eyes widen. "Lachlan, I was *kidding*."

"Pity, I'm not."

CHAPTER SEVEN

KATYA

The flight this evening is my last hope. No way will an airline let a beat-up, hysterical woman on a plane. I plan to make a scene. Find a police officer. Show him my bruises and make him help me.

"Just keep the veil lowered until the end of the ceremony," Nadia, who arrived early to help me get ready, says when the sixth application of her powder foundation won't hide the yellow and purple star-shaped bruise on my cheek.

The bright blue eyeshadow, that makes me look like a clown, barely hides the red blister above my left eye.

I'm no stranger to punishing bruises. Despite ballerinas looking graceful and delicate, rehearsing and practicing is brutal on our bodies. Male dancers don't always catch us when we're flung in the air. Like football players who beg to go back on the field with a concussion, I have the same drive and don't want to be sidelined. I've shown up to rehearsals with cracked ribs and purple, swollen ankles wrapped in perfect, pretty satin to fool instructors.

It made me tough. The pain in my face is laughable. The terror rising in my throat is fear that I will end up in Russia. Married to a monster who will beat me daily.

I take one last look at my bruised cheek, swollen eye, and split lip, wondering what my father will say when he sees me. My stomach twists, thinking he won't care. He's that far gone.

The wedding gown Papa picked out is nothing short of a monstrosity. The glittering ballgown weighs at least twenty pounds from all the beads, and has long, sheer sleeves to cover my arms. It's July, and I feel like I've been shoved into an oven. I'm so itchy, and my body is sweating profusely underneath.

I don't care, really. These discomforts are the least of my worry.

Nadia, who proclaimed herself my maid of honor to get on the property to help with my makeup and dress me, lowers my veil. The tulle is stiff and thick with appliques. It's hard to see through and having use of only one eye isn't helping.

Nadia steadies me down the stairs where Papa waits in what looks like the same white suit he wore the day my mother brought me here at age twelve. A wild feeling of déjà vu hits me, and I question if the last eight years really happened.

"You look beautiful, Katya," he says with a taut jaw and signals one of his many henchmen to open the front door.

"My name is Katriane," I mumble.

"You are going to be the Mayor of Moscow's wife. I suggest you go by Katya if you want any respect from Russian citizens."

I don't plan for this to get that far. But unless a miracle or the apocalypse happens, I'll be married in less than an hour. I'm sure someone can help me dissolve that. Even if I make it to Moscow, I doubt Rahil will want to consummate the marriage.

My throat tightens, thinking of that vile man on top of me. Taking my virginity. He doesn't deserve my special gift. My virtue.

I ride next to Papa in his vintage white Rolls Royce, on our way to St. Agatha's. Papa never converted me to Russian Orthodox, so I cannot marry in his church. He doesn't talk to me. A caring father should prepare his virgin daughter for what to expect on her wedding night. My mother isn't here, my sister is missing, and Maya never warmed up to me the way Yulia had. Perhaps Papa knows Rahil has no plans to bed me.

I glance over and see he's texting someone!

My heart ticks up when I realize the driver has wandered onto a back road in Astoria. "Where are we?" I ask.

"There was a barricade on Mayfair Street. A cop directed me to this road," Papa's driver answers freely.

"Just get there," Papa hisses. "They cannot start without the bride."

I let go of a ragged breath and lean back on the sticky leather seat, but shoot forward when we're rammed from behind.

My bouquet goes flying as I use both hands to stop my throbbing face from smashing into the front driver's seat. The car is so old, there aren't seatbelts in the back.

"*Chyort!* What in the fuck's sake?" Papa spats and wrenches around. With a hand tucked inside his jacket because — of course, he brought a weapon to my wedding — he gets out.

Maksim, who escorted the Rolls Royce with Papa's Town Car, also gets out, a team of skinny, frightened-looking *bratoks* following him.

Behind us, the doors of a black Mercedes with tinted windows swing open, and four men dressed in black hop out. Towering above everyone is...Lachlan O'Rourke.

I push out of the car and realize no one is guarding me. Or even paying attention to me.

Story of my life.

I can make a run for it.

With so many people surrounding the cars and the drivers arguing, Lachlan approaches me.

"Katriane?" His deep, velvety voice strokes my soul. "Are you all right?"

My chest pounding, my thoughts fly into a whirl that he called me by my real name. He remembered. He paid attention to me last week. I feel an intimacy between us, even with so many dangerous people close by. Unable to breathe, I lift my veil.

"Hello, Lachlan."

Seeing my bruises, the enforcer's eyes narrow into frightening beady slits. "Who *fucking* did this to you?" He reaches for his gun.

The humidity in the car must have melted Nadia's attempt to cover my bruises. Even though we painted over my discolored skin, I can still feel my swollen cheek and jaw, not to mention my split lip.

I see the depth of Lachlan's concern while his terrifying, obsidian eyes pierce Papa with a coldness I can feel. "It's nothing."

"Did your father lay a hand on you?"

Lachlan O'Rourke is rumored to be insane, and I worry he's reckless enough to gun down *the pakhan*. Maksim and his *bratoks* will shoot back and kill Lachlan. That makes me want to vomit, the idea of him dead. Because of me.

"No." I lower the veil, not bothering to tell him it was my soon-to-be husband who beat me senseless when I caught him with his mistress. Lachlan probably thinks the same as other powerful men, that I'm a piece of property and nothing more. "I'm fine."

Papa finally notices Lachlan hovering over me and rushes to my side. With a sneering once-over, he hisses, "Back off, enforcer. I do not know what your driver is pulling here, hitting my car."

With another man awash in thick, rumpled, auburn hair at his back, Lachlan, rasps, "Do you *want* to get

53

married, Katriane? Who bruised your face?"

"Her name is Katya. And bruises, what bruises?" Papa asks, pulling me close enough to feel the gun in his jacket. "You have no idea what you are talking about, enforcer. Go back to whatever hole you live in. Griffin Quinlan, control your boss."

"No one controls me," Lachlan drawls. "Not even you, pakhan."

With Maksim guarding Papa, I'm shoved back into the sweltering car. Papa follows, complaining about the damage to his precious metal rear bumper as we drive away.

"This is your fault," he yells at his driver. "You should have just run through the barriers. I am *pakhan!* No one tells me where I can and cannot go."

"Yes, sir."

The church spire comes into view, and my stomach violently flips. I wonder if I threw up all over this ugly gown would Papa still make me get married in it? Pride has me controlling my body. Another part of ballerina training. Ignore pain. Ignore illness. Perform. Look beautiful. Don't complain. But that control is in service to get what I want. Which is to be on stage, dancing. Right now, all I want is to get out of this situation in one piece. Rahil beat me under my father's roof. I can only imagine what he'll do to me in Russia.

Not happening.

Damn, what if I'd told Lachlan I *wasn't* all right? He'd lose it and start shooting. I heard Maksim sent his men to kill Lachlan's brother, the Irish Underboss, months ago. All members of my father's Bratva are unhinged these days. I can't live with someone's death on my conscience.

We arrive in front of the church, and I tune everything out, turning robotic.

Papa helps me out, smiling for anyone watching. There are no cameras, though. Nadia, who rode with Maksim, snakes up to my side with a reassuring smile. I am a pawn in her game, too. I am the distraction she and Rahil need, so they can continue their love affair and have their babies. She won't help me in Russia.

Papa enters the church and grumbles at the vacant pews. "No one comes to see the pakhan's daughter marry?"

I want to answer: *Oh, you mean the daughter you made sure everyone knew you didn't care about all these years?* Or the near-empty church is from my father's violent missteps since Stasia disappeared. Those tirades stripped him of the respect he once had in this city.

"The roads are barricaded all over Astoria, pakhan," Maksim placates him. "The fair."

Something tickles my brain. The driver said the same thing about the roads. I may have taken a blow to the head, but I recall the annual street fair isn't in town until next week. I remember, because I love the fresh crepes from the French chef's truck every year.

Who put those barricades up?

Did Lachlan cut off my driver?

Those insanity rumors might be true.

"When...when do I sign the marriage license?" I ask, my breath going shallow, a sense of doom settling in.

"After the ceremony," Maksim answers for Papa. "The priest needs to sign it." With Grigori Laskin exiled to Siberia, Maksim has barely left Papa's side.

The slow drone of organ music fades, and the haunting, opening notes to *Here Comes the Bride* start. Nadia gives me another assuring nod over her shoulder and steps down the aisle, holding a bundle of calla lilies. Papa grabs my arm instead of me taking his. I fist my bouquet of blood-red roses with both hands, palm sweat soaking the satin-wrapped stems. I feel like I'm being dragged, but I don't care.

I get to the altar, but it's as if I'm not there. Rahil's eyes are on Nadia, not his bride. The priest says something, but it's all white noise. I jump when Papa wrenches my right hand from holding the bouquet and places it in Rahil's.

"Disgusting sweaty palms," he barks and roughly wipes his left hand on his suit.

"I sweat a lot," I murmur.

He leans toward me and hisses with awful breath, "Moscow gets ice-cold for many months, especially if there is no heat."

"No problem." I roll my eyes.

"You disrespect me?" he brazenly hollers.

The priest stops the mass, and a hush comes over the church. I glance at Papa, who looks furious, like he wants to slap me himself.

"Yes, I'm disrespecting you." I whip my veil flap over. "Do you think anyone who does this to a woman deserves respect?"

"No," a deep voice from the back of the church booms.

Lachlan O'Rourke stands there, dressed in a suit and tie. Was he wearing that before? I hadn't noticed. A *sea* of men stand behind him, assault rifles pointed our way. A scream tears from the choir balcony as men with guns crawl up there, too.

"What is this?" Papa yells and reaches for his gun.

"I wouldn't do that, pakhan." Lachlan struts up the aisle, like it's *his* wedding.

He comically reminds me of the scene in *Dirty Dancing* when Patrick Swayze dances toward the stage with an entourage behind him while Baby watches him.

No one puts Baby in the corner. The iconic line never felt more realistic.

No one puts Katya in a wedding dress against her will.

This must be a dream. I can't believe this is happening.

"You're outnumbered," Lachlan says, beaming with pride. "Only twelve men outside, pakhan? How sad."

Griffin Quinlan follows Lachlan on the left, pointing his rifle at Papa. A man I don't recognize on his right aims at Maksim.

I've kept to myself since I arrived in Astoria—a scared twelve-year-old girl ripped from my angelic life in France and dumped onto Papa's estate—but I know you *don't point a gun at the pakhan*. The same goes for the Irish and Italian Dons.

"I have twenty trigger-happy souls in here and *thirty* more outside. Your men have been rounded up and are being held at gunpoint. You lose this one, pakhan."

"What do you want, enforcer?" Papa says smugly, thinking this is an opportunity to negotiate something more favorable.

It's always about *him*!

"I want her," Lachlan barks, his gaze turning to me. "Katriane is marrying *me* today."

Even I gasp, along with the captive audience. I wasn't expecting *that*. The look of bloodlust in his eyes grabs me by the throat. Despite the terror running through me, despite the aches and pains, my body physically reacts to Lachlan.

He's the most handsome of the O'Rourke brothers. And that scar on his left cheek makes him more striking.

"Listen, you slimy *buckeroo*." Rahil pushes me out of the way so hard that I tumble onto my ass.

Lachlan roars. "That's the *second* biggest mistake of your miserable life, *fuckeroo*. The first one was bruising such a beautiful face."

From his jacket, he takes out a massive handgun and, without moving a muscle in his face, Lachlan aims his gun at Rahil's head.

The thud of a bullet breaking through skull echoes through the rafters, the sound only broken by Nadia's screaming. "Rahil!"

The spray of blood hits me, my dress speckled with the kind of deep, crimson ooze that comes from the brain.

"How dare you!" Papa whips out his gun.

"Don't do it, pakhan," Griffin sneers. "We have a code between us. We don't kill made men."

"That scum who hurt your daughter isn't one of us." Lachlan gently lifts me off the floor and fastens me to his side.

Nadia whimpers over Rahil's body, but no one else moves.

Lachlan whispers to the man on the right I don't recognize, and next, he and the others are dragging Rahil's dead body off the altar, guns aimed at Nadia to be quiet.

"I'm sorry your dress got ruined," Lachlan whispers, plucking a red rose from my bouquet and sticking it in his lapel. Staring down at me with a teasing grin that makes him look even more handsome, he says, "Now we match. How about you marry me? You're not a bargaining chip for anyone. And no one—" He brushes my face with the most tender touch I would think is impossible for such a brutally dangerous man. "—will ever hurt you again."

"Stop!" Papa yells, waving his hand, but puts his gun away. "This is not necessary, enforcer. Don't make me call your father."

"*My father* isn't in charge anymore," Lachlan barks. "And no one, not him *or* my brother, tell me what to do. I *want* Katriane."

His words send shivers through me. The romantic in me wants to believe we made a connection last week, and he's here because he has feelings for me. But I doubt a man with so much rage and who kills for a living can feel the kind of love I want in a husband.

He's rescuing me. My own plan to stop this wedding failed.

I take the bullshit ring Rahill gave me and throw it on his corpse. "Yes, I'll marry you, Lachlan."

CHAPTER EIGHT

LACHLAN

"You may now kiss the bride," Father Edward sputters, not meeting my eyes since I just committed murder in front of him.

He must be figuring out that Father Patrick's loose lips about my confessions aren't a result of nipping at the communion wine.

My men keep their guns trained on the crowd while Katya stares at me with glassy eyes and a blood-soaked wedding dress. It pains me to look at her face with all the bruises. I've been hit many times by eejits who dare to take a swing at someone my size. They don't live to do it twice, but I know what a punch in the mouth feels like. I'm a tough, hardened son of a bitch, but Katya is delicate. She must be in fucking agony.

Dueling instincts war in my head to not touch her, but another one, stronger, more visceral, wants to claim her. Plus, grooms kiss their brides. And Katriane *is* my bride.

Mine.

I lower my head because she's so tiny compared to me. "I need to kiss you," I rasp, and I wait for horror to flood her already bloodshot eyes.

Instead, they flare with a need that women can't hide from me.

"Okay." She delicately closes her eyes, one of them red and inflamed.

Her top lip is split and scabbed over. Anger fills me, but her smile, waiting for my kiss, sparks arousal through me. Slowly, I lower my mouth to press my lips to hers.

I softly kiss her, holding her face with my rough, bloodied hands. Our joined lips feel like the sky opening up after a vicious thunderstorm, making way for rays of sun that glow and bathe us in light. I'm awakened by this kiss. Brought back to life, better than new, but now more dangerous because I have a wife to protect. Fuck, now I get why my older brothers look more feral than ever these days. Adrenaline soars through me, and I feel like I can lift a fucking car. Okay, I can probably already lift a small one, now I might be able to toss it like a plastic toy.

Katya's eyes flash open when I growl in pleasure. "That was..." She swallows, looking at me. "That was nice."

I've interrogated enough people to know when someone is telling me what I want to hear. "It was, little one."

Holy fuck, it really *was*.

She clears her throat while the priest rambles quickly to end the ceremony. "That was my first kiss."

"Good girl." I lean in and whisper, "Mine, too."

*

I scratch out the name Rahil Nikitin on the marriage certificate and write in my own after Katya signs hers. I have to ask her what she wants to be called. I've only known her as Katya, but last week she told me her real name. I want my wife to be comfortable with me.

With the marriage certificate in my fist, the shaking priest backs away. I shove the license at Griffin. "Make sure this gets filed with *my name*." I want her to be legally mine.

"Aye, boss." Griffin folds it and puts it in his jacket.

This marriage can be temporary or forever. I had no plans to take a wife, but Katya needed me. Plus, she plans to move to London.

"We cleared the church out, and the clean-up team is dealing with both the dead body and that hysterical woman. Koslov and his men are gone, too," Connor Quinlan reports, holding an AR-15 against his chest. He's on loan from Riordan as a favor to his older brother, Griffin.

Everyone looks shocked at what I just did. My phone buzzes, and I'm guessing it's my brother, Kieran, with an angry text about my *shotgun* wedding. Seeing it's a call from him, my breath stills. Wow, he's *so* mad he can't even type.

"Alo," I say into the phone, all gruff.

"What in hell did you do?"

"As usual. Whatever the hell I want. Did you just meet me?"

"Alexei Koslov is parked outside my gate. He's demanding a meeting."

"Since when do you —"

"Get your ass to Divona right now." He uses the code name for our family home that sits on a tributary off Astoria Harbor.

My da christened it with the name of the Gaelic goddess of sacred springs and rivers when he built it. Its monolithic size and breadth are the symbol of O'Rourke power. Naturally, Kieran claimed it for himself when Da passed down his crown.

"Aye, your highness." I do what the fuck I want, but I respect Kieran is my king.

"And bring your wife." Kieran ends the call, muttering Gaelic curses.

I smile. He called Katya my wife. Taking the pakhan's daughter by force will need some smoothing over. Guns and threats get the immediate job done. Those are my skills, my specialty. But negotiations and additional maneuvering are sometimes needed to cement deals.

That's Riordan.

Glancing at how damaged and in pain Katya looks, however, I consider blowing off my brothers and putting her on the helicopter waiting in the church parking lot. Resume my plan to tuck her away in the new family safe house on the Canadian border in Upper Michigan. Then I read the incoming text and hear the whoosh-whoosh-whoosh of blades chopping the air overhead.

Fuck, the helicopter is leaving.

Kieran: That's my bird. Not yours. Ten minutes, Lachlan.

Inside Griffin's Escalade, I turn to Katya, thinking she'll be looking down. No, her eyes are right on me. On my lips, actually. Did she like my kiss? It did something to me, but we're about to enter another phase of this battle. I have to stay strong. Sharp.

"Thank you." She leans in and hugs me.

Warmth runs through my veins where ice-cold brutality usually flows. "You're welcome. You're my wife now, but what shall I call you? Katya or Katriane?"

She thinks about that. "I don't know. Everyone knows me as Katya. I'm used to it by now."

She could be my Kitty Kat. A little meow sounds in my head, and impure thoughts fill my brain. *Pussy.* "Katya it is," I whisper, and tuck her hand inside mine.

By the time we reach Divona, Alexei's outdated Town Car sits in the courtyard, the engine still running. Griffin opens the rear passenger door for my little wife, still in her blood-stained wedding dress. I hop out the other side and quickly wind my arm around her waist. She's pliant in my hold, walking willingly by my side.

Sergei, leaning against Alexei's trunk, gives me a sly smirk and lets me pass without incident. But he barks something in Russian to the other men who came with Alexei *and* Maksim. *Bratoks* who only know anger and violence.

My men are well-trained and deadly, but disciplined, not controlled by hatred.

I walk proudly toward the kitchen door with my wife, the woman I saved from a life of hell. She moves gracefully with her head held high. Riordan waits for me in the kitchen, his arms folded across his chest. His face is unreadable as far as his thoughts about what I've done. If we weren't brothers, I'd report to him as underboss. But we all report directly to Kieran, and I only take orders from him.

"Rior," I address him in a pleasant manner like I didn't just light the fuse for war with the Russians. "This is my wife, Katriane O'Rourke."

His cheek ticks up, respecting my boldness. "Nice to meet you, Katriane. Do you..." Riordan steps closer. "What happened to your face?"

"The man Koslov was forcing her to marry beat her up last night," I answer for her and plan to be her voice as much as she needs me.

"Jesus." Rior lowers his head. "I'm sorry."

"I don't want to be any trouble," Katya whispers, sounding embarrassed.

"Shhh, little one." I stroke her chin softly. "You're *not* trouble. You're my wife."

Riordan snickers. "Never thought I'd hear those words come out of your mouth, Lachlan." He is one of the few people who knew I wanted to be a priest. "Alexei is *furious*. He wants her back."

"The marriage license is being filed right now. She's mine." I tug her next to me.

"Welcome to the family, Katriane."

"Oh..." She sounds surprised, like that part hasn't hit her. "Thank you. You can call me Katya."

"Let's hear Alexei out." Riordan gives her bloody

wedding dress a concerned once-over. "Do you want to change your clothes?"

"I have nothing else with me."

"Then, considering the circumstances, wearing a wedding dress splattered with the blood of a dead man who hurt you might work in our favor."

Our... My strategic-thinking brother is already on board.

I follow him to Kieran's office, where I hear yelling in both Irish brogues and Russian accents. For a second, guilt fills me. Since returning from the training camp, I swore an oath to fix problems for my family. Eliminate them. Not make them again after the disaster I escaped at age eighteen. With this marriage to Katya, I've broken that promise.

Riordan throws the door open, and the room, filled with my three other brothers, turns silent as I usher Katya in.

"Katya, you are getting an annulment *right now*," Alexei fires. "I assume you didn't violate my daughter and consummate the marriage on the way over here, you animal."

"Hey!" Kieran barks, standing in front of his desk. "You do not call *my brother* names in *my goddamn house*."

"I can handle a little name calling, Kieran." I wave him off. "Is that all you got? *Animal?* You *dare* call me an animal when the man you forced her to marry did this to her." I point to her damaged face.

Alexei glances at his daughter with cold blue eyes. If I know this man and his backward thinking, he wants to blame her. He looks around at five O'Rourke men who clearly think differently and wisely says nothing.

"I thought so," I grouse at him.

"The man I chose for her was helping me find my daughter." He bemoans, "My *other* daughter. Have you all forgotten Anastasia is still missing? Now the team Rahil gave me is leaving for Moscow. Katya is all I have left. Give her back to me, and I promise, the next man will not lay a hand on her."

I don't believe him for a minute. "She's *my* wife now."

"Enforcer…" Koslov tilts his head at me. "You do not want a wife. We all know your past. Your history. I appreciate you playing knight and shining armor to my daughter." He turns to Kieran. "With all due respect, King O'Rourke, a marriage between my Katya and *anyone* needs my approval. You *know* this."

Kieran exhales, and I hate that he's considering Alexei's words. We live by a code. He *can* force me to annul this marriage. "Lach," he says to me with dread in his voice.

I pull my gun and shove my wife behind me. Alexei takes out a knife and Maksim makes the deadly mistake of aiming his gun at Kieran. That has the rest of the guns in the room clicking to life.

Katya shakes, holding on to me from behind. I worry she's been raised to be so compliant that she'll pull away and run back to her father, rather than watch a room full of alphas fight it out. Over her.

Priscilla, Riordan's wife, who I didn't even notice because there are so many hulking O'Rourke men in that office, steps forward, speaking Russian. Alexei stares at her in amazement.

Fuck, she's blowing the secret we all agreed to keep about her.

"Pris," Riordan cries out, and goes to grab her.

She changes to English, but speaks in that sexy Russian accent she used as an undercover FBI agent for months. "Close your mouth, pakhan. You are not going crazy."

"*Pasha?*" Maksim slurs.

"Da," she taunts them.

"Not anymore," Riordan barks, pulling her to his side with his free hand. "Her name is *Priscilla O'Rourke*."

"And before that I was Priscilla Cage, FBI," she announces in the Irish brogue she freely speaks with now because she is one of us.

Alexei pales, looking sick, but Maksim snaps. He lunges for her. Before anyone gets off a shot, I take out his left kneecap. Just his leg because I *can't* kill him. The same way he can't kill me.

The room erupts in chaos. Eoghan and Balor leap in front of Kieran with their guns trained on the pakhan, which is another *massive* violation.

"*Quiet, everyone!*" I point my gun at Maksim's head. "You, suck up the pain, you pussy. Priscilla, don't."

"It's okay, Lachlan." She bravely defies me. "I'm part of this family. I protect what's mine."

She swaggers up to Alexei wearing jeans and a black blazer with a white tank top underneath. Wisps of rich, dark hair brush her long neck, and I never would have recognized her as the high-heeled, ice-blonde Russian submissive she transformed into for the undercover assignment to nail the Koslovs. She now works with Griffin and Connor, investigating for us. Even gets her hands a little bloody when the mood hits her.

My brothers and I made a pact to protect her identity especially since she's pregnant. But she just outed herself. For me. For Katya, who she *just* met.

"You were spy?" Alexei mutters, furious.

"Aye," she taunts him. "You ordered the death of three federal agents. I was undercover gathering evidence. The D.C. office has audio and video against Grigori, but he fled."

Alexei shrugs. "That had nothing to do with me. You can't prove it."

"Ah, but I can. I also have wire transfers from you to

Grigori for the mercenaries he paid to gun them down. I lived in that house for three months. I had access to his computer."

Alexei's lips quiver briefly. "You would have turned them over."

Priscilla removes her jacket to show arms scarred from first-degree burns. Scars similar to Riordan's from diving into the burning building to save her.

"I spent weeks in the burn unit after Grigori tried to kill me. *Me*, after I told him who I really was." She slinks back next to Riordan, who pats her stomach, identifying her as pregnant. She was already untouchable, but pregnant spouses walk on water. "The FBI didn't promote me like I wanted. Why should I help them when I can make better use of this evidence?"

Only... She's bluffing. She never got that evidence. Alexei seems to believe it, though.

"Now, get the fuck out of here, pakhan." I take over, not wanting to put anyone else at risk. "Don't even think of making a move on my family. That now includes *your* daughter, my wife. Her name is Katriane O'Rourke. Don't forget it."

"I saw you murder Rahil," Maksim whines, now on his feet, hobbling, holding his bleeding knee.

All over the carpet. Kieran will have a fit. He's a savage, but likes nice things.

"Half of my *bratoks* saw you." Alexei folds his arms across a white suit. "We are owed something."

I know enough how things work, and he's right. Seeing Maksim is out of commission, my bullet ricocheting around his knee, I groan, "I will cover for your enforcer."

"Lachlan!" Kieran barks.

Before I can argue, I'm shot down. Not literally, though.

"No. Lachlan stays with us," Eoghan protests

vehemently. He is probably the *deadliest* out of all of us because no one would expect a Harvard lawyer to pull out a knife and slit your throat in a contract negotiation.

"I'll personally help your team find Stasia." Balor steps forward and adjusts his glasses, looking at my wife. "Katya is our sister now."

She gasps from behind me, and I turn to stare down at her. She looks terrified, and it enrages me, what she's been through. Glancing at my family, the 'crowd' I grew up with, I see for the first time how overwhelming so many people with the same last name in one room can be.

I'm used to it. I'm third born, but five more kids filled up this house after me. A bulk of my childhood memories include me, Kieran, Riordan, Eoghan, and Balor beating the hell out of each other. Or rather, the four of them trying to beat the hell out of me.

Katya grew up with one sister. How alone that must have felt. Feeling protective, I hold her even tighter. The O'Rourkes will have to come in small doses. She's overwhelmed. This is not the sassy girl I talked to last week outside the church. That girl intrigued me. This girl is shaken up, understandably so. I need to make her feel safe. Considering I spend my life making people feel the exact opposite, I'm out of my depth.

"I'll walk Alexei and Maksim to their cars." I glance at my brothers and wonder who I want to take my place protecting my wife. The choice is obvious.

"Priscilla, guard Katya for me."

"Aye," Priscilla agrees heartily, and stands at my wife's side.

"After you, pakhan." I open the office door.

Alexei shakes his head and pushes Maksim, who's still whining and seething, hopping on one foot. "Get the fuck out of here and get your knee looked at."

Outside, Sergei puts Maksim in his car. His smirk hints at a crack in the brotherhood armor. Is there a silent mutiny happening within Koslov's Bratva? In front of his Town Car, Alexei stares at my suit covered in blood.

Plucking the rose from my lapel, he leans in. "Is it too much to ask that you leave my Katya untouched? When you get over yourself and tire of her, I want her back as pure as she is now so I can..." He stops talking when my expression turns murderous.

Katya wants to be a dancer. I will let her go to that conservatory in London because this is just a temporary respite that saved her life. I will give her the independent life she wants.

I don't know what love is. I understand craving and obsession, but it's not the same thing. I get lusting after something, but after the thrill of the chase, I feel nothing.

Katya can't stay a virgin, though. The more ruined she is by my cock, the safer she'll be from her father trying to marry her off to another scumbag business partner to save his fledgling brotherhood.

I whisk the rose back from Alexei, and let the stem dangle between my front teeth. "Sorry, pakhan. Your daughter is my wife. It's my right to deflower her. If she consents to me, I'll be taking her nightly."

Alexei scoffs a laugh. "I raised a good girl. She won't want you."

"*You* didn't raise me," Katya contradicts her father from the kitchen door.

I spin around and smile at my brave little bride strutting toward us.

"My *maman* raised me. Then Yulia, who you killed." Face bruised and a bloody wedding dress, any other princess would fall apart. Not my bride. She isn't afraid of her father, the most powerful man in the Bratva. Or me, given how she looks at me. Sliding her hand into mine, she adds, "And you have no idea what I want. And if I want Lachlan that way..." Our eyes meet and my cock strains against my tight suit pants. "Then that's between him and me."

She invites a kiss with her eyes, and I bend to take her mouth. Fuck, maybe I won't let her go to London. I brush my lips against hers. This ache I feel cannot be denied much longer. This itch I couldn't scratch will be satisfied by her nails down my back while I fuck her so hard, she will never want another man inside her again.

Seeing her flushed cheeks and glassy eyes, I sneer at Alexei, "I need to get *my wife* to a doctor, thanks to your neglect."

It hits me out of nowhere—*he's* my father-in-law. All I've been able to see is how Katya will fit into my family. Shite, I'm also part of hers.

I'm connected to the Bratva.

And it's fucking falling apart.

CHAPTER NINE

KATYA

"You need a doctor," Lachlan says, cupping my chin gently when we're back in his brother's house, surrounded by his family.

Glancing at all the faces, I struggle with the names. Some I remember, some I don't. There are so many of them. Gulp, my name is technically O'Rourke now.

It's so surreal. I'm married to *Lachlan* O'Rourke. His stare carries so much weight, and the depth in his eyes makes me feel like he can swallow me whole.

I should be terrified of him. I'm not out of immediate danger. I'm just in a different spider web.

Yet, I feel utterly safe, encased in a warm, soft cocoon. And the way his eyes crinkle in the corners with mischief suggests he'd love someone to try and pluck me away from him.

"I'm fine. I know how to treat bruises," I answer him when my silence makes him uneasy.

Lachlan's upper lip curls into a snarl.

"From dancing," I clarify quickly. "It's hard on the body."

"Ewan's wife, Darcy, got her RN and can call in meds," Griffin offers.

"Thank you. I just want to take all this makeup off. Can we go..." My legs go weak, realizing I can't go home.

"My house. You're coming with me, little one." Lachlan's hand around mine tightens. "I assume I can take my wife home, my king?" He stares at Kieran.

He grins. "I'll even give you a few days off for a

honeymoon."

Honeymoon. I stiffen. Will he want a real wedding night? This is not a real marriage, as far as love. But he is my husband. I said I do. I signed the marriage license. I told my father I'd give myself to him. If he wants to take my virtue, he has the right. Do I have the right to say no? Looking at him, the body of a God, and the face of a warrior, scarred and rugged, I'm not sure I want to say no.

"Where do you live?" I look up at Lachlan.

"You'll see where *we* live." He may not have planned to marry anyone like Papa said, but I feel he's all in on this fake marriage.

My body tingles, my nerves reaching the surface. This horrible dress pinches me, reminding me I don't have any other clothes. From the corner of my eye, I see my father getting into his Town Car. Maksim's men helped him into his truck and drove off a while ago. He needs a doctor more than me.

"Give me a minute." Grabbing the gown's thick skirt, I run past an older woman in the kitchen who gawks at me in my blood-splattered dress. "Papa!" I yell.

He stops and spins around with a wide smile. "You came to your senses, Katya."

"No." I halt. "I mean, I've not *lost* my senses, Papa. But I *want* my clothes. All my things. Maya packed everything up for the flight tonight."

"You are not taking the flight tonight, are you?" He folds his arms.

The O'Rourkes offered to help him, but he's sulking because he didn't get to call the shots. He's an old-school proud man. Being pakhan has distorted his perspective on life.

Lachlan probably won't hesitate to buy me whatever I need, but I feel like he's done enough. I had access to a bank account that I assume Papa will close.

"I am married to Lachlan O'Rourke, but I am still your daughter. I am still a Koslov by blood and name. You may have considered me invisible all these years, but people in this city know who I am." Lifting the skirt of my blood-stained gown, I add, "Do you want me roaming this city shopping for clothes looking like this, with bruises on my face? Advertising that you tried to sell your daughter to a monster?"

Warmth spreads across my back, and a low chuckle rumbles from Lachlan's chest. "Nice, little one," he whispers in my ear. His support means so much to me.

Papa's cheek twitches. He wants to be feared in Astoria, but not for the wrong reasons. All leaders, Kieran O'Rourke, Papa, and the new head of the Italian mafia, all need respect.

"Your bags will be dropped off," he relents bitterly.

"*I'll* pick them up." Lachlan rests a possessive hand on my shoulder.

"Right, enforcer. Your lair is one of the best-kept secrets in this city."

Lair? He didn't tell me where he lives. Where *we* live.

"I'll go put the third-row seats down in my car." Griffin brushes past me.

Car... I have always been driven around and don't have a driver's license.

"Are you ready to leave, little one?" Lachlan whispers in my ear again, his warm breath tickling my skin.

"Yes," I say with a straight spine. I'm married to an enforcer, a man who eats brutality for breakfast and spends the night terrorizing people. He needs a strong wife.

Lachlan steers me to Griffin's massive SUV. The weight of the day finally hits me. All morning, the thought of that plane ride to Russia with Rahil made my stomach churn with terror. But now, I'm heading 'home' with my 'husband.' Not a madman who hurt me, just a...psycho who shows an unusual amount of kindness toward me.

Nerves still shake my soul, but for a much different reason. Being alone with Lachlan has my heart pounding.

The sun sets off in the distance, red and burning hot. It was a gorgeous day, but I missed it. Lachlan puts his arm around me but doesn't look at me. He and Griffin chat in hushed tones. I pretend not to listen, or be interested. Does he automatically trust me?

We reach my father's estate, and it looks so different. The feeling I had coming to this massive, haunting compound eight years ago hits me. I breathe in and out. But the words, *let me go*, don't pass my lips. They're not even on the tip of my tongue.

When Griffin gets out, Sergei, Maksim's second-in-command, struts up to the car. Lachlan lays his arm across my lap. "You're safe, Katya."

Griffin and Sergei chat for a moment, their faces absent of stress. Sergei barks something in Russian, and three men bring my suitcases to the back of the SUV. When the rear door snaps shut, the feeling I'm owned by Lachlan solidifies really fast.

The guards at the gate watch us as we roll down Papa's driveway. Griffin gives a wave, smiling, while Lachlan stares straight ahead, his lips flat.

We live on the border of Long Island City, but Griffin heads north. Just when I think he'll turn onto a street with fancy homes, he doesn't. Glancing up at Lachlan, I understand. He doesn't look like a man who would own a fancy house all by himself. His brother, Riordan, lives in a penthouse. But we passed the only high-rise in Astoria miles back.

After a couple of turns, we're on a winding, one-lane road with a thicket of tall trees on both sides. Griffin sharply cuts into a driveway that I would have missed.

His Escalade climbs a steep hill, and I watch with anticipation for the house that will appear when we crest the incline.

Lair. Papa called where Lachlan lives a lair.

I gasp, seeing the sprawling one-floor home constructed of mostly vertical glass panels.

"You live here?" I point. "In a house of glass? Off a public road?"

Lachlan chuckles darkly. "Little one, there are cameras everywhere and there's a guards' cottage hidden in the brush with a rotation of men who patrol the property. That glass? Bullet proof." He brushes my sore cheek. "You are safe here."

Just being with him, I feel safe. But it makes sense that this place is surrounded. He's the O'Rourke Enforcer, a major target.

Griffin stops his SUV, and Lachlan pats his shoulder. "Thanks, brother."

"I'll help you unload the suitcases."

"I got it. She's *my* wife." He keeps saying 'my wife.' The words fall easily off his tongue.

Lachlan gets out and then comes to my side to open the door. After I gather all the layers of the heavy, beaded dress, he helps me out, and swaggers to the back of the SUV. His smooth movements feel natural, practiced, and rehearsed to show his confidence and strength.

Rehearsed.

I can rehearse for my conservatory audition now. Will Lachlan let me? I'll wait to bring that up when I fully understand how this is going to work out between us.

The rear door pops open, and Lachlan smiles at me. "A lot of bags," he comments wryly.

"I was supposed to move to Russia." I hold my stomach, the horror I narrowly escaped settling in. "It's all my stuff. If it's too much—"

"It's not too much," he says, low and throaty. "I have plenty of room."

All I see is one floor. A rustic bachelor pad. He's one person, so I didn't expect anything tremendous. "If you say so."

"I say so." He grins, taking bags out one at a time and stacking them on the gravel drive. "You'll see."

As if this is the most normal thing in the world, Griffin backs up and leaves us.

With several cases stacked and tucked under his arm, Lachlan boasts, "I'll come back for the rest." He brushes the small of my back and steers me up a set of slate steps.

"Do you spend a lot of time here?" I ask.

"Aye, why?"

"Seems so off the map compared to the rest of Astoria." I glance down and marvel at the beautiful stone walkway.

We get to the front door, and Lachlan takes out a key from deep in his pocket. I'm figuring this is not a 'smart home.' I understand technology and how phones or anything computer-related can be hacked into.

Phone... I don't have a phone anymore.

Lachlan opens the door and stares at me in my wedding dress. "Why not, right?" Laughing, he scoops me up with his free arm.

Giggling, I say, "We're married."

"We are." He carries me inside, and everything glows from the sunset flooding the entire home.

The walls on the back of the house are all glass as well. It's so unexpected.

"Are you hungry?" he asks, lowering me then puts down my luggage.

"A little."

"Kitchen is here." He points to a floating woodgrain island, rustic looking cabinets, and red retro appliances.

I wander to a window facing the back of the house, and my breath catches, seeing water far below us. "We're on a mountain? I didn't know Astoria had mountains?"

"We're on a high elevation. I wouldn't call it a mountain. There's a small patio below. I sit out there and listen to the water."

I glance around. "Where do you...sleep?"

"In my bedroom," he answers all gruff.

I swallow. "Where will I sleep?"

"In the spare room."

"Oh..." I'm half relieved, half disappointed.

"Did you want to sleep in my bed? Tonight?" he asks, sounding surprised.

"That's probably not a good idea. This isn't a real marriage, is it?"

"We said I do in front of a real priest." He twitches, saying that. "I kissed you. We signed a marriage license. This marriage *is* real."

"But we're not..."

"I married you so that vile eejit couldn't hurt you. And to punish your father for daring to give you to such a piece of shite." He reaches for my shoulder, where a delicate tendril of my hair sits. "You're a Bratva diamond."

I shake my head. "No, Stasia was his diamond."

"If you don't want to be here..."

Instead of on a plane to Russia with an animal, I'm in a house overlooking Astoria Harbor with a gentleman. I grip his suit jacket. "I want... I want to be here with you." Considering the alternative.

"I understand. There's no need to be afraid."

"I'm not afraid." Strength returns to me, and my voice

grows tough. "I'm overwhelmed. That's not the same thing."

"Aye."

I press down on my temples aware my face is a mess with ugly makeup that covers worsening bruises. "Why? Just tell me why you did this?"

Lachlan hesitates, his palms flat on the island's counter. "Last night, I saw your fiancé. The man you were supposed to marry came out of a strip club. He was drunk and banged all the strippers."

I'm not offended. Nadia, however, would have been. "He had a pregnant mistress and gave no indication he wanted to be intimate with me."

"Men always want sex, Katya." He reaches to touch my face again, anger brewing in his eyes. "I thought banging strippers the night before his wedding was the worst thing about him. If I'd known he'd done this, I might have murdered him last night. Spare you this horrible day."

"I *had* a plan, by the way. I wasn't waiting to be rescued."

"What was your plan, little one?" He folds his arms, smiling at me.

I understand alphas. My father is pakhan, for crying out loud, and beasts of men roam freely in and out of my house.

"My plan was to make a scene at the airport. My father didn't shelter me. I know what's going on in the world." I stand up to Lachlan, but I'd have to jump to smack him, something I think he'd enjoy. "Everyone is on edge at airports. I was going to run to an officer and show off my bruises."

Lachlan rubs his chin. "In the terminal where your father has a private plane? I'm sure he owns those TSA officers."

"Private plane?" Why hadn't I considered that? "I would have figured something else out. I'm not stupid or helpless."

"I never thought for one moment you were stupid. East Side Performing Arts doesn't accept stupid people."

"You know where I go to college?"

"I know everything about you. Have for some time." He inches toward me. The heat coming off him warms and excites me.

My throat constricts. "Why?"

His handsome face, even with that scar, goes expressionless. "I'm not sure. I live on instincts, and I had an instinct about you. My gut told me to watch you." He deftly removes my veil. "Watch *out* for you."

The stalker aspect sends my guard up, but also thrills me. I never thought I'd be attracted to danger. Falling for the Irish Enforcer is dangerous. Even if this murderer is my husband.

"Okay. But what were *you* doing at a strip club last night?" I fold my arms, mimicking him.

Lachlan's jaw tightens. "I went there to relieve the kind of stress that torments my life."

I have no right to question what he did before he became my husband, or even after. This isn't a marriage based on love.

"Again, thank you." I turn around. "Can you please unbutton this thing for me?"

He breathes against the back of my neck. "I didn't go inside, Katya. I went home and planned the murder of the man who hurt you. I found that satisfying enough, knowing you'd be safe. And as long as my name sits on a marriage license, I will not be frequenting strip clubs any longer."

I consider his confession, and I believe him, because he has no reason to lie to me. "Okay. I trust you."

"Mmmm." He deftly undoes one button at a time on my dress until I feel it give way from my body. A pleasant humming changes to a deadly growl. "Katriane... Your *shoulder* is bruised."

"That's a fall I took at school. Not Rahil."

"Still, your skin is all red." He drops his hands. "I'm getting you ice and ointment for your lip."

"How long can I stay here, exactly?" I hold the loose, scratchy fabric against my chest. I'm dying to get out of this ugly thing and toss it.

"Katriane..." His Irish accent, mixed with the French-rolling r pronunciation of my name, makes me swoon. "I didn't want you with that man." Not exactly a declaration of love. Not even close. "You are *my* wife now. You can stay here as long as you want. But I put the question back to you. How long do you want to stay?" He strokes his chin, rough with dark stubble. "You mentioned an audition next month to finish your studies in London."

It crystalizes now. He sees this as temporary. That suits me. I never wanted to stay in Astoria. *Maman* brought me here. I had no choice. I fought for the choice to determine my own future.

"I appreciate that you listened to me. No one really listens to me. Except, my sister." My voice gets low, worrying about her so much.

Lachlan hovers over me. "Have you heard from her again?"

"No." I catch my breath to show strength. "So...this is all temporary until I leave for London? *If* I leave for London. I'm auditioning against other dancers."

"*I* can get you into that conservatory," he boasts. "I can give you anything you want and need. But you need to have a full grip on the situation. You are valuable to your father. London is only an ocean away, he can get to you there. Are you truly a virgin?"

I gulp down the lump in my throat. "Of course, I am."

"Good girl." His mouth lingers above my swollen lip. "Before you leave for London, we will change that."

CHAPTER TEN

LACHLAN

I leave Katya blushing with quivering lips while I collect the rest of her suitcases. I still can't believe Koslov tried to give his daughter to that pig.

Katya wanders around my living room, holding her wedding dress up against her chest. My heart pounds, thinking of what's underneath, and how it will feel against my bulky, scarred body. Am I too much for her? Will I hurt her? She's tough, though. Dancing gave her both grace and strength. What she lacks in stature, she makes up for in power.

Fuck... I'm a big guy, and when I take a woman to bed, I need someone sturdy, someone who can handle me. Even if bruises like the one on her shoulder come with the territory.

I bet I can be a little rough with her. My cock swells so thick, so fast, I get dizzy from all the blood draining away from my brain.

"Lachlan..." Katya's voice drags me from dirty thoughts that sent my mind inward.

I didn't realize I was staring at her. "Right. I'll show you to your room."

"I'll take that small bag for now." She steps toward a blue and white case, but her foot catches her dress, pulling it down. She's not quick enough to stop it from snapping to the floor. Her hands quickly cover tiny, naked breasts. She's got adorable curves too, thanks to a tiny waist. She's sexy as fuck. But I can't help chuckling at the white cotton panties that come up past her belly button.

"That's not very encouraging. My husband laughing at my body on our wedding night."

"I'm not laughing at your body." Feeling bold, I swagger up to Katya, impressed that she doesn't shirk back in horror. I reach out to touch all the skin she's showing me.

As her lawful husband, I have permission to put my hands on her. So long as she doesn't scream or flinch, I'm dying to test those boundaries. My blood stirs in a way it hasn't in a very long time. My heart starts a steady beating rhythm I've never felt before.

I kill without taking an extra breath. Yet, Katya's nudity has *my* body doing things I'm totally unfamiliar with.

I trained myself to shut off lust and desire when I wanted to be a priest. Then after I killed Father Eamon, and my da sent me to Ireland, to a camp where I learned to be a heartless murderer. Indulging in the flesh was how those maniacs soothed the rage of taking people's lives. Only, that felt hollow after a while.

Katya's warm brown eyes stay on mine as she gasps loudly when I brush my hand on a taught stomach. I slide my fingers down toward the top of the waistband of white cotton briefs. I have a fucking sense of humor. I'm always cracking my brothers up. Why not act that way with my wife, who deserves to know the real me? "These are cute."

She looks down at my hand gripping her panties. "They're comfortable. I don't have anything lace or silky, or those thongs, I know men like. But if you want that—"

"No," falls from my lips. *Well, maybe.*

"Oh."

"You don't have to change anything for me, Katriane." I let go of her panties when way too much blood pumps to my groin. My body reacting this strongly is a nice surprise, spurred by her greedy smile to please me.

"Good. Neither do you."

"Good to know." I wouldn't expect a Bratva princess to be *that* disgusted with me, an enforcer. Especially since her father's enforcer is a fucking mess.

From a chair that sits in front of the massive stone fireplace, I whisk off a crocheted blanket from our grandmother in Ireland and drape it across Katya's narrow shoulders. My sister sent a decorator to stage the place, but Shea-Lynne added small family mementos.

"I'll show you where the thermostat is," I tell Katya. "You're free to control the temperature here."

"What about you? How do you prefer it?" She bites her lip. "The temperature."

My heart pounds. Is she flirting with me? "I learned to control my feelings, my emotions. I can take anything. Extreme heat, extreme cold. Nothing affects me."

Yet, this ninety-five-pound woman here is setting my body on fire and I can't stop it.

Leaving the hideous wedding dress on the floor, which I *will* burn later, mostly because it's evidence of a murder, I steer Katya to the second largest bedroom. It sits on the other side of the house, far away from mine.

Lair. Her father called my home a lair.

We joke about Balor having a Batmobile and a Batcave, all while I'm the one with the house carved into a mountain. But I do envy his sweet, rare Lamborghini Murcielago.

"This is fine." Katya steps inside the bedroom and points to the sheer wall of glass. "No drapes in the bedrooms?"

"There are shades inside the glass that can be lowered for the sun in the morning." I show her the remote. "You don't have to worry about human eyes. No one can see inside."

"The view is incredible. What is that?" She motions to a lighthouse in the distance.

"Sands Island. Party boats circle it a few times a day in the spring and summer. The water is shallow and ices over in the winter."

"I never knew any of this existed."

"Most people don't. That's why I built my house here."

"Do you spend much time here?"

"Aye." I show her how to raise and lower the shades. "No one except my men and my brothers know where I live. Oh, and my cleaning lady."

"No need for that." She shrugs. "I can clean."

"I have plenty of money. You're my wife. You don't need to clean."

She drags a breath deep into her lungs. "You said we should… You know. Get on with our wedding night." She goes to lower the blanket.

"Wait." This is moving too fast, even for me.

Her touch last week ignited a fever in me. Made my obsession feel real. Finding out Alexei planned to hand her over to that disgusting piece of garbage, led me to that church today to steal her for myself.

She's a Russian princess, even if Alexei slighted her for years. She grew up with money and privilege. But she has dreams for herself. I like that. Like her better for it.

"Let me guess," she says. "You like it rough."

She's been in college for three years and must understand men to a degree. She's also Bratva and has been exposed to ill-mannered, untamed animals who work for her father. Many probably boast about their whores around her. Alexei acted like she meant nothing to him, so his bosses probably followed his lead.

Arseholes.

"Aye. It will be rough at first." The grittiness in my voice sends a blush across her cheeks. "But I'll give you time to adjust. You'll be very pleased with me in bed." I hint at my willingness to go slow with her.

"I see." She tosses the blanket off, offering herself to me. "Shall we get started?"

I study her body again and soak in what it does to mine.

Approaching her, I caress her face. "You were brutalized by a man last night. I won't subject you to any more trauma." My hand sweeps down her neck and next, fuck, my finger is circling an erect, pebbled nipple.

"Oh." She bites her lip, turned on by my touch. "Mmmm."

That soft feminine moan makes me lose my mind. I drop my hand and step away.

"Clean the blood from your neck." I swallow, wanting to put my hands around her throat to feel her pulse. Feel how alive she is. "Do you need help unpacking?"

She pulls the blanket back around her shoulders, shielding that delightful little body from me. "Not tonight. I'm tired. And...a little hungry. Maybe tomorrow we can put everything away. Lachlan, are you serious about letting me go to the conservatory in London, if I get in?"

"I am," slips out easily, followed by a cloud of dread. Then she'll be gone. Why does that bother me?

"I need to audition in a month. Then the judges decide a week or so later."

"I can persuade them." I grin.

Her eyes slip closed. "I prefer to get in on my own merits."

I think of how she danced two years ago in that gazebo. "How long have you been dancing?"

She shrugs. "Feels like forever. In Troyes, a local woman taught basic ballet. But when I moved here, Papa enrolled me in formal classes. Probably to get rid of me for a few extra hours."

"But you dance beautifully." My hands ball into fists. "I've been watching you, Katya. You deserve that spot in London."

"It's a paid scholarship for tuition and living expenses."

"Even if it wasn't, I'll pay whatever you need beyond the scholarship." I amble toward her again. "Either way, I can get you in there. Get you away from here. I can even have you enrolled under a different name, so your *Papa* never finds you."

"I don't want to look over my shoulder the rest of my life."

"You can stay married to me, or I'll give you a divorce when you go to London. I'll send you there with a guard. No one will bother you."

"Okay." Her cheeks redden.

That damn blush just fucking does something to me. She sits on the bed, bouncing to test the mattress that's never been used.

"Get dressed and meet me in the kitchen," I tell her. "I'll make you something to eat, and you can tell me all about your plans after you graduate."

Plans I will decimate if I decide I want her to be a real wife.

CHAPTER ELEVEN

KATYA

It takes me a few minutes after Lachlan leaves the room to realize I can drop the blanket again. My heart was pounding, and I felt every thumping beat when his fingers fondled my nipples. It's like nothing I've ever felt. I found it incredibly sexy that *my husband* is the first to touch me there, and it excited me.

Lachlan's reaction, however, confused me. He said at the church, our kiss was his first. My brain is wrapping around everything, and it's hard to keep it all straight. Lachlan O'Rourke isn't who I expected him to be.

He's...gentle. And thoughtful. To me, anyway.

I close the bedroom door he left open. The room is very basic, a rustic yet elegant design with a simple double bed and a crisp-white down comforter. The blue and cream quilt with matching pillow shams look untouched.

An open door across from the bed leads to a bathroom. In there, I get a gander at myself in the mirror. Nadia's attempt to cover my bruises failed miserably. Most of the eye shadow and foundation are gone. I look like a boxer after several rounds with a heavy-weight.

If anyone doesn't care what my face looks like, I bet it's Lachlan with that gigantic scar across his cheek. Now that we're married, I can ask him how he got it. All kinds of crazy rumors float around Astoria. From a knife fight with ten men, to stupid theories like one of his brothers did it when they were kids.

I won't ask him tonight, though.

I run the hot water and wipe the blood splatter from my skin with a warm washcloth, as Lachlan told me to do. Finally, I remove what's left of the pathetic makeup job. Bruises always look worse a day later. I'm not surprised by the purple blemish across my right eye, and the blue and yellow splotch staining my cheek. My upper lip is just one big scab. These bruises, poorly hidden under makeup, ignited Lachlan's kill switch and set this day in motion. How will he react to seeing them fully exposed?

Releasing the matronly bun that held my veil, I brush out all the disgusting hairspray and drape my hair across my shoulders. Because of that bun, and the veil being so thick, there's no blood in my hair, thankfully.

Nadia had packed a tote with clothes for me to change into for the plane ride. From that bag, I remove and put on my velour tracksuit. I skip the bra and pull a tank top over my head. My knuckles hitting my lip remind me of what I look like on the outside.

When I open the bedroom door, the smell of something cooking on the stove grabs me and my mouth waters. I turn the corner and, in the kitchen, Lachlan sets up plates with food. Looking up at me, his face tightens, but he doesn't mention my bruises.

He's removed the blood-covered suit jacket and moves about the kitchen in an unbuttoned white dress shirt. It dangles in front of his trousers, both speckled with Rahil's crimson sins.

"Grilled cheese?" he says, ignoring my face. "I don't know how to cook much else. I don't really care about food. It's fuel, and I eat whatever, wherever. I work nights and usually end up in the diner at some point to just fill my stomach."

I remember seeing him there a few weeks ago and how it made me feel. Now here I am, married to a man who seemed so far away at one time.

Climbing up on a stool, I say, "That's okay. I know how to cook. Yulia," I choke back a sob. "Papa's housekeeper, who was kind to me for so many years, taught me to cook and bake."

He pushes the plate toward me. "Give me a list of what you want, and I'll have it added to my grocery list."

"I can't shop for us?" I exhale and wait for the sandwich to cool down.

"Not alone."

"Papa said I only needed a driver because no one wanted to hurt me."

Lachlan snorts. "Either your father is stupid, or..."

"Or I am?" I fold my arms. "You can say it."

"Naïve. Not stupid. There's a big difference." He studies me, his eyes gently creeping across my face.

"I guess it was naïve of me to think I could stop myself from being taken to Russia."

"Your father obviously kept you sheltered. I don't think less of you, having to be rescued."

"You could have started a war."

"An all-out war between your father's Bratva and my family benefits no one. My father, Isabella's late father, and your father forged a workable truce years ago. The real enemies are people who steal and try to hurt us. We all have them. That's my job. To enforce the rules of doing business with the O'Rourkes."

"You sound much saner and more put together than Maksim. The guy foams at the mouth half the time when he talks."

"Because he's a fucking tool." Lachlan lifts his sandwich to take a bite but stops to stare at me. "Sorry."

I shake my head. "Don't censor yourself around me."

"You're a lady. We don't let filth drip off our lips like Neanderthals around women." His lips curl into a smirk, like he's considering another kind of filth to speak around me. "My father always respected my mother."

I learned from the friends I'd made at school that a man whose parents had a strong marriage would make a good husband. "Still, this is your house." I finger the warm sandwich and salivate at the cheesy goodness.

"This is your house now, too."

I chew quickly and put the sandwich down. "You keep saying things like that. Lachlan, you did me an enormous favor, but you don't have to stay married to me." I sit up. "If I get into the conservatory, I'll move to London, and you won't have to deal with me anymore." I watch his eyes for a reaction. But he's trained to keep his emotions off his face.

"*Deal* with you?" He bares his teeth, hungry for my answer.

I nibble on the sandwich, considering my response. "If I'm accepted into the conservatory, I'm almost guaranteed a job with a premier touring company. I prefer that. I want to see the world." I hop off the stool and twirl. Spins are easy, but I don't know my surroundings too well and slam into a wall of muscle.

"Easy, little one," Lachlan gruffly hisses.

From his open shirt, I feast on curved pecs, and a chaos of ink etched into his warm skin.

"I'm not little." I stand up to him because he seems to like it.

"Compared to me, you are."

Lachlan is *gigantic*. What would it feel like if he were on top of me, pounding into me? His delicate hold suggests I'm fragile in his arms. I can't go making promises of being tougher than I am. I can take a lot when it comes to punishing dance routines and practice sessions. I put my body through hell on a near-daily basis.

Rough sex with a man like Lachlan O'Rourke is something else.

"Do you call *every* woman little one?"

"I called Kieran's wife, Isabella, little one when I met her."

"I heard you refer to your brothers' wives as sisters."

"We don't use 'in-law.' If you have our name, you're part of this family." Lachlan strokes my cheek. His touch ignites a fire in my belly that sends pools of heat between my thighs. He stares down at me like he's affected, too. "As of this afternoon, your name is Katriane O'Rourke. You are one of us."

My lips tingle, thinking of that kiss at the church. The one that bound us together for life, according to God anyway.

What if my husband is really the devil, though?

*

With the warm grilled cheese in my stomach, exhaustion pulls me under. Feeling faint, I almost tumble off the stool.

Lachlan reaches over the island to catch me. "I got you. Time for bed."

When I'm steady, he swaggers around to my side and lifts me up. Next, he's carrying me down the hall, and deposits me into that empty spare room. Spare, I was Papa's spare. I hate feeling like this.

"Lachlan?" I say his name.

He purrs, "Katriane?"

"You don't love me or anything, right? That's not why you did this."

His posture stiffens, and he just stares at me, his eyes moving across each bruise with a heated gaze I feel. Heat from anger, though. "Aye. You don't love me either," he rasps.

"I don't know you. But in the few hours we've been

together, you've proven to be honorable and kind. I'm..." I reach for his hand and gasp at how big it is compared to mine. "I'm proud you're my husband."

"I'm a murderer, Katriane."

"So is my father. I understand the world we live in. It doesn't bother me if you kill people. Just don't hurt me."

His hand tightens around mine, and he lifts it to his chest. "Never. I will never hurt you. We don't hurt women." Despite his scar and scary size, Lachlan is utterly gorgeous. He has a head full of thick black hair and his sharp jaw, long nose, and round, gray eyes make him easy to stare at. I can drink him in.

"Can you kiss me goodnight?" My heart pounds again, remembering what his mouth felt like on mine. "You said we'll eventually have sex. We should start with a kiss."

I expected to spend a horrible night on a plane to Moscow and then ushered into a cold house where Rahil would have beaten me some more.

Lachlan keeps a steady gaze on my mouth. "Your lip."

"Yeah?" I consider other girls in school talking about how their boyfriends beg for blow jobs.

Lachlan's thumb gently brushes the fleshy part that's not throbbing. "I don't want to hurt you."

"When you kissed me earlier, I felt something." I drag in a breath. "Something...nice. Not pain."

"What *did* you feel?"

I can't say that my panties got damp. The whole situation was overwhelming, to be rescued and then claimed so viscerally like that.

I bring his hand to my stomach. "Butterflies, here. I wasn't expecting it. Are you saying you felt nothing when we kissed?"

"I didn't say that." He backs me against the wall next to the bathroom. "I'm a man, and you're a beautiful woman with a strong, sculpted body. You stood up to your father, and you're not afraid of me. I felt something I've never felt before." Bending down to take my mouth, he whispers, "Let me know if this hurts."

The air rearranges around me with *this* kiss. Heat rising in my blood, I sputter, "Doesn't hurt."

"Good. Now open for me, little wife."

At least he's not calling me little one. One. Short for No One. I am his wife, so I open for him, and his tongue finds mine. I've never been kissed with tongue, but my body knows what to do. Lachlan deepens the kiss, and it's perfect.

He tilts his head side to side each time, gently sliding his velvet tongue against mine with a little more force. A growl echoes from deep inside his chest. It's a butterfly frenzy in my stomach this time. My heart thunders against my ribs like it's trying to come out of my chest. I can't feel Lachlan's chest because he's hunched over me, but something stiff and long in his pants presses against my stomach.

I grip his massive biceps to pull him closer so our bodies fit tighter together.

Lachlan hisses when I lean into his erection. "*That* is from kissing you."

"I understand how sex works. I just never..." I clear my throat.

"I'll make your first time good. I promise." He cups my chin.

The way he's looking at me, and his manhood tenting his trousers, suggests he wants to rid me of this burden right now. Then what?

I'm not a fool. I know men like him have whores and mistresses. They use women's bodies to release tension and aggression. Their wives are for show. But that's not our arrangement. Not our deal. Yet, I'm in the devil's lair, and he's wearing a grin that melts me like molten lava.

"We should slow down." He steps away, veins in his neck ready to burst. "You've had a long day. And I want you fully healed before we…"

"Before we consummate?"

"Are you agreeing to make this marriage a physical one?"

"You made a huge sacrifice. If you're good to me and treat me well, I'll give myself to you."

He stalks toward me, backing me into the wall again. "I asked if *you* want us to be physical. Not what you think I want."

Perhaps I'm not seeing all this as clearly, or as dire as I should. Perhaps my bruises look a lot worse than they feel, or I'm in denial about what happened to me.

But he's right. If I'm not a virgin, my father has little use for me.

"Yes, I want us to be physical." I gently brush Lachlan's chest, his skin warm under my fingers. All these tattoos and scars intrigue me.

"Good." Lachlan's lips seal over mine again and without breaking contact, he rasps into my mouth, "I own you legally, but I want to own your body, too."

I consider arguing the owning part, but then he deepens the kiss again, his tongue stroking mine more passionately. He's not being as gentle. I don't mind the pain. It makes me feel alive. I thought I'd have to shut down and go numb.

Now all I want to do is feel.

CHAPTER TWELVE

LACHLAN

I've been crouched in a corner with bullets flying around me. I've been under a car that mowed me down. I've been trapped beneath a boat, gulping my last breath. My thoughts were always crystal clear, like the sheen of ice on a lake.

With Katya's body pressed against mine and the way she's kissing me, my thoughts splash around in a puddle of mud. I don't know what the hell I'm doing.

I never expected anything so soft and delicate could wreck me. I'm brutal in bed, don't know any other way to be. As fragile as Katya feels, there's a sexy strength in her grip. She's a physical powerhouse to dance the way she does. She'll need to channel that strength to handle me.

I vividly imagine and even *feel* my cock sliding into Katya based on the way her warm mouth feels.

At the training camp my da sent me to, I learned how to control my heartbeat. And emotions. Skills I excelled at because they came naturally to me. My lips on Katya destroy my defenses in both areas. My body feels like it's on fire, and my cock throbs painfully hard.

I'm a hammer for Kieran, and strike at the nails he and Riordan point at. I don't ask questions, and I give every arse-beating two hundred percent.

When Katya and I take this further and make this marriage a real one as far as pleasures of the flesh, I don't see how I'll easily bolt out of here when I get a call to deal with someone.

Katya is mine until she goes to London. And she

wants to spread her legs for me. That makes her extremely brave in my book, not shirking away like a waif. It makes me want her more. Test how much she can take. Life is tough. She needs thick skin to survive.

When Katya's moans turn sharp, my brain recognizes the sound of pain and not arousal. I pull off and she holds her lip. "Sorry, I was so into that kiss." She blushes. "I forgot my lip was bruised."

I push my forehead against hers. "No. I'm sorry. You're hurt. I need to be careful with you." This feels so different, holding back and not pouncing on something I want. "You need some sleep." My cock stirs as I gaze at my wife, who is rightfully mine to do with what I please. But she's hurt, and I'm not an asshole to women.

Katya throws herself against me with a gripping hug. Banging into my erection, she looks down, pink coloring her cheeks. "You're so sweet."

"Not always, little wife." I tug on my hard cock and step back before I scare her away.

Hiding her embarrassment, she looks around at the spare bedroom, barren except for a bed and tall bureau. "Okay."

My heart pinches, and I stroke my chest, wondering if I had a ministroke. I just don't get these fucking loopy feelings. "You can sleep in my bed tonight if you want." The words come out of my mouth in a seductive tenor.

A gorgeous smile forms on her bruised lip. "Are you sure?"

No. "Very." I take her by the hand.

She's mine and in the eyes of God to-boot. I said my vows right on the same altar where I listened and worshipped Father Eamon. With Katya's hand in mine, my marriage to her is the only thing I put my faith in now. My wife. And protecting her.

In my room, she glances around. "This looks

very...basic. Not too different from my room."

"I come here to pass out."

She holds her throat. "Do you mind if I just sleep in my track suit?"

"So long as you're comfortable, little wife."

"What do you sleep in?"

"Nothing."

"Oh." She loses her breath and gives me a once-over. "Don't change on my account." The hint of mischief in her voice tugs at my groin.

"Katya." I snap my belt off. "You need to be very careful with me. I'm not a giant teddy bear. I'm a dangerous grizzly who loves the smell of blood. You're my wife and I'll always respect you. But I will not be toyed with when it comes to sex." I lower my pants and briefs until my cock hangs heavy between my legs.

Stunned, she stares at my cock. "Oh..."

"Let's take all of this one day at a time." I remove my shirt, the fabric tearing when I yank it off my body. After kicking the pants away, I stand there. "Go ahead and look. This is me." I run a hand across all my scars and tattoos.

"You're...beautiful." She breathes heavily. "You look so...tough and strong."

"I am. No one will ever lay a hand on you again. You're mine now. With my name. That alone is protection."

Her stare wrecks me. I've never backed away from a female gazing at me while my cock is hard. I'm in unfamiliar territory. The day must end for a new one to start as I begin this journey with my new wife. My new life. Breaking her heated gaze, I move toward my bed.

Lifting the covers, I say, "Now get in my bed, and let's get some sleep."

She pulls back the covers to get in on the other side,

but I drag her against my chest. It just feels like the right thing to do. To hold a wife who's had a rough day, to say the least.

Even though I'm the one who looks like I lost a fight with a cheese grater.

*

I wake up on my stomach, my cock painfully hard.

Since I haven't had sex in a while, I've been coming in my sleep and waking up in messy sheets. I change them daily. Fuck, I'm actually throbbing.

I close my hand around my dick, the touch lighting me up. I groan, the pleasure in it taking my breath away.

A face forms in my mind: blonde hair, chocolate eyes, and a sweet smile. A smile on a mouth I'd love around my cock right fucking now. A vision of Katya Koslov kneeling before me in her bloody wedding dress, taking my cock down her throat, shoots into my brain.

Katya! What I did the day before rushes back at me. I'm married. I married Alexei Koslov's daughter. Fuck. Without opening my eyes, I breathe in her sweet scent.

As if drugged last night, I passed out after a few breaths holding her. Lying here naked with a hard cock next to a wife, my brain is completely rearranged, from pushing away the urge to fuck to craving it.

I'll toy with her beneath me. Destroy her for anyone else. The way I get excited from a man's pain, I'll salivate at my wife's pleasure from my hands, mouth, and a stiff cock. It's about ego, and mine is as big as Astoria.

Licking my lips and holding my cock, I turn my head to watch my wife sleep. I want to come picturing those lips, bruised or not, around my cock. Her fucked-up face angers me, but her strength turns me the fuck on. How tough she really is when she dances like a feather in the wind.

But Katya isn't next to me. The scent sucked into my

lungs came from her tracksuit jacket left behind on the bed. I reach into the nightstand for my gun. Not caring that I'm naked, I open my bedroom door with my Glock drawn. Calling out to her will give away that I'm awake. I step down the hall, the carpet fibers tickling my feet.

I smell…coffee.

After the hallway, the living room and kitchen are one in an open floor plan. The light from all the windows hit me. Sun streams in, like a spotlight.

Katya turns around and nearly drops a carafe of steaming black silkiness. "Oh. You're awake. Don't shoot. But it is decaf. Why do you have decaf?" she asks and doesn't address why I'm naked.

"I have no idea. Mix up with the grocery order, I guess." With my gun resting against my thigh, I strut up to her. "I woke up, and you weren't there."

"You were sleeping so nicely." Her tight, white tank top doesn't hide nipples that have hardened to thick nubs after she's had a look at me. "And you were…um…groaning a little."

"What?"

She pours me a cup, and I thank fuck for the kitchen island to hide my cock that is now so hard, it's leaking with pre-cum.

"You were on your stomach, moving your hips." She hands me the coffee. "Like you were having an erotic dream."

The vision hits me. My dream. I dreamt I fucked Katya right there on the church altar, her bloodied wedding dress pulled up, so I had access to her sweet cunt while I was completely naked. But instead of that Russian piece of shite bleeding out next to us, it was Father Eamon with a bullet hole in the head.

Then I cut off his dick and set him on fire. Felt very biblical.

I sneak a look at my cock, bobbing, breathing like he has a heartbeat. He wants Katya because she's mine.

She's ours!

I put my Glock on the kitchen island since she's not afraid of guns. "What is your schedule for these rehearsals you mentioned?" I ask to remove thoughts of me fucking her from my brain so I can form sentences.

She runs a hand through the crown of glistening blonde hair, twisted into one of those loose sexy braids she makes. "Starting next week, I rehearse every day with a choreographer. The audition is next month, remember?"

"Aye." I stare at her coffee mug that is the same as mine, not realizing I had a set. The utterly normal act of two people having morning joe is a stark reality strangled by how she actually ended up here.

Because I killed her fiancé.

"Rehearsals start at nine a.m. and go until around five p.m." Stress lines form over her cute nose.

I stop my sip midway to my mouth. "What?"

"I have to figure out how I'll get there. Papa's driver used to take me."

"I'll drive you," I say without a second thought. "And pick you up."

"Thank you." She looks around. "Where is your car?"

"I have three. They're in the garage." I have to think about whether or not she needs a guard. "Whatever you need, I'll take care of."

"I don't want to be a burden."

I roughly put the mug down. "You're not. Never think that."

"Okay. What's your schedule?" she asks as if I don't hurt people for a living.

"Nights. Usually."

She nods thoughtfully. "That means you need to sleep

during the day."

"I used to have breakfast with Riordan every morning before going to sleep."

"I won't get in the way of that. I'll take an Uber back and forth. If you're okay with someone picking me up here." She bites her lip. "But I don't have a phone anymore. Papa took mine away last week."

"I'll get you a phone. And Riordan's got a wife now, so I don't meet him anymore. I'll take you and pick you up from school. I'm strong, Katya. I've gone twenty-four, even thirty-six hours without sleep."

"Really? You slept soundly last night."

I think about that. Could the stress of what happened eclipsed what I normally deal with on the day to day? Did killing the man who hurt *her* tire me out that much? It takes a lot to bring me down.

"Then you'll sleep while I'm at rehearsals?"

"Aye."

"Okay." She perks up, looking excited. "Then when we get home, I'll make you a nice dinner before you go to work."

"Sounds like a plan." I throw back the entire mug of coffee, ignoring the burn in my throat. I round the island to pour a fresh cup when Katya gasps.

"Um, Lachlan. You're still naked." She stares at a full-frontal view of me.

Fuck, how did I forget that? Why does it feel so natural to be with her like this?

Her eyes glance at my dick, still hard. "Do you want me to take care of that?"

"Take care of what?"

Her warmth closes in on me. "Do you want me to make you...come."

"How do you know that word if you're a virgin?"

"I'm twenty. I have cable and streaming. Plus, girls at

school...talk." She bravely stares at my dick. "Although, I don't think anyone in my class has ever had anything that...big."

Fuck, I have to consummate this marriage. Ruin her, so her father can't abduct her and sell her to someone else. I need to keep her secure. That means violated, dripping with my cum. And with a big fucking smile on her face because she loves it. Loves me.

Can she? Love me?

Can I love her?

I take her by the arms and squeeze, testing how much she can take. "Let's get something straight here, Katya."

"Did I do something wrong?" The fear in her voice guts me.

"No." I pull her against my chest.

"Lachlan, you're still naked. And...stiff."

"I won't *make* you blow me," I blurt. "Ever."

"You wouldn't have to *make* me."

My eyes flutter with those damn sexy words coming off her lips. I stroke her chin, the bruises on her face enraging me. Whoever I thought she was is so completely wrong, it frightens me. Unless I saw what I wanted to see. A frail victim, I could protect. But Katya's no victim. She's bold and strong. Daring to take me on.

Fuck, I like that.

I take her hand and lay it on my cock. The electricity in her touch nearly brings me to my knees. I never came last night, so I'm close to exploding.

"You're so warm. And thick." She breathes heavily, staring down at my cock.

I jerk off, using her hand. Groaning, stars pop out behind my eyes and my hips start to move. "Christ, that's good."

With one tiny hand on my cock, her other hand strokes the planes of my abs. "You're so beautiful, Lachlan." She brings her mouth to kiss my chest, her full wet lips puckered against each bulging ridge.

"I'm gonna come, Katya. Let go."

"No way."

"It's gonna be messy."

"I'm not afraid of a little mess."

"Aw fuck." My climax erupts as I tilt my cock up, hot cum squirting from the slit and flowing down the side coats her hand and mine.

"Wow," she moans, her eyes glued to the cream show I just put on for her with my throbbing dick. She's not afraid of the stickiness and the lewdness of what I just did.

"Let me clean you up." I pin her against the sink, my excess cum wiped up on her ass in that delightful track suit as we wash our hands together under warm water.

The smell of her hair takes me back to my past, a time in my life when I felt innocent and hopeful. It's fresh and clean. All I've felt for years is wrecked and dirty.

Turning her head back to catch my eyes, she whispers, "Was that good?"

"That was the best hand job I ever had." I turn off the water and dry her hands along with mine.

Katya sounds too good to be true.

That's when things go spectacularly wrong.

*

My front door opens, and I reach for my Glock. I shoot, emptying my clip, I'm so wired, leaving gaping holes in the wall.

"Lachlan!" Griffin hits the floor. "Check your damn phone. I sent you a text that I was stopping by about that lowlife's brother who Priscilla deboned the other day."

"Oh, geez!" Katya rushes to Griffin and helps him stand up. "Lachlan! Go put some clothes on."

The way she orders me around stills me,

105

then…fuck…arouses me.

Griffin gets to his feet and stops my wife from picking up his phone. "I got it." He sneaks a look at me standing here with no clothes on. "You guys are getting along, aye?"

I should be mad at him, but he's my top lieutenant and aside from my brothers, my best friend.

"We are." Katya shrugs like this is all no big deal, like I *didn't* just riddle my wall with bullets.

"I have to go see a cardiologist to make sure I didn't have a heart attack just now." Griffin keeps his eyes off me. "I'm checking in with the guards. Meet me down there."

"10-4, Quinlan," I say, not covering up. It's my damn house! "Get someone to come up here and patch these holes."

"Aye," Griffin says, leaving and not looking back.

Katya comes up beside me, gawking at my new bullet-riddled wall. "Nice shot. Good grouping."

I stare down at her again, amazed at how nothing scares her. "Are you hungry?"

"I am." She nods.

"Let's get dressed, and I'll take you out for breakfast." I think my word is final, but I catch Katya touching her face.

"Um." Pain shows in her eyes.

I halt my steps. "Unless you're concerned being seen with bruises." Not that anyone would think I gave them to her. It's well known how we treat our women.

She straightens her spine. "No. I don't mind. I'm sure what's happened has gotten around the city. I won't hide."

I stroke her hair. "Good girl."

"I'll go put some clothes on." She looks down. "That aren't so messy." With mischief in her eyes, she saunters down the hall toward her bedroom.

I get to my room and dress easily since most of my clothes are black. Black pants, black shirts, and a long trench coat. But it's July, so I swap out a white T-shirt and a light jacket. I never leave home without two guns and a knife, so I always need some kind of coat.

I return to the living room to find Katya dressed in a light green dress with a cute denim jacket over it. Her hair is in a high ponytail and when she turns to me, she smiles with a face full of bruises sitting on her skin like a badge of honor.

I need a tough woman, and fuck, she's made of iron.

I steer her to a short breezeway that leads to my garage. I use my phone to unlock the door and it opens with a sigh. The smell of rubber greets me as overhead lights flash on in succession, brightening the three-bay garage.

"We'll take this car for breakfast." From my phone, I pull up the Vette's icon and start the engine. It hums to life.

"Wow, a Corvette." She sounds so enthusiastic, it's fucking addicting. "You fit into this?"

"I had it specially built for me." I step to the passenger side and open the door for her. Before Katya gets in, I say, "I always open this door for you. Do you understand? Getting in and out."

"So chivalrous."

"That and it might be unsafe. I don't expect you to see what I see. To watch out for danger the way I do. That's my job. Not yours. I protect *you*."

"Like I said, chivalrous." She gets in and strokes the leather dash. "This is gorgeous."

"It is now." I run a hand across her shoulder. "Now that you're in it."

"Thank you." She sounds sad.

"What?"

"Do you really find me attractive, or are you just being nice?"

Her question hits me. "I don't find you attractive."

She exhales, fingering her bruised lip. "That's okay. You clearly didn't marry me for my looks."

That's a minefield because she's right. I planned to marry her because she was being sold to that disgusting prick. I decided to *kill* him when I saw her fucked-up face.

"Katya," I growl at her.

"Yeah?" She looks at me with huge glassy eyes.

I crouch down. "I find you fucking beautiful. And not just your face. You're sweet and graceful. You're kind and decent." Then I lower my voice. "As soon as your lips heal, I can't wait to see this pretty mouth wrapped around my cock." That mouth tips open and it's too much, so I softly close it. "As I was saying. You grew up with wealth and privilege, but you seem so very real. Like my sister."

"You seem very down to earth, too." She rests her hand so easily on my knee. "As far as growing up with money."

"Kieran soaked up the king's role, moved into the mansion we grew up in. His wife drips with diamonds. It's a show of power. I get that. That's not me. I keep it real."

She nods. "I felt the same way about Stasia. She was Papa's diamond. I had no illusions that I'd live her life."

"I think we're going to get along perfectly." I drop a kiss on her forehead and close her door.

I slide into the driver's seat, carefully folding my bulky body behind the wheel. After tapping an icon on my phone, one of the garage bay doors opens. The hot sun shines through the windshield, blinding me for a moment, and I feel exposed. Seen.

I've kept my entire existence in the shadows. My past ticks like a bomb waiting to go off and hurt my family. In less than twenty-four hours, I've opened myself up to someone who can not only steal my sanity, but might very well steal my heart.

CHAPTER THIRTEEN

KATYA

During a big breakfast at the diner, Lachlan tells me about his mother having MS and twitches while talking about it. When I ask when I'll meet her, he doesn't respond.

We stop at a pharmacy, and he shuts off his car's engine. "Do you need anything? That special ointment for your lip should be ready."

"I don't think I need anything else." Maya had packed up my entire bathroom. "Can I come inside with you?"

"Of course."

I stay put and let him come around to open my door. It's a simple gesture, but for the first time, I feel important. I *am* important to Lachlan. I'm his wife, and that means something to him. Even if it's just symbolic. Even if I'm just his property. Men are very possessive about what belongs to them.

We get inside, and he nudges my arm. "Do not leave here without me, okay?"

I get chills. "Okay."

He walks off, and it hits me hard. How Lachlan fully supports me auditioning for the London conservatory and my daily rehearsal schedule. He even agreed to drive me back and forth to school every day. My only worry is I'm penniless and completely dependent on him. But if I'm picked to attend the conservatory, I'm guaranteed years of work, dancing on the grandest stages around the world. I can make a living and completely support myself. I won't need anyone. That plan made perfect sense, especially knowing Papa had no use for me.

But Lachlan has a use for me, and with a tool that will break me in half. Good heavens. How in the world will that fit inside me?

I got plenty tingly jerking Lachlan off, standing in his kitchen stark naked. When I changed my clothes after our little hand-job interlude, my panties were so damp, I had put fresh ones on.

The way his cum bubbled and poured from his manhood was such an erotic turn on. His eyes closed, his head thrown back with chorded throat muscles, he looked vulnerable and disconnected from the world. I was his only bridge. I like how that felt.

I wander into the feminine product aisle. Perhaps some lubricant to feel sexy and slick will work when we... I get dizzy thinking of that massive body on top of me.

I find a brand I'd heard of, but I don't have any money. How do I ask Lachlan to buy it for me? Maybe he won't mind.

"Hang on, don't ring me up." Lachlan's deep voice sails over the aisles, finds me, and tears into my soul. "I need one more thing."

I watch the top of his rumpled, dark hair amble toward the aisle I'm in. Panicking, I step behind a cardboard display when he turns the corner. What could he want with the feminine aisle? He stops short at a rack of...condoms. A shiver goes through me. He's buying condoms.

For a moment, my heart hurts, thinking he keeps a steady woman on the side, a mistress, and they are for her. He found the display with such alacrity and confidence, an unthinking mental practice. Clearly, he does this *all the time.*

Irrational jealously fires through me.

But Lachlan pulls a box off so roughly, the peg falls out. He sneers at the boxes spilled on the carpet and walks away. When he's back at the register, I check out what brand he picked.

Durex Extra *Extra* Large.

Ultra Ribbed for Her Pleasure.

I'm mesmerized when a shadow crosses over me. I look up and there's Lachlan, holding the box he took from the rack, staring at me. "Oh, there you are."

"Um...I was further down the aisle. You didn't see me."

"I didn't?" His scarred cheek ticks up, like he can't believe he missed me standing there.

"Okay. Confession," I whisper, feeling busted. "I hid. I wanted to give you privacy."

"I see." He fists the box in his hand. "I grabbed this, but I came here to put it back."

Mixed emotions flood me. He changed his mind about sleeping with someone else. "Oh."

He smirks and says gruffly, "The guy at the register told me they have the bigger box count now." Stroking my hair, he says, "I don't have any at the house. I don't sleep with women there."

His seductive promise tightens my throat. "Ever?"

"Never."

I let go of a breath. "You mean you bought those for me? For us?"

His jaw tightens when I say *us*. "Of course, they're for you. *Us*." Leaning down at me, he adds, "I have no intention of being unfaithful to my wife."

"Me neither. I mean, to my husband," I say, getting choked up. "I would never..."

"I believe you." He reaches around me, his scruffy cheek brushing against mine. "I think." He whisks the lubricant away from me.

My body sears hot. "I saw and felt how big you are. I thought maybe I'd need a little help."

"I'll buy that if you want." He strokes the outer rim of my sore lip, his touch miraculously making me feel better. "If it will make fucking me easier for you."

"I don't know. I've never done it before."

"I know, little wife." He stares down at me. "I'm dying a little more each time we touch, thinking of how bad I want to push inside your tight cunt and *really* make you mine."

His shockingly graphic confession makes my center throb. "Will you go easy on me?"

"I'm not sure I can." He grins deliciously, holding a mega pack of condoms. "It's been a really long time for me."

That's how he didn't realize his favorite condoms now come in a jumbo pack.

*

We walk in silence to Lachlan's car, his arm draped across the small of my back. Him saying he's not sure he can be gentle with me because he hasn't been with a woman in a long time weighs heavily on mind. But also has my body buzzing with need. Preoccupied, I almost miss the large banner on the plate-glass window to my old dance studio.

CLOSED

Stopping short, I press my hands against the glass. "Oh, no."

"What?" Lachlan comes up behind me.

Our reflection takes up almost the whole window. My tiny body superimposed with his looks romantic. "This is where I took dance lessons. Miss Theresa taught me ever since I moved here." I crane my neck up. "Why is it closed?"

Lachlan shrugs. "I don't know."

"I don't understand. It was open a month ago. I stopped by to tell Miss Theresa about my audition for the London conservatory. She made a video recommendation for me." My breathing goes shallow. "She didn't die, did she?"

"I don't know, little wife." He pets my head, then gets on his phone.

"What are you doing?"

"Follow me." He takes my hand and leads me down the narrow alley to the back of the studio. "Balor, Miss Theresa's Dance Oasis on Mayfair. Why is it closed? Okay, call me back. Oh wait, there's an electronic lock on the back door, can you—" He's interrupted by a click as the knob turns.

"We can't break in!" I look around. "Miss Theresa lives here in Astoria. She might come by and see us."

"It's not breaking in. It opened on its own." Lachlan winks.

Curiosity itches under my skin that maybe there's a clue inside to why she closed down. I follow Lachlan as if I have a choice, because he's holding my hand. He's always holding my hand.

The smell of the varnished floors hits me, reminding me how much I miss coming here. After *Maman* brought me to Papa's, this was the only place I didn't feel so alone. Stasia was a moody teenage girl who didn't have time for me in the early years. We got closer later on. For a long time, this studio was the only place I felt happy, and where I could be myself. And now it's gone. I double over with emotion, struggling to breathe.

"Katya?" Lachlan soothes my back with a meaty hand.

"I'm all right. This studio closing feels like such a loss. Like someone died."

Lachlan's phone rings. "Yeah, Bale. Uh huh. Thanks. Any cameras still hooked up in here? They're turned off?

Okay. Talk later." He puts his phone away. "Miss Theresa's husband retired, and they moved to the Hamptons."

"Really?" I scratch my head and wonder why she didn't mention it to me when I saw her last month. "That means she's okay?"

"Apparently."

"I'd like to go see her. I've been to the Hamptons with Papa and Stasia. You can give me a driver, or I can take the train to get out there."

Ringed and tattooed, Lachlan's middle finger rests at the base of my throat. "You don't take a train by yourself. I'll take you. My sister lives in East Hampton."

"Oh! Maybe we can spend weekends there visiting her."

He frowns. "Actually... We don't *hang out* there. We don't want to draw attention to her. But we can visit Miss Theresa if you want."

"I'd like that." I look down at the blonde-wood floorboards.

"When you're healed, we'll go see her." He strokes my ponytail.

"Right." I consider my bruises and what she'd think.

"Are you ready to go home?"

"Sure." I let him lead me out the back door, but stop. "No. Actually, can I..."

"Can you what?" When I don't respond, he cups my chin. "Never be afraid to ask me for something. I'm your husband."

"When I would stop by, Miss Theresa let me do a routine for the class." My gaze cuts across the room and a memory dissolves of me in a line of other pre-teens. Many whose mamas forced lessons on them. Lessons I adored, lessons that became my salvation.

Much like Lachlan is now.

At times, I felt I was the only student who wanted to be here. Miss Theresa saw that and gave me the most complicated parts for solos. It helped me. My heart swells at how she shaped me. I don't think I ever really thanked her.

"Can I do a short routine I showed the little girls when I came here?"

"Of course." He squeezes my shoulder and steps away to lean against the mirrored wall.

The light coming in from Mayfair Street stills me. "Oh, we're still trespassing."

"No one will bother you. Even if a cop shows up, I'll—"

"Lachlan! You can't hurt a police officer!"

He barks a laugh. "We own the police in this city. Dance for me, little wife."

"Okay." I place my shoulder bag on the floor, but Lachlan picks it up and holds it against his chest. It's one of the few purses I had and found it packed in one of my suitcases. Nadia had collected my wallet and passport earlier that day. She must have dropped them off after dealing with Rahil's body. They ended up in one of the bags. All my credit cards and the little bit of cash I had in my wallet were gone, though.

It doesn't matter. I'm penniless but married to a rich man who says he'll give me anything I want.

Standing in the middle of the studio, I fall back into a time when I was so happy to be here. It's not hard to reach. I'm happy now, too. Lachlan's made me happy. Or is it that I just feel relieved and safe? I never felt in danger before. Papa surrounded his compound with guards and guns.

Maybe I fooled myself, never thinking he'd do what he did to me.

I sneak a look at my husband, and my breath leaves me

116

how handsome he really is. The compassion in his eyes guts me. How can this man, who's so kind to me, be a *murderer?*

I close my eyes. And the routine ingrained in my head takes over as I move through a set of classic dance steps. I swish my feet back and forth, then lift my hands over my head like a halo. With space around me, I feel a little daring. I let my edgier side shine through. I don't have impressionable young girls or my teacher here. But there is someone I wish to impress.

I bend in half, my butt sticking out toward my husband. Peeking at him between my calves, I see him smiling. A little too much.

I flit across the floor in leg lifts and hops. Ending in a twirling tornado of a dozen pirouettes followed by a row of leaps in a tight circle, my legs easily spread wide.

Lachlan moves to the middle of the dance floor on the other side, softly clapping.

I smile and find myself directly across from him. Feeling silly, I say, "Stand right there."

He wiggles his big feet in big shoes into the varnished floor, being playful.

I kick off my back right leg and barrel toward him. His eyes go wide, and when I leap, his giant arms catch me. I'm so high up, it's dizzying. I've never had a catch partner so tall. But I'm not afraid.

Lachlan lowers me as I slide down his body. He's warm, and the friction is electric. When our heads come together, he kisses me. Deep and sultry.

"I like this," he rasps. "I didn't think I'd like this so much. The way you kiss me, like your mouth was made for me. You taste so sweet and soft. That I can be delicate and not brutal, like the world I live in when we're in this bubble." He releases me, and his eyes go dark. "It's easy to become heartless and lose touch with humanity. I... I was facing that, you know. Going to the dark side completely." He easily opens up to me.

"I watched Maksim go mad."

"It's called bloodlust. It's got a chokehold on Maksim for sure. That and all the drugs he's polluting his body with. I know people think I'm insane." Lachlan scrubs a hand down the back of his neck. "There's one central focus to our world. We protect my brother, Kieran. That includes his reputation. He expects me to do my job ruthlessly, but I can't be unhinged. I want to be feared, not despised and considered inhuman." His voice goes emotionless. "I never planned to get married."

My breath sticks in my lungs. "Never, ever?"

"No." He peers down at me, his lips twitching. "I wanted to be a priest."

Shocked, I say, "Really?"

He was the altar boy not named in the article. *He* was there when the boy's father accused the priest. *He* was there when that man died.

Then the priest died, too.

Lachlan's hand strokes my throat, and I feel so utterly at his mercy. "Really. Not marrying came with the life I originally wanted."

"That meant you planned to go your whole life without sex, too?"

"Aye," he says easily, but his fingers tighten around my neck.

"And I guess when you decided you would not be a priest—"

"I didn't decide. It was taken from me. I was sent away."

"To where?"

"Too many questions, little wife." He brushes his mouth over mine. "My past is dark and brutal. You're sunshine and goodness. Don't concern yourself with my past. Just worry about today and tomorrow."

Yesterday, I was almost forcibly married to a man who beat me. Today, I woke up married next to another man, who killed him.

What in the world will tomorrow bring for me?

CHAPTER FOURTEEN

KATYA

I sleep in Lachlan's bed again. Turns out he's a fan of *The Big Bang Theory* like me. We laugh at the same punch lines. The guy has a wicked sense of humor. He's smart, too.

When a movie previews after the show, I say, "I've been wanting to see that. Can we watch it?"

"Of course." He sits lazily on his California King, shirtless with black sweatpants. God, he's beautiful. Even with the scars all over his body. So very male and strong. I feel so safe with him.

"Thank you," I say, getting up. "I'm going to make popcorn."

Balor dropped off a new phone for me, and I ordered microwave popcorn from the app Lachlan uses to get his groceries. One of Lachlan's guards picked it up and left it on the doorstep. I microwave the popcorn and bring it back to the bed. Sitting up with his warm ivory, damaged skin, Lachlan looks perfect against the rough texture of the tufted, black leather headboard.

"Are you okay with me eating in your bed?" I ask him, holding the bowl in front of me.

"Are you a messy eater?"

"No," I answer quickly. "Will you be mad if I drop a few kernels?"

A dark eyebrow arches into his forehead. "You'll have to test me." His voice is laced with carnal temptation.

I climb in and playfully drop a few on the bed. "Oh,

"Bad girl." He picks up a dropped kernel, but instead of putting it back in the bowl, he pops it into his mouth. He teases me with those full lips folding in the snack. Before I can pick another bite, he reaches in, and I think he'll eat that, too. But he lifts it to my lips. "Open for me, little wife." His deep voice pulls at my core.

I do and let him drop the popped corn on my tongue.

He growls. "Show me that tongue again."

I chew and swallow. "What?"

He picks up another piece of popped corn. "Open."

Feeling bold, I slide my tongue out. The bowl is pushed aside and he pulls me under him. His knees spread, creating a pocket for me to lie under him without being crushed, but I'm fully caged. He tugs down the thin strap of my tank top, exposing a hard nipple. I gasp when his lips close around the aching nub.

"You're fucking sweet," he groans into my skin.

"That feels so good, Lachlan."

Saying his name, lifts his eyes to me. "Your face looks like it's healing." He strokes my sensitive cheek. "Good."

The ointment I've been putting on my lip has sped up the healing process and the ice packs I rotate on my eye and cheek have brought the swelling and bruising down. "I like the way you look at me."

"I like the way you look at me. With no fear." He lowers his mouth to me and sips from my lips. "Is this okay?"

"It's so okay."

Low and throaty, he says, "You like kissing me?"

"I do." I let him devour me, and it gets wild, like a pack of firecrackers going off all at once. His velvety tongue strokes mine in a carnal rhythm. Somehow, I know what to do, to kiss him the way he wants. Even how to close my mouth around his tongue.

His eyes fly open, and he squeezes my hips. "What

time do you need to be at school tomorrow?" he asks with his hard length rubbing against me.

I know I told him, but he's got a lot on his mind. "Nine a.m. We'll need to leave here around eight."

He glances at the clock. It's coming up on ten p.m. "I'll need more time than that."

He rolls back, but keeps our hips touching. At one point, he puts his arm around me, feeding me on and off.

When the movie starts, he gently kisses my forehead. "I really like kissing you, and I want more of it. I want all of you, Katya."

I never thought I'd feel like this, considering how I ended up in Astoria...

CHAPTER FIFTEEN

KATRIANE - AGE 12

"Sommes-nous déjà là, maman?"

"En Anglais, ma petite fille."

"Are we there yet, *Maman*?" I grip the car's headrest from the backseat where we're both sitting to see out the front window.

"Soon. Do you remember I told you to be a good girl today?"

"Oui."

"*Yes*, Katriane. Yes. You *must* speak English from now on."

"Yes, *Maman*." I learned English from my tutor, but *Maman* and all our servants speak French.

"Soon you will learn Russian," *Maman* mutters, a shaking hand in front of her mouth.

"Russian?" I glance at her.

"Oui," she whispers, then looks out the window suddenly. "Here! We are here."

The driver slams on the brakes. "Ma'am, we have a problem."

He signals for her to look out the windshield. At a gate in between two tall stone columns, three men in suits approach the car carrying guns. They must be fake. Who walks around carrying guns like that?

"Let me handle this." *Maman* rolls down her window.

"This street is private property, Miss. Tell your driver to turn around," a man with sunglasses says, pointing his gun at the ground.

"Is that thing real?" I ask, but *Maman* quickly

shushes me.

"It is very real, child." The man looks inside the car and stares at *Maman's* legs.

Maman is beautiful, and many men pay attention to her. "I'm here to see Alexei," she says, pinching her skirt upward.

"Pakhan *Koslov* is busy."

"Tell him it is Loria."

"Ma'am, he does not see people without appointments."

"I have something better than an appointment." *Maman* unbuckles my seatbelt and lifts me onto her lap. "I have his daughter."

My heart jumps into my throat. "Que, *Maman*?" She told me my papa was in heaven.

"*Shhh*, Kat." She squeezes me. "What is your name, guard? I *will* get in touch with Alexei. He has enemies in this city, yes? I bet *they* will grant me an audience. Do you want to be the man who turned his daughter away, only to be handed over to an enemy?"

"*Maman*," I whisper, and her fingers tighten around my waist even harder. "You're hurting me, *Maman*."

The man looks at me, and when our eyes lock, he steps back. He speaks into a microphone at his wrist, like I've seen our guards back home in Troyes use. I don't understand what he's saying. The words sound rough, and his voice is deep.

Must be Russian...

He drops his hand and opens *Maman's* door. "Come with me, Miss. You and the child. Tell your driver to leave."

"No problem," the driver mutters, pinching his collar.

"Hold my hand and do not say a word, Kat," *Maman* hisses at me as the guard helps her out of the car.

The driver opens the trunk and more men wearing

suits and carrying guns take our luggage. I glance around and beyond the now-opened gate, a paved driveway curves up a hill like the yellow brick road in *The Wizard of Oz*.

Father. Whoever lives here is my father? I'm so confused.

Maman holds my hand and walks with her head held high, past even more men with more guns. She's so beautiful with her long dark hair always brushed and styled so nicely.

I hear static as we walk by more guards as they frantically whisper into walkie talkies. They don't look at *Maman*. They *gawk* at me. We climb the steep hill toward the massive house for what feels like forever. Pretty pink trees line the upper part of the driveway, and white flowers sit in painted boxes beneath every window.

More men in dark suits stand in front of a majestic house made of stone. I'm amazed at how big it is. Long, really. Tan and brown with fancy windows and black shutters go on forever. A man in a white suit steps out from behind the long line of men in black suits.

He doesn't smile and *doesn't* look at me. His eyes are glued to *Maman*. I peek up and see she's smiling. But I don't think she's happy. Her hand is sweaty in mine and crushing my fingers.

The man wearing white yells at the guards, and they scatter down the lawn to where we walked from. *Maman* keeps strolling, but the man we're here to see holds up his hand.

"Loria." He says her name harshly. "You shouldn't be here. My wife…"

"Your wife is dead." *Maman* bows her head. "My condolences."

The man's eyes land on me. "Who is this?"

"This is your daughter, Alexei."

I feel dizzy. *Maman* told me so many times Grandpapa was all the father I needed. But lately, he and *Maman* have been arguing. Then two days ago, one of the maids started packing all my clothes into a suitcase.

"Do you know how many *shlyukhas* tell me this?"

"You dare to call me a whore? In front of our daughter? You told me you loved me. That *I* was the only woman you—" She stops talking when the man takes a step toward us.

"*Quiet*. My daughter is in the kitchen having lunch."

"Your *other* daughter. Katriane is your daughter, too." *Maman* smooths her dress. "I learned I was pregnant months after you...you told me it was over."

"You could have at least given her a Russian name."

She holds my hand against her chest. "Call her Katya. She's only twelve, Alexei. Here is her birth certificate. I gave her your last name and listed you as the father because you *are* her father." She shoves a brown envelope at him.

Guns click all around us when *Maman* touches him, but he screams something to them in that yucky language, and they back off.

"What do you want, Loria?" He pulls her close to him, and I shudder with fear when she gasps.

Maman drops my hand. "We are here to live with you."

I tug on her dress. "*Maman?*"

"Shhh, Katya." She winks at me. "Alexei, I gave you time to mourn the wife you had no love for. A wife you were forced to marry at eighteen."

"You make dangerous presumptions." The man who *Maman* says is my father lets her go and looks at me, clutched to her skirt. Our eyes lock, and he's the meanest man I've ever seen, but a few seconds later, his eyes soften on me. "Yulia!" he yells over his shoulder.

Still clutched to my mother's hip, an older woman in a

gray dress appears on a covered porch.

"Da, sir?" She curtsies to him.

He speaks to her in that language I don't understand. Whatever he's saying draws a shock of surprise on the gray woman's face. "Bring the child inside the house."

Maman relaxes and gives me a little push. In French, she says, *"It is all right, Katriane. He accepts you. We'll be fine now. We're home."*

The man makes squinty eyes at her like he understands what she's saying.

"Come with me, little girl." The woman named Yulia reaches for my hand.

"Go, *Katya*," *Maman* stresses the strange name again.

Yulia's hand is warm and envelops mine. When we go inside the house, it makes me dizzy, it's so big. Scary large pictures line the walls of a hallway. It smells funny, too.

"I want to go home."

Yulia holds my chin. "I think you are home, child. Your mother is leaving now."

"Que?" I spin around and see the man in white dragging *Maman* by her arm down the driveway. "Where is she going?"

The man in white shoves her in a car, yelling something at her. And then the car drives off.

She's leaving me!

"Maman!" I scream and break away, my fingers slipping through Yulia's tight hold. I make it out of the house and run down the hill, but I trip and skin my knees.

A man in a dark suit picks me up. *"Privet,* kid. Be careful."

"Laissez-moi passer!" I scream for him to let me go, but he grabs me and pulls me back up the hill.

Yulia hurries to me. "Take your rough hands off that

child. Oh goodness. She is hurt. Give her to me."

The man in the dark suit lets me go, and Yulia pulls me against her chest. She's soft and smells sweet. Like sugar. "She left me! *Maman* left me. Is she coming back, miss?"

"Yulia. Call me Yulia." She holds me, shushing my tears. "Perhaps she will be back tomorrow. Come now, let me look at your cuts." Yulia brings me back inside the house and into a bathroom. "Your name is Katya?"

"Katriane," I say with emphasis on the r.

"*Français?*"

"*Oui.*"

She speaks French to me as she tells me it will be all right, that no one will hurt me here. She cleans my wounds, the strange smelling liquid cooling my cut. But then a wicked sting makes my legs kick.

Yulia smiles at me, and steers me out of the bathroom. In the hallway with the scary pictures, her lips go flat seeing the man in white who waits for us. The nice woman holds me against her chest. She says something to the man in that other icky language. When he reaches for me, Yulia, holds me tighter.

He barks something to her, and she releases me a second later. Yulia bows her head and scurries off. I'm terrified to be alone with this man.

He stares at me, his eyes narrowing to slits. His cold fingers slide under my chin as he turns my head from left to right. "A doctor is on the way."

"My...my knees are fine, sir. That woman—"

"Not for your knees. To test you." His hand sweeps across my cheek. "You look much like my mama. Still, I need to be sure. Come, I will introduce you to your sister."

"Sister?" I squeak, asking him. "I have a sister? How old is she?"

The man in white glares down at me. "Fourteen. How

old are you?"

"Twelve, sir," I say on a painful swallow.

His eyes slip closed, and he pinches his jacket's lapel where *Maman* shoved papers into his pocket. "Follow me." He steers me deeper into this massive scary house. "Are you hungry?"

"Um. No, sir."

He stops and stares down at me. "You may call me Papa."

"Wha... Why, sir?" I feel like this is a bad dream.

"Because I am your papa, as your mother said."

Maman, where is she? I'm afraid to ask, afraid of everything, so I just whisper, "Okay, sir."

The man walks ahead, and I follow him through twists and turns in the huge house. I don't know how I'll remember my way around. We turn a sharp corner, and there's a wide staircase with red carpeting like I've seen in movies. Is that what this is? Am I on a movie set?

When the man climbs the stairs, the whooshing of his pant legs drowns out any sound I would make following him. It takes him a moment to realize I'm not behind him. I can't move.

"Child?" The man stares curiously at me from over his shoulder.

"*Maman* said I do not go upstairs in a stranger's house."

"I am not a stranger. And this is not a strange house. I am your father, and you live here now."

I feel dizzy. How can this be happening? Yesterday I woke up in my bedroom in Troyes, the sun shining and birds chirping, eating my favorite breakfast with Grandpapa, the person I loved with all my heart after *Maman*. Now, I'm stuck in darkness with a strange language and smells. I don't like this. I don't want to be here.

A man holding my suitcases appears at my side. He speaks to the man in white in that language again.

"Da," the man in black says, and jogs up the stairs past the man in white.

"Those are my suitcases."

"He is bringing them to your room. Yulia will get you whatever else you need." The man in white turns and keeps walking.

I follow him since all my clothes and toys were brought to the second floor.

Muffled music fills the narrow hallway, and the man in white throws a door open. "*Anastasia!* Lower that awful excuse for music."

I wonder if he's speaking English so I can understand.

"Oh, Papa." A girl with beautiful long blonde hair like me comes to the doorway. She's wearing jean shorts and a bright, flowery top that sits off her shoulders.

I self-consciously pinch the tips of my plain tan coat, feeling awkward and out of place. Her legs are long and smooth. She's only two years older than me, but she looks so grown up.

Maman doesn't let me shave my legs yet, and they are very hairy. A sister. I have a sister? Maybe she'll show me how to shave my legs.

"Who's that?" Anastasia points at me.

"This is your sister, Katya." The man uses that name I don't like.

"What?" Anastasia's eyes bulge. "Is she adopted?"

"*Nyet.*" The man shakes his head. "Anastasia, go wait in my office. I will explain everything to you. You are old enough to know the truth."

"When the song is over." The girl slams her door shut.

I giggle. I'm only twelve, but I can tell whoever this man is, he's very powerful. He lives in this big, nice house surrounded by men with guns. But his daughter isn't afraid of him.

Maybe I don't need to be afraid of him either.

The man who says he's my father turns to me. "Your room is there." He points to a door across from Anastasia. "Yulia will help you make it however you want. Go."

"Go?"

"To your room."

"What... What about school?" I was really looking forward to my second year in *le collège*.

The man rolls his eyes. "Yulia will take care of that."

"And the doctor you mentioned?"

"I do not think I need the doctor." He brushes a hand down my cheek. "I believe you are mine, Katya."

"My name is Katriane, sir." I feel dizzy again, and I might throw up all over this ugly carpet.

"In this house, with me, you are Katya. Katya Koslov."

I feel the walls close around me, and I force pretty music into my head. When Yulia held me, it felt nice. She smelled nice. I miss her. Where is she? Seeing the man waiting for a response, I curtsy. "Yes, sir."

"Oh gawd, don't curtsy to him. He thinks he's a king already," Anastasia comments, leaving her room. She walks with a spring in her step, so comfortable around here. If she's comfortable, maybe I can be comfortable, too.

"You're a king?" My papa is a king? Does that make me a princess? I'm starting to think differently now about all this. Who doesn't want to be a princess?

"Da, I am pakhan. People bow to me and respect me." He folds his arms. "You will do the same."

"Yes, sir." I bow, wondering who will bow to me if I'm a princess. "Will Yulia be in my room soon?"

"Da. Whatever you need, Yulia will take care of it." He turns to walk away.

"What about you? What if I need something from you?"

"Like what?" His cold blue eyes make me shiver.

Like love? This man is supposedly my father. My friends back home in Troyes have nice fathers. They sit on their papas' laps and get hugs. Something tells me this man hasn't hugged anyone in a very long time.

"Nothing, sir." My father is a king, and kings are very busy. "I won't need anything from you."

CHAPTER SIXTEEN

LACHLAN

"Lachlan, are we grabbing that guy or not?" Griffin knocks me out of my thoughts.

Thoughts that have not stopped firing through me, reliving how I kissed Katya in my bed last night, and how close I came to fucking her. She felt so warm, and my body seized with a fiery lust I've never felt before.

I'm hard all the time now because I can't stop thinking about my wife.

Sitting in an alleyway, staring at the back door of a dive bar, I say, "I'll snap his neck."

This guy I need to hurt isn't our usual troublemaker, someone who got in bed with us and then fucked us over, knowing the consequences.

This is what we call a civilian.

"He deserves to have his neck snapped." Griffin shifts his gaze to me. "He's blabbing all over the city how some brunette with scarred arms castrated his brother. People are going to put it together that it was Priscilla."

Feeling rage, I push out of the car. Five minutes later, we're in a field behind the bar, and the guy's neck is under my shoe.

"*Lachlan* O'Rourke. That's the only name you need to concern yourself with. Your brother raped that college girl and got what he deserved. Don't make us cut off your dick, too, *and* your tongue."

The lowlife rustles for a breath beneath my foot.

"That's blood in your throat, mate," Griffin mocks his pain. "Blink twice that you don't want to lose your pecker *and* your tongue." My lieutenant laughs and looks at me. "He agrees."

I lift off the rat, but he stays on his knees, coughing up blood. I give him one last smack in the head before walking away. No one goes after our wives. We've already taken out one Italian underboss and five Russians.

Griffin and I get back to his Escalade and head to the diner.

I placed a call to Riordan about what happened, and I felt the stress in his voice. He's proud of his wife, who's hungry to dispense the kind of justice she couldn't as a Fed. But she's pregnant with his wee one.

I'd love to be a fly on the wall when he tells her she's got to scale her shit back. If I see him with a black eye, I'll know her response.

I think about Katya and how feisty she is. She may not throw a punch like Priscilla, but those legs... Those fucking gorgeous, strong legs can do some damage to my nuts.

After ordering a hungry-man omelet for myself and a few pastries to go for Katya, I look up at Griffin, dying for an opinion on how I feel about her. How much I like her, something I didn't expect. Because I didn't think I had it in me to actually feel anything. I was obsessed. That's about greed and pride. But this is more.

For years, I took out my cruel needs with anonymous women who only saw a giant man and the promise of a big dick to get them off. Then I pushed sex out of my mind and threw myself into darkness, letting my body release on its own while I slept.

Things seem upside down now. I'm hesitant, because I worry I'll get attached.

"Katya wants to live in London," I blurt when Griffin has a mug of coffee halfway to his lips.

Her plans have been rattling around in my head. Looking forward, I figure once she's settled, and I know she's out of danger, I'll give her a divorce. Let her find a real husband. Someone who will marry her for love. But thinking of someone else touching her drives me crazy.

"Why?" Griffin asks, then takes his sip.

"There's a dance conservatory she wants to attend. She auditions next month."

"Does she have a shot?"

"I'll make sure she gets in." My stomach twists, thinking of what I'd say to each judge in the dark alley I drag them to. "I want her to have this. She's wanted it more than being married to me."

"People's goals change when they're in love."

"I'm not in love." Am I? No. "I'm not husband material. I can be killed any day."

"You?" He pats my arm. "You're like a cat, Lach. You're not going anywhere. She looked happy that day I caught you standing there naked. She didn't go shrieking into the corner like I'd expect a little waif like her to do," Griffin rattles off with humor.

"She's happy to be safe." I dilute the connection we have because it makes little sense to feel so real. "It was marry me or the animal who rearranged her face." I tighten my fist around a mug of black coffee, thinking of that vile swine hurting her.

"You care about her. Nothing wrong with that." Griffin digs into his food and says nothing more.

"She sure is sweet." I shift in my seat, and I assume that tiny, virgin cunt tastes sweet.

Fuck, I get dizzy just thinking about it.

Life's a wild ride, and all I can do now is strap in and see where this roller coaster takes me.

CHAPTER SEVENTEEN

KATYA

On the first day back to my rehearsals, Lachlan drives me to school in his dark green Grand Wagoneer with tinted windows. It rides like a tank and feels safe, as if a giant gun is strapped to the roof.

We listen to the radio, and he lets me choose the music. To get in the mood for my routine, I find the classical station on his satellite radio.

Lachlan's eyebrows go up, but then he settles into his seat. "This is nice."

"Right?" I close my eyes and breathe.

"You have a healthy knowledge of classical music, I bet. For your dancing?"

"I do." I sit up. "I have a Pandora account with hundreds of songs. If it's okay, I'll play some of it when I'm cooking dinner."

"What do you mean, if it's okay?"

"It's your house, Lachlan."

"It's our house. We're married."

I smile. "You know what I mean."

He turns to me with a serious look. "And did you not understand what I mean?" His powerful glare slices through me.

"I guess I don't. I appreciate what you're doing, and I like it when we kiss, but...are we in a relationship?"

Lachlan looks away. "Marriage *is* a relationship. We live together. You like sleeping in my bed, so yeah, I guess we are. We'll just take each day as it comes before your audition." The words flow off his tongue, thoughtful and deep.

I think they surprise even him. Like he just realized what we're doing. We had an explosive start. Clearly, this was a spur-of-the-moment decision after seeing Rahil the night before. Lachlan acted on instinct, and so did I by saying yes.

But Lachlan appears to *like* me, likes kissing me, likes holding me at night. I like him, too. How can I not? Look what he's done for me? Everything about him takes my breath away, and that confidence he has makes him a twelve on a scale of one to ten.

I'm just afraid that massive cock will hurt me and put a damper on things if we take this further.

"Maybe we shouldn't put a label on this," I say, sorting through my thoughts.

"Exactly." He kisses my hand. "I've always been the square peg trying to fit into a round hole."

I giggle. "Well, you're so big."

"You have no idea, little wife." He strokes his chest.

I have *more* than an idea. I held that massive muscle between his legs. Made it come all over my hands.

We listen to the music in silence for the rest of the drive. When we get to my school, Lachlan cuts off a line of Ubers dropping off other students.

"You can let me out here. The school is very safe. Papa's driver didn't come inside." When Lachlan growls, I reach over and kiss his cheek. "Trust me...um."

"Um?" He holds my face.

"I was wondering what to call you. You call me little wife."

"Do you like it?"

"When you explained it, I did like it because you made an effort to come up with something." I smile. "Is there a nickname you'd like?"

"I've never been in a relationship. This is new to me. I'll let you decide." He pecks me on the nose.

That's something I'll have to think about. "You need some sleep. You have circles under your eyes." And blood stains on his hands, which I don't ask about. I lean over and kiss his eyes. "I finish up around five p.m."

"I'll be right in front of the school."

I glance around. "Sometimes the spots are blocked off."

"I'll be right here. No one blocks me." His voice gets dangerously low. "Wait for me to open your door." He pushes out of the car and lets me out.

"Bye, and thank you for driving me." I hug him.

"Do you need money?" He breathes against my neck.

Dread kicks me in the gut. I only found a few singles in my school bag. "I guess."

Smiling, he takes out his wallet and hands me a wad of twenties. "Here."

"That's too much." I peel off one twenty.

"Take more."

Exhaling, knowing what lunch costs around here, I snag a few more. "Happy?"

"To take care of my wife? Ecstatic."

"Me, too. Now that I know if I want water, I don't have to sip from a dirty fountain." I kiss his cheek, catching the corner of his mouth.

His warm wet lips slide over mine, and we sink into a passionate kiss. I want him to rest, and yet I'm charged up. I might miss a few steps and get hurt. I pull away, or I'll never leave him.

His protectiveness borders on obsession, the way he's so intense about everything. But I like it. I went from thinking no one cares about me, to feeling so precious to a man who married me out of vengeance, and now can't stop kissing me.

*

At five p.m., I approach the main entrance's double doors, and a hulking body dressed in black lurks inside.

138

Lachlan.

"How did you get in here?" I lift my ID badge. "You have to key in."

He grins.

"Did your brother, Balor, get you a fake badge?" I pop my hands on my hips.

He slides a keycard out of his pocket. "No comment. If something happens to you, I have to get in here."

My heart jolts, thinking how protective he'd be if he *loved* me. I suspect the same passion he directs toward his job, he would show to me.

He lifts my bag and throws it over his shoulder. "This is heavy."

"It's all my dancing gear. I assume it's okay to use your washing machine."

He glares at me. "The cleaning lady will do your laundry."

"I don't mind doing the laundry."

"Do you know how to use a washing machine?" he asks with humor.

"I can figure it out."

"I'll show you. And if you want to wash my clothes, too, I won't argue. I admit, I go through a lot of shirts and pants from all the blood."

"Good to know."

He puts me in his double-parked SUV. A man yells that Lachlan's been blocking him in. But when my husband turns to face the guy and snarls, he backs off.

"Asshole," the guy snaps, walking back to his car.

Lachlan lunges, but I grab him. "No. Don't. This is Manhattan. I know you, Papa, and the Italians don't have the same influence here."

"Wise. No, we don't." He strokes my braid. "And I have you with me. I have to consider that now. Although..." He takes out his gun and points it at the guy with a howling spit of laughter.

I watch from the rearview and giggle when the guy hits the ground. I open my window and shout, "Next time, don't call my husband an asshole."

"Good one. *No one* tells me what to do," Lachlan says, getting into the driver's seat and pulls away.

But bumper-to-bumper traffic locks our car in a middle lane as we come to a standstill. A tractor trailer tried to make a U-turn and tipped over. Cops are diverting cars to a side road, but it's a slow go.

A muscle cramp hits me and without thinking, I shoot my leg forward onto the dashboard and stretch it. "Ack."

"What?"

"Cramp. Hamstring."

Lachlan drags my leg into his lap and massages the sore muscle. I changed into silk shorts and a tank top for the ride home because it's so hot. Lachlan's hand on my skin heats me up even more.

I lean on the passenger door and let him work me. "God, that feels good."

His eyes fly to mine. "Keep going?"

"Yes."

He leans his long body toward me. "Pay the massage fee."

I laugh and kiss him. But something sparks, and he opens up to me. Next, we're making out like teenagers. Not that I ever kissed anyone as a teenager, and he's almost forty.

But it's hot and intense. My tongue swipes across his lower lip. A rush of salty and sweet flavors bursts into my mouth. I want to taste his entire body. I imagine his warm, wet tongue is his cock, and I swirl mine around it, sucking it in between my lips.

Lachlan curses under his breath. "Bad girl."

The energy in the car shifts, and with the faint piano

concerto humming from the radio, I use the rhythm to kiss him.

Lachlan's throat vibrates, and he's revved like an engine. "Keep kissing me," he rasps.

I tug him closer by the jacket he always wears, my arms bumping into the gun. "I feel that."

"I want to feel more." His body twists as his hand trails up my leg. "So smooth."

"I shave every day. I'll need to buy razors soon."

"I'll buy you whatever you need." The rough pads of fingers inch under my shorts. "You're warm *and* damp." He's referring to my panties. "Is this okay?"

"Yes, keep going." My center clenches from the contact.

"You're consenting for me to touch your wet cunt?" he breathes against my neck.

I shudder as his finger brushes against my sex. I grasp his neck and pull him closer to me as his finger traces my slit with delicate caresses.

"Fuck, little wife. I can *feel* myself inside you."

"Does it feel good?"

"Mind blowing."

"I… I want that. I want you to take me. Make me yours. Only yours."

A finger slides inside me and my womb clenches immediately, a rush of electricity zipping through me.

"You're coming, aren't you?"

"God, yes. Don't stop." I writhe against him.

"Fuck, you're so wet. If we were home, I'd lick you clean."

His hands are so big, I can't see what he's doing exactly. The finger inside me stretches me, and his thumb is rubbing my clit.

"Keep stroking me, just like that." I'm so slick and aroused, I feel something dripping down my thigh.

"Is this your first orgasm?" He peers at me.

"No," I confess. "I figured out how to make myself come."

He growls, "Now you have me for that."

Aware that I'm satisfied, and he's not, I say, "When we get home, I'll take care of you. Or I can do it now." I lick my lips, wired from the aftermath of what he did to me.

"Fuck, yes." Lachlan reaches for his belt, but car horns blast behind us.

We fogged up the windshield, and when I wipe the dampness away, I see the road has cleared.

"Hold on, little wife." Lachlan screeches into drive and takes off.

CHAPTER EIGHTEEN

LACHLAN

As I race home, wild, inappropriate thoughts fire through me.

I'm hard as a rock, feeling how wet and tight Katya's cunt was. I'm worried I'll hurt her. I'm worried this is moving too fast. She's young and inexperienced. I'm older and know better. She had hopes to marry for love someday, and I never intended to take a wife.

Yet here we are, married and completely hot for each other. I lived my life like a fuck machine, brutalizing women nightly when my schedule allowed for it. Since I watched her dance that night, Katya moved into my brain, and the desire to keep up that filthy lifestyle vanished.

I pull into my garage. "We're home."

I stroke that long braid. The glistening different colors weaved together fascinate me. I want her. I want to be inside her. I consider how much I should tell Katya about my past before she lets me steal her innocence. What I did to Father Eamon and Charles Foster.

Is Katya my reward for such strict obedience after I fucked up?

I was forced out of Astoria for what I did to Charles Foster and sent to a training camp for killers after I murdered Father Eamon. I learned the kind of brutality most men can't handle. And when you're programmed to kill, how can you love?

How can hands that squeeze the life out of a man, or snap bones like twigs be gentle with a wife? I don't know how I'll balance going wildly feral every night and then try to passionately make love to Katya the way she deserves. Some nights, I might just hold her down and fuck her senseless.

Out of pure guttural need.

Inside my kitchen, I stroke the delicate parts of her face that have healed. "I have to meet Griffin at eight p.m."

She sneaks a look at the clock on the stove. "Right, duty calls." The disappointment in her voice guts me.

I consider what will take more time? Fucking her? Or telling her my screwed-up past?

CHAPTER NINETEEN

KATYA

What do I really need to know about Lachlan if we'll only be married temporarily? I know that I want to have sex. With him. We're married. Legally. There's no shame in it. If I get into the conservatory and decide I want a life of freedom to travel with a dance company, I'll face that when it happens.

Right now, I want to give my husband what he wants from me. What he needs from a wife.

With dried sweat making my top sticky, not to mention how soaked my panties are, I say, "I'm going to take a shower first, if that's okay."

"I don't mind a little sweat," he says, low and throaty.

"It's my first time. I want to...look nice for you. Smell nice." My heart pounds as I watch him consider my words.

He lays a kiss on my forehead. "Go shower, little wife." Lachlan radiates masculinity and power.

My blood warms the way he gives these little orders. "Yes, sir." I plié into a curtsey.

Feeling his eyes on me, I strut down the hallway toward Lachlan's bedroom, where I've been sleeping and showering. I strip out of my shorts and tank top, while toeing off my flip flops. Stark naked, I stare at my body, lithe and slender. Does Lachlan think I'm too tiny for him? Will he be too careful with me?

I quickly wipe my makeup away and unravel my braid while the water gets hot. The warm spray soothes my shoulders as I rinse my hair. Washing my body, I reach between my legs and jump, feeling sensitive there. I've touched myself before and reached that blissful place, bringing on a peaceful sleep. Lachlan touching me exploded in my veins.

I'm wired and want more of that.

With my father giving me no indication that he would arrange a marriage for me, I figured somewhere along the way I'd meet a man and fall in love. I expected to be my own woman and make my own decisions because my father ignored me. Ironically, it's my husband now who is giving me a chance to live my dream.

What about love?

Lost in that thought, I shut the water off and slide the glass shower door open to grab a towel. Lachlan stands there holding the towel open for me. Our eyes lock and I let him see me. All of me. Without words, he wraps me up and lifts me into his arms. Kissing me, he carries me to his bed.

My warm, wet body hits the mattress. "I'm getting everything wet."

"Who cares." He kisses me deeply, our tongues tangling.

"We have to hurry, right? You're meeting Griffin?" I squeak.

"I changed my plans," he says, his voice thick with lust. "My wife comes first."

I press my lips to his and breathe deeply. "You're so sweet. But you should be naked, too. You already made me come. I want to make you come."

His chest heaves, and he bares his teeth like a wolf. "I won't say no to that." He sits up to pull his shirt off.

He strips and stands in front of me, naked. God, he's gorgeous. His hard, thick length juts out and bobs from the apparent weight of the thing.

Stroking himself, he growls, "I want your mouth around my cock, right fucking now."

146

Sitting up on the side of the bed, I lean forward to lick the plummy tip. The feel of velvet on my tongue has me slipping it entirely into my mouth.

"Fuck, Katya," he groans and throws his head back. "Oh yeah, baby."

"Keep going?" I ask, licking the underside, my tongue running over thick veins.

Ribbed for her pleasure.

Don't need that in a condom with these ridges that will hit my nerve endings perfectly.

"Aye," Lachlan rasps, fingering my wet hair. "Don't stop."

I work him with my mouth as much as I can. Miraculously, I get my lips around him and focus on my breath. Relaxing my jaw, I let him slide all the way in until the tip bumps the back of my throat.

"Aw fuck," he moans. "Aye, keep going. Right there."

I suck hard, the friction warming his skin.

"Katya, I'm gonna come." He grips the base to remove it from my mouth.

I listened to girls in stretching clinics when they think I'm meditating, how men love coming in a woman's mouth. I grip Lachlan's butt and lock my lips around the shaft.

"Oh, yeah, Katya. That feels fucking amazing." He throws his thick biceps over his head while his hips rock. "You wicked, little wife, take my cum down your throat."

Warm, salty spurts hit the back of my throat, and I swallow it all down.

Lachlan roars with pleasure, and I smile, proud I got him to this point. He's ridiculously handsome, brooding, and smoldering. I reduced him to a moaning maniac!

At an event last year, I heard a couple of women whisper how they'd love to be thrown down by him and just…fucked. Yet, here I am, getting him off in our bed. Just me. Only me.

He pulls me up and crashes his mouth down on mine. When he pulls away, a sense of loss startles me.

"Keep kissing me," I say, leaning back on the bed, reaching for him. "Hold me."

Shuddering, he says, "I think I need to be held, Katya. That orgasm blew me away."

"I blew you away. Literally."

"Ha." He stretches out over me and his right hand winds around my waist. "This feels so good."

"I know." I play it off to keep things fun and light between us.

We're just having a good time until… Until I leave, I guess. One way or another.

"Will you make love to me now?" I say, and feel him tense.

"Make love?"

"Um, I'm not comfortable saying…fuck," I whisper.

"You're adorable." He strokes my chin and then kisses me. "So sweet and innocent. But Katya…" His voice turns low and dangerous. "You said it yourself. This is temporary. Don't fall for me."

"I fall enough at school," I joke to match his humor.

"Katya, I'm serious. I'm not built to be the kind of husband you deserve."

I process his warning. "Okay, so you're scary. But you protect your family." I run my fingers through his thick, dark hair. "You're not hurting innocent people."

The ache in his pessimism hits me unexpectedly. It's only been a few days, and I've made it clear I'm leaving. Sounds like *he* doesn't want to fall for me. Lachlan doesn't strike me as a man who can handle being told no. Or simply doesn't take no for an answer. I can't turn this into some romantic fantasy. When it comes time to live the life I want for myself and not be hidden away in some enforcer's lair because it's too dangerous to come and go as I please, or live with a guard up my ass, I'll need to walk away without any regrets. I cannot look back.

I'll heed his advice and keep my heart out of this. "So, it's not making love? It's...fucking?"

"Aye. I'm a lot older than you, too. I have to be careful with you." He cups my breasts. "These are so fucking sexy."

"They're not too small?" I'm a b-cup when I'm PMSing. They're barely mounds. Just little bumps with pink nipples.

"They fit you perfectly. They fit inside my hands perfectly." He massages me and then goes back to work on me with his mouth. Sucking my nipples, he slides his fingers into my folds. "Fuck, you're still wet."

"Making you come with my mouth really turned me on." I bite my lip.

He grins. "I'll let you do it whenever you want."

"Lachlan, do you want to make love to me?" I shake my head. "I mean, be inside me, make us *both* feel good?"

"Aye, I do, but..." He crushes me.

"But?"

He sits back and strokes himself. "I don't want to hurt you."

"You won't." I take the hand not stroking himself. "Every touch you've laid on me has been gentle. Firm, but gentle. I'm not worried at all. I trust you." I lick his fingertips.

"Fuck, I'm so hard again already."

"Are those condoms nearby? I'm not on birth control."

He gets off the bed and digs into the top drawer of his dresser. "Thank fuck for that bigger box." He tears it open and comes back with one in his hand.

"Show me how to put it on you."

He growls again, liking the power I'm handing over to him. I want him to feel powerful right now. I want to give him the control, and I have no intention of changing who he is. "I want to taste you first."

I'm pretty wet, but I'm not going to pass up feeling his tongue on my clit. "Please!"

He gets down on his knees and buries his head between my legs, running his tongue along my opening. "So pretty."

I rock my hips against his mouth, my tensions building immediately again. "Don't stop."

"No way. I'm not done with you," he groans, sucking harder, cresting the wave with me even though I'm so sensitive.

I lose track of time, but I see him rise to his full height. The light from the bathroom shrouds the front side of him in a gray shadow. It hits me. The man in my thoughts when I masturbate. The faceless mammoth with bulging muscles and a raspy voice. It was Lachlan I fantasized about.

Standing there, he smiles down at me, lost in pleasure. I'm embarrassed that I've wanted him all along and didn't know it. I wanted a hulking, broody devil of a man. Me, the little virgin.

"Here, help me put this thing on." He bites the wrapper with his teeth.

My fingers deftly roll it onto his long, thick length. Sheathed, I stroke him and shudder at how slick the surface is.

Lachlan gently pushes me down and climbs on top of me. He kisses me while positioning himself against my quivering slit. "Tell me you want it."

"I want it so much."

He pushes inside me. "Fuck," he groans as his cock fills me, spreading me open, connecting us.

A pinch deep inside me is followed by a burning sensation, but the friction from his cock soothes that ache with a pleasure I never expected.

"I felt that. Does it hurt?" He looks down at his cock, slowly easing out of me. "Fuck, I made you bleed."

I don't suppose the Irish Enforcer cares about blood on his dick. "It doesn't hurt."

"Damn, this is sexy as hell. Me claiming you. Being your first." He strokes my cheek. "I want this to be good for you, baby. You're my wife, it's my job."

He grabs my butt, and using his thighs to control his weight, he shoves himself deeper inside me.

"I can't believe you fit! How big *is* it?"

"Funny you should ask. I measured it once to win a bet." He leans forward. "Nine inches, fully erect. But fuck, I feel bigger."

"It feels bigger than nine inches." I wind my hands around his neck. "Did you win the bet?"

"Aye. By a lot." He pumps with such velocity as he grips the headboard. His powerful body sings, and his abs ripple as he takes me harder and deeper.

He looks so beautiful on top of me like this. Everything about him is sexy. "I'm there. Do you want me to come?"

"Please come inside me."

"This feels so fucking good." His words set off a wave, and I throb against his thick length, dragging along my sensitive nerves. "I'm coming."

"Me, too." I hug him, and I love that we're so good together like this.

He breathes and kisses my lips. "I'm gonna say something right now that might scare you."

My heart seizes. "Yeah?"

"I killed a priest..."

CHAPTER TWENTY

LACHLAN

Katya's face doesn't move when I tell her my greatest sin. After a moment, she holds her stomach like she's going to vomit. Ironic, that with all the blood on my hands, crimes she shrugged at, killing a priest is oddly a deal-breaker.

I locate the nearest wall I can punch a hole in. I would never hurt my wife. Or strike any woman.

Flushed, Katya chokes out, "There's something *I* need to tell you."

I thread my fingers through her wet hair and tug her face so she's looking up at me. "Go on."

"Stasia told me you killed a priest and to stay away from you." She smiles. "I watched you kill Rahil. And I still married you. What does that say about me?"

I let go of her hair, or I'll pull the strands right out of the roots. "It means you're brave." The trust I feel for her is insane.

"Can I ask why you killed the priest?"

"He was hurting children." My answer has always been that simple.

She doesn't look shocked, and that is the greatest travesty, the worst PR the church suffers. Numb indifference. "Is that where you got this?" Her fingers brush against my scar.

That morning in the sacristy flashes at me, and I close my eyes. "No."

"I looked up the priest's murder, and there was something about a boy's father who accused him a year before. That man died in a confrontation. Did Father

Eamon kill him?"

"I did."

She clutches her chest.

"That was an accident, though. He was my friend's dad. He'd already slashed Father Eamon and did this to me." I finger my scar.

Katya shrieks. "That's where the scar came from?"

"Aye. We... There was some shoving back and forth. Lots of yelling and blood. I pushed Charles Foster, and he hit his head." I leave out that I went to plunge the knife he used to cut me into his chest. Father Eamon stopped me. Didn't want Charles to die, even though he cut us both pretty badly with that damn knife.

Katya looks breathless. "I'm so sorry. And no one knew you were there?"

"My da got me out of it."

"How?"

"The usual way our fathers intimidate people." I stand up to get my blood moving. "But he flipped when I killed Father Eamon. I did that one deliberately. Calculating. And premeditated. All on my own. Me. That wasn't a sanctioned O'Rourke hit I carried out. Da worried me killing him would unravel how he protected me from paying for Charles Foster's murder. He feared a special prosecutor would investigate the death of a priest who'd been stabbed by a father, who also ended up dead. A death I witnessed. He worried it all would click for someone." I take a breath. "I was in my first year at Fordham. And since I was failing, Da pulled me out and sent me away."

"Where?"

I stare at my wife, caught between not knowing what information about a secret Irish training camp I can trust her with, or what my heart can handle telling her about me.

153

"You don't have to tell me. This is just temporary between us." Her words shock me with the cruel reality that I may feel more for her than she feels for me. I don't like not being in complete control of this relationship.

"That's not why. It's hard to talk about what happened to me there."

"There?"

"A training camp."

"Oh..." She bites her nails. "I heard Papa mention those. He recruits *bratoks* from camps in Russia and Syria. I saw the result of those camps day in and day out, and I understand places like that, what happens there."

"Not like this, little wife. It was hell. Beatings to the point of exhaustion, testing to see how we fought back. Extreme heat, then cold, no food, no water for days. I may have been this size and had a father who murdered people, but we lived like little princes, my brothers and me. I wanted to serve God. I didn't adapt well at first."

"I'm so sorry. No one should have purposely hurt you." She straddles my lap and wraps her legs around my waist.

"That's what the instructors get paid for. It wasn't personal, I realized that eventually."

"How long were you there?"

"A year."

Her breath hitches, and she stares into my eyes. "Did you kill anyone there?" she asks with too much enthusiasm, proving she really is a Bratva princess who grew up in our world.

"Not there." Another memory pops into my head. "After I got back, Da sent me to MIT to kill a guard who failed to protect Balor from being beaten up by some bullies. I didn't want to do it. I'd heard the guy was outnumbered, but I learned at the camp not to question orders. My da amped me up, though, explaining my *job* is to protect my brothers. No one threatens my family."

Katya throws her arms around me. "God, you're so wonderful. I can't believe my sister told me to stay away from you."

"Want to hear something even more ironic?"

"What?"

"My brothers told me to stay away from you."

"But we're married." She looks adorably offended.

"Before." I take out my phone and show her all the pictures I've snapped of her. "I've been obsessed with you since that night we spoke." I let her take in my words, waiting for a look of disgust.

Instead, she rubs my cock. "I find that very sexy." She climbs on top of my growing erection.

"Fuck yes, I want you to ride my cock." Christ, we can't keep our hands off each other. "But first, sit on my face."

"Your face?"

"Aye. I want to make you come while riding my tongue."

"I'll crush you."

"Do you really think that?"

"How will you breathe?"

"Don't worry how I'll breathe. Just concentrate on fucking my face hard enough so I can't breathe. I'll suffocate on your cunt any day of the week." I drag her to my face, her wet pussy coating my entire chest.

I won't shower for days now. I want to hurt someone while smelling my wife's cunt.

"Oh!" she gasps when my lips clasp on to her clit.

"Dig into me, baby. Grind my face with that sweet cunt."

She gives my tongue a fucking sweet lap dance, and in a matter of minutes, she's screaming my name.

When she collapses, I roll her over and kiss her.

"What changed your mind about staying away from me?"

I stroke her mouth. "One look at these lips, and I knew my cock would look so good in them. It was an order I couldn't obey."

CHAPTER TWENTY-ONE

KATYA

The next couple of days, Lachlan and I fall into a
routine. He drives me to and from school, we get home,
have amazing sex, eat dinner, and have more sex. I fall
asleep on his chest, and wake up to the feel of him
sliding down my panties and him making me mindless
until I have to get up. We shower together, fuel up with
coffee, and the routine starts all over.

It certainly isn't boring.

Lachlan's explanation of all the bloodshed in his past
doesn't change how I feel about him. He seemed
relieved to confess to me like he does at church.

During a break at school, I get a text from my
husband:

Lachlan: Kieran wants us at a fundraiser tonight.

Me: Tonight? That's short notice.

Lachlan: That's my brother.

*Me: I need a new dress. There's a boutique a couple of
blocks from school. I can leave now.*

*Lachlan: Fuck. I'm dealing with something. Wait for
me.*

Dealing with something is code for beating the crap
out of someone. I picture him holding a man by the
throat with one hand and dictating into his phone

about a fancy party with the other.

Me: I'll be all right walking two blocks myself.

Lachlan: I said, wait for me.

Me: I SAID, I can do this. You're working. I'll text you when I get to the store.

Lachlan: ...

Me: I may be small, but I'm fast.

Lachlan: ...

Me: I can leap over someone.

Lachlan: ...

Me: And scream pretty loudly. I'll be fine. I promise.

Lachlan: Aye. Use the credit card I gave you.

I feel like something shifted, and he trusts my judgment.

Lachlan: I want photos from the store.

Me: I said I'll text you.

Lachlan: I want photos of the dress.

Me: Any requests? Long or short?

Lachlan: Short.

DEAL WITH THE DEVIL

Me: Easy access or challenging?

Lachlan: In between. I like a challenge, but not to the point, I'm tearing it by the seams.

Me: Are you sure?

Lachlan: No, actually I'm not. In fact, not too short either. You're mine. No one sees what's mine.

Me: I don't want anyone to see me the way you do.

Lachlan: …

This may get too deep and dirty, and I have another dance set to run through, but I can't stop.

Me: Panties or no panties?

Lachlan: Fuck, I think I just killed this guy…

It's bizarre, but I laugh.

Me: For real?

Lachlan: No comment.

Me: No panties means easy access.

Lachlan: Just don't let it show you're NOT wearing panties.

Me: It will be my secret.

Lachlan: OUR secret.

*

In a boutique on Fifth Avenue, the saleslady helps me select a pale pink chiffon A-line cocktail dress with a jeweled bra-cup top that sits right above my knee. Taking a photo with the mirror, I send it to Lachlan, and he sends back a thumbs up *and* a tongue emoji. Giggling at what a good time we're having, I amble to the shoe section and try on a pair of nude strappy espadrilles.

The saleslady packs everything up and says, "That comes to 1,879.42."

I freeze, feeling embarrassed. Lachlan didn't tell me what to spend or what not to spend. Dread and anger fire through me, being so dependent on a man. First my father, and now my husband. I'm beholden to him, and I don't like it.

I don't think he sees me as a burden, but I have to figure out how to be more of my own woman in this relationship. Or am I fooling myself that it's even a possibility when married to the Irish mob?

I haven't gotten to know my sisters-in-law, Isabella and Priscilla, yet. Priscilla works for the Quinlans and has maintained some independence. Isabella's twins are due soon and she spends most days in bed. I found out she started a foundation and runs it from an office in that huge mansion.

I relax, thinking Lachlan might let me dance for a living and make my own money. Make my own choices. If we stay married.

From my school bag, I take out my wallet, blushing. "My husband gave me his credit card."

"No problem." The sales lady takes it from me without batting an eyelash and runs it through.

A high-end store like this probably has lots of customers whose husbands pay for everything.

With the wrapped dress hanging up, and the shoes in a box, the nice woman hands it all to me after the receipt.

"Here you go. I hope you'll come back for another event."

I'd explained the dress was for a fundraiser, just not which one, because Lachlan never told me.

"Is it okay if I stay here until my husband comes to pick me up?"

"Sure. You can sit there." She motions to the leather slipper chairs near the front of the store.

I sit and text Lachlan where I am, but he strolls in the door a few seconds later. "*There* you are."

My heart races. "How did you find me?" I expect he'll say process of elimination since this is the only high-end boutique near my school.

"There's an app on your cell so I can find you."

"Really?" I tighten my fingers around my new phone, unsure how I feel about that.

"Is that a problem?" He folds his arms.

"I wish I would have known," I say softly. "Not that it matters. I have nothing to hide from you."

He leans down and brushes his lips against my cheek. "It's for your protection, little wife. It's so I can always find you and get to you if you're in trouble." His words give me chills, reminding me I married a very dangerous man, who probably has enemies lined up to hurt him.

Now they can hurt him by hurting me.

"Is this yours?" He points to the wrapped dress hanging from a stand.

"Yes. I bought shoes, too." I reach into my schoolbag. "Here's the receipt. It was a little pricey."

He shoves it in his pocket without looking at it. "Doesn't matter. You're my wife. You can have whatever you want."

"I'd like another kiss."

He growls. "I want more when we get home."

"Do we have time?" I put my arms around him and

161

kiss him.

He breathes against my neck. "That tight cunt of yours is ripening my stamina, so we might be late."

"It's our first event together." I clear my throat. "Your brother was angry that you married me. I don't want to get you into further trouble with him."

Tossing my dress over his shoulder, he puts his other arm around me. "I like trouble."

*

The minute we walk into The Orchid, a very high-end venue, I feel like the biggest idiot.

This is a black-tie event. I should have bought a floor-length gown. Not a cocktail dress. I tug my husband's elbow. "Lachlan, you didn't tell me I needed a gown."

Unflinching in his black suit and burgundy dress shirt, when he should be in a tux, he says, "I didn't know either."

Swallowing, I pull him back. "I can't go in like this. People will laugh at me."

He narrows his eyes. "I'm pretty sure everyone in that room knows who I am. No one will *dare* laugh at my wife."

I roll my eyes. "Okay, not to my face."

"You're a young, beautiful woman, Katya. Your dress is fine."

I want to argue that he's treating me like a child, but Lachlan O'Rourke isn't a glamour-ball regular. "How often will we have to attend these things?"

"I have no idea." He shrugs. "But after tonight, I'll tell my brother—"

"Tell your brother *what?*" Kieran appears from behind Lachlan.

My husband dwarfs most men, but Kieran stands only a couple of inches shorter than his younger brother. Dressed in a sharp, black tux, with his dark hair slicked back, he's breathtakingly handsome.

"Where's Isabella?" Lachlan asks, putting his arm around me.

"Ladies' room with Priscilla. My sons are sitting on her bladder." He gives me a pleasant once-over, then stares at his brother. "No tie?"

"I'm not a tie guy." Lachlan brushes off his brother with a refreshing independence.

When Kieran looks me over again, I say, "I'll help Isabella tonight, too."

And hide in one of the stalls.

"Thank you. She's looking forward to seeing you." As if he has eyes behind his head, Kieran turns around.

Isabella elegantly glides toward us, dressed in what looks like a wedding gown of jeweled white satin with sheer cap sleeves that sit off her olive-skin shoulders. The empire waist displays her visibly pregnant stomach right under a belt of Swarovski crystals.

Wow.

I'd met her before at the private swim club our fathers belonged to. She was always petite, and now she's carrying two sons of a man just as tall as my husband.

I tug my own stomach, wondering what carrying Lachlan's child would do to my body if we take things that far. Ballerinas are supposed to be lithe and graceful. Code for ultra-thin. Would I recover my shape enough to dance again? Casting agents are brutal, carrying scales and measuring tapes around.

I dismiss all that and relax, because my marriage is temporary. I think. Lachlan said we'd take it one day at a time. It seems to depend on me. Whether I get picked to attend the conservatory.

Staring at Lachlan's family, my heart flutters at the lonely life I've led. And the one I'll live after this, if I go to London.

"Katriane," Lachlan saying my full name snaps me out of my head. "Isabella said hello to you."

"I'm so sorry." I hold my chest, and something makes me kiss her on the cheek. "Hello, it's nice to see you again." I exhale. "I'm sorry for your mother. And your father." I lower my head. Goodness, she's an orphan!

"Hello, Katya. And thank you." Isabella sounds as nice as I remember. Her elegance astounds me. And she's a queen. She's my queen if Lachlan considers Kieran his king. "And thank you so much. It's crazy, isn't it? Here we are, sisters." Her hand in mine, she gives it a squeeze that wrecks me.

"I know. And you look amazing," I say, hiding my emotion.

"So do you. I love that dress." Her warm eyes soak me in. "I can't wait until I wear something cute like that again."

Kieran winds his arm around her and kisses her cheek. "Don't count on it."

"That's because he's a caveman and wants to keep her pregnant." Riordan, in a tux identical to Kieran's, struts up to us with his wife. "Hello, Katya. Good to see you again."

"Hello, Riordan." I bow my head to the underboss and recognize Priscilla from my wedding day. She's wearing a blue dress with long sheer sleeves and a stunning sapphire necklace. "Hello, Priscilla."

When she notices my eyes lingering, she rubs her arm. "Burn scars."

"Oh, I'm sorry. I just thought with the summer heat and everyone wearing strapless dresses..." I trail off, catching her husband hand her a glass of what I'm thinking is water, because she's pregnant, too, although she doesn't look it.

"Let's get to our table. It's in the front. I paid extra,"

Kieran says, putting his phone in his jacket.

"Is the dais too expensive these days?" Lachlan's hand easily winds around my waist.

"That's just audacious," Kieran answers, steering his wife that way.

From inside the ballroom, my father struts out, startling me. I didn't even think he'd be here, but that was dumb of me. As pakhan, he holds just as much power and prestige as Kieran O'Rourke. These fancy galas were never my life, except for an afternoon party here and there. He brought Stasia to all these evening events, or came alone.

"What is this?" he barks at me. "This is how you dress for a black-tie event?"

"I..."

He grabs me by the arm. "You're embarrassing me."

The sudden invasion of a man touching me other than Lachlan pops a shriek from me.

"Get your fucking hands off my wife." Lachlan lunges for my father, but Riordan snaps his arm down.

"Lachlan, that's *the pakhan*," his brother warns, sending his family into strange territory.

"I don't give a fuck if he's the pope." He shrugs off Riordan. "I said, let go of my wife, *pakhan*."

My father's fingers loosen around my arm, but I hide how he hurt me. Lachlan might gut him with the knife he's got on him.

"I hold *you* responsible, enforcer. You stole her from me, and next, you parade her around in a joke of a dress?"

It happens quickly—Kieran and Riordan flank Lachlan, a wall of O'Rourke men blocking my father from me.

"I *am* responsible," Lachlan sneers. "But I didn't know this was black tie. I didn't ask, because I don't care. I don't answer to anyone but Kieran."

"It's no big deal." Kieran defends me. "Alexei, do you honestly think anyone will criticize one of *our* wives?"

"I want to talk to my daughter."

"No," Lachlan bites out.

"You can't keep her from me, enforcer."

"Watch me, *pakhan*."

CHAPTER TWENTY-TWO

LACHLAN

"What's going on?" Riordan asks me in a private bathroom for megadonors.

"What do you mean?" I zip up my fly and strut to the sink to wash my hands. We've been here for hours, and my patience for this nonsense has worn thin.

"You and Katya. You're acting like you have feelings for her."

My head snaps up, and I meet my brother's eyes in the mirror. "She's my wife."

"I can see you like saying that for effect, but is she more than a possession to you?"

Anger roils through me. "That's my business."

"That's where you're wrong, Lachlan." Riordan gets in my face. "Kieran bought Isabella from her father, and the Cosa Nostra lost both the don and underboss. That reinforced our power in this city. You stole the Russian princess in a shoot-out. That makes us look reckless. People are talking, Lachlan."

"They're talking about *your* wife, too. And I took care of it."

Riordan exhales. "Thank you."

I push him against the wall. "You never say thank you to me. I'm not hired help. We're one. Brothers. And Priscilla is my sister now."

"I appreciate you feel that way about my wife. But *your* wife's father is foaming at the mouth to get her back. She's all he's got to bargain with."

"That's why we have to work harder to find Stasia."

"Balor is coming up empty." Riordan shakes his

head. "I don't get how a twenty-one-year-old princess who left town with no money can allude his tracking."

I close my eyes and worry she's dead. That will destroy Katya.

Changing the subject, I say, "Katya is not Alexei's to bargain with anymore. She's my wife and her own woman. She's auditioning next month to get into a London dance conservatory. If she gets in, she's going."

"You're moving to London?" The vein in Riordan's neck nearly bursts. "Does Kieran know this?"

"I'm not going anywhere. This is what she wants. I'll hire a bloke from Waterford to guard her." The words come out of my mouth easily, but something feels off.

He exhales. "Good. We've been hoping you'd come to your senses and let her go."

The words being said out loud give me a sudden and uneasy feeling about Katya being alone in the ballroom.

"With Grigori out of the country, the brotherhood is falling apart," Riordan continues to talk business. Shit we used to discuss every morning at breakfast. Now I get info dumps while taking a piss at a gala. "You're giving Koslov the green light to attack us. You stole his daughter. Our bluff to hand over those wire transfers that we don't have won't hold."

"That poor girl was going to live a life getting beat to shit every night. Excuse me if *I* know what it's like to be sent away somewhere I don't want to be."

Riordan's guilt wafts off him. "I know what you're saying. You also know how powerful Da was back then. How ruthless. Neither Kieran nor I could talk him out of what he did." He grips me by the jacket, surprising me with the physical contact. "I see the way you look at her. You're lying to yourself if you're just going to let your wife go off and live on another continent. What are you doing?"

"She has to pass the audition."

"You didn't answer my other question. Do you have real feelings for her?"

I put my hands on the counter, annoyed to face what I've been denying. She's gotten under my skin. The way she makes me feel brings out another side to me. It's new and terrifying, yet when I'm inside her, I feel more alive than ever.

"She's a pleasant wife," I mutter and eye my brother with a look that signals he back off.

"Right there. Your face, when you said that. I know you, Lachlan. You feel something for her."

"I'm falling for her, all right!" I roar and strut past him.

I stomp through the lobby to find my wife and bring her the hell home.

CHAPTER TWENTY-THREE

KATYA

"I told your father it was a mistake to marry you off to Rahil," a voice trails over my shoulder while I sit at our table listening to fundraising goals for tonight's charity.

Lachlan is with Riordan somewhere, and Priscilla just took Isabella to the ladies' room again.

"Hello, Maksim." Feeling this was planned, I give him my best annoyed glower. "Clearly, Papa doesn't listen to you."

I resist a huge laugh at how pissed off he looks using a cane to walk.

"He will when I'm his underboss." He shoves the cane down and grabs the chair next to me. My husband's chair.

Big mistake...

I know very little of how my father runs his brotherhood, but I want to believe he wouldn't elevate Maksim to such an important role. If something should happen to the pakhan, the underboss takes over. Unless a council votes to have him removed. For Maksim, he'd have to be killed, because he'd never let go once he had that title.

"Good luck." I stroke the back of my neck and stand to go find my husband, but Maksim's cold fingers close around my upper arm.

"This is the *second* time tonight someone has touched me without permission." I try to pull away, but he's too strong. "Lachlan was ready to tear apart Papa but got talked down off the ledge because *he's pakhan*. Do you want your other knee blown off?"

"I hear you want to live in London."

My throat goes tight. "That's no secret."

Maksim laughs. "I know Lachlan O'Rourke very well. There is no way he will let you go."

"That's none of your business."

"*I* will let you go."

"What are you talking about?"

"Say the word, Katriane. Cry out that you want to come home. My entire *brigadier* is outside."

I glance out the floor-to-ceiling windows curtained by blue velvet drapes and go rigid. Men in dark suits with ear pieces surround the venue. "What did you do?"

"What I have to." He pulls me closer. "If you agree to marry me, your father will make me underboss."

"He said that?"

Maksim's right eye twitches. "Not exactly. But when I tell him your sister is dead, he will."

"What?" Bile rises in my throat. "What makes you think that?"

"We would have heard something by now."

I debate if I should mention the postcards. When I say nothing, he continues.

"Your father will get his ass back in the driver's seat once I tell him he can give up looking for Anastasia, the ghost, and that you have agreed to leave Lachlan to marry *me*. Then you go to London and—"

"My *wife* is married," Lachlan says, hovering against Maksim's back.

"Is that a gun, or are you happy to see me, O'Rourke?" Maksim sneers, letting me go.

"Ask your knee how a bullet felt." Lachlan glances out the window. "Call off your dogs. I'm taking *my wife* home."

"She just agreed to marry me, so why don't you—"

Maksim groans in pain. "What the fuck is that?"

"The tip of a knife in the back of your neck. One hard jab, and you're paralyzed. Katriane agreed to no such thing. Did you, my sweet, little wife?" He eyes me with a wide, confident grin since he couldn't have heard our conversation.

He trusts me.

"I most certainly did not agree to marry this snake." I stand up straight. "He wants to use me to convince my father to make him underboss."

"Maybe you should have thought about that before Alexei gave her to that scumbag I murdered," Lachlan taunts Maksim.

Gasp. Then he and I wouldn't be together. "I'd like to go home, Lachlan."

"Aye, my sweet wife." He puts his knife away, but leans into Maksim's ear. "I may have married her to get her away from that vile animal, but she and I are turning out to be very compatible. Her cunt weeps for my massive dick every night and every morning. Snooze, you lose, asshole."

I blush from Lachlan's graphic confession of our sex life. But I get how alphas are.

"I asked her nicely to be my wife." Maksim spins around, reaching into his jacket. "I have the means to just abduct her, you know."

Lachlan bellows a laugh. "Try it. I'd love a legitimate reason to slit your throat. Wives are off-limits and automatic death sentences. No meetings needed for permission to kill. Dante Caruso, the Italian underboss, dared to hurt Kieran's wife, and he's worm food right now."

"We'll see, Lachlan." Maksim struggles to keep upright with his cane.

"You won't be seeing *anything* if I decide to blind you

with acid." Lachlan takes my hand and kisses it. "Stay the fuck away from my wife."

Maksim stalks off, and Lachlan smiles, watching him. Until his grin drops. I follow his gaze and see his brothers, Kieran and Riordan, standing there. He looks away and stares down at me, his eyes burning with passion. Dark possession lurks deeper inside than ever before.

Does that mean he won't let me go to London, like Maksim suggested?

*

We drive home, listening to a piano concert. Lachlan parks his Corvette, and when he opens my door, he carries me all the way to the bedroom.

He lays me down on the bed and drapes his massive body over mine. "You looked beautiful tonight. You're too young and lively for a matronly floor-length dress."

"I'm nearly the same age as Isabella," I say, and open for his hungry kiss.

"She's pregnant and married to the king."

"Do… Do you want children?"

He stops nuzzling my neck and studies me. "Do you?"

"I hadn't thought about having children yet. I'd like to dance professionally for a few years first."

He feathers my cheek with his ringed, tattooed fingers, then closes his hand around my neck. "Then you shall dance professionally first."

I swallow, feeling the tension under his hand. Did we just agree to stay married? He said nothing about having kids with him, though. But I feel so strongly he implied that.

The idea of a child of my own fills me with joy. And to raise it with its father… Something I was denied. I want to ask a few follow-ups, but I really want him inside me more.

He slides off me and undresses, giving me a show. A few other men showed up in suits and not tuxes. Even though my father lost his shit on me, there were a few other women in knee-length cocktail dresses.

Piece by piece, Lachlan removes his clothes, black pants, black jacket, and the burgundy shirt I picked out disappear in a matter of minutes. All pulled off by thick, rough hands, inked-up with a skull and roses. Death and love.

Lachlan loves to kill people.

"Stand up, my precious little wife." His deep voice thrills me. "Turn for me."

I do and shudder, feeling him unzip my dress. "I hope I can wear this again."

"Me, too." He soaks my bare shoulder with his warm, wet lips. "You looked so beautiful. Fuckable."

The sequined cups and thin straps didn't require a bra, so when the dress slides down my body, I'm there in just a tiny, white lace panty I bought at the boutique as well.

Lachlan doesn't just sip from my lips. He drinks me down like I'm the last drop of water he'll ever taste. Or like I'm the blood he needs to maintain his evil image. He claims me with those lips, his tongue, and his hands gripping my waist with bruising strength.

I catch a breath as his tongue circles the tip of mine. "So sweet," he drawls, his fingers brushing against my sex.

My body jerks from the contact, I'm so wired and sensitive.

"Open for me." But he doesn't wait and pries my legs apart.

I'm boneless and beguiled, unable to think straight. "I want you to lick me."

"Aye, beg for it, little wife."

"Please."

"Please, what?"

"Please lick me."

"Please lick your *what*..." he growls.

My heart thumps. "Please lick my cunt."

He brushes a thumb across my sensitive clit. "This cunt?"

"Yes."

"Or is it my cunt?"

"It's yours. I belong to you."

"Fuck yes, you do." He brings a dewy finger in front of my eyes. "See how wet you are? How wet you get for me?"

"You do that to me."

"And you do this to me." He pushes his erection against my thigh, its wet tip smearing my skin. He nuzzles my neck, sinking two more fingers inside me. "This wet cunt is such a tease. I want to feel you so bad."

"You do feel me."

"I mean fuck you balls-deep without a condom." His eyes burn dark. "But I don't think I can stop once I'm inside you. I want to empty myself into this sweet cunt."

My head fights to think about my cycle, which often gets messed up from intense ballet training. Should I take the risk? Perhaps I should wait until I'm bleeding and then pay closer attention. But I don't want to wait.

"It's okay," I sputter, not caring. The fullness of his fingers inside me is mind-blowing.

He pulls them out and licks them clean, flicking his tongue. "Time for me to worship your wet pussy with my mouth." He peppers my neck with kisses and moans, his hot breath fanning my skin.

"That feels so good." I arch my back as he sucks on each nipple. "I can't take it."

"I want you crazy and dripping before I shove my cock inside you." His dirty talk brings me to another level of enjoyment.

He moves down my body, and when his hot mouth clamps down on my center, my hips jerk. With his lips around my clit, I'm pulsing in seconds. I moan so embarrassingly loud that I slap my hand over my mouth.

He kisses the center of my palm. "There's no one for miles, my little wife. Yell as loudly as you want. Everyone who saw us tonight knows I've claimed you. That you're mine." He sounds so primal.

I want to squeeze his head with my thighs for relief, I'm so sensitive, but Lachlan tears me apart, piece by piece, with firm lips and long, rough fingers probing me. I dig my nails into his hair. The more they become one with his scalp, the more he moans, pushing his hips against the mattress, humping it.

He sits up, looking like Adonis, with sculpted shoulders and thick biceps, stroking his massive length. His eyes flutter. "Fuck, you have me so sensitive. I may not last long. Are you sure I can come inside you?"

"Yes, please. Please take me bare."

"I love hearing you beg for it." Lachlan pushes the crown of his manhood against my entrance. No matter how many times we have sex, it's still a slow go. But the way he smiles entering me inch by inch, he doesn't mind easing inside a little at a time.

My center gives way, and he easily slides all the way in. I'm *that* wet.

"Aye, that's what I needed." Lachlan props up on his knees and grips my waist. Groaning, he gives a heavy thrust, knocking the wind out of me. It's slow, but he gets so damn deep, filling me and hitting every nerve ending.

"That's so good. Don't stop." I start to spiral.

"That dripping cunt of yours is soaking my balls. You're so fucking wet for me." He pushes in and out.

How did we get here? He saved me from a horrible man and married me to spite my father. Yet, deep in my bones, I think he cares about me now. This feels like more than just sex.

"Christ, this is so fucking hot." His hips shift, and he takes me on an angle that hits in places that make me see stars.

Everything below my waist shudders.

"That's right. Come on my cock. My dick belongs only to you. You're the only woman I want to fuck, Katriane. Only you. Fuck..." He groans and shatters inside me.

"I only want you, too, Lachlan." I drag my nails down his back, but I'm not strong enough to break the skin.

"I'm coming." His cock jerks so violently, it stretches me even more. "You're mine," he growls in my ear. His lips drench my shoulder as his teeth dig into the skin.

I hope it leaves a mark. I want to be branded his.

My ears are ringing from my heart pounding so hard, but I think I hear him say...

Forever.

CHAPTER TWENTY-FOUR

KATYA

A few nights later, I wake up in the early light to find Lachlan sweeping past the bed and into the bathroom. The door clicks shut and a few seconds later, the shower is running.

I'd heard cheating husbands come home and shower immediately. It seems implausible Lachlan would do that to me, but he said I was naïve about my father. I won't be naïve about my husband. I get out of bed and creep into the bathroom to say good morning. See if I notice anything suspicious. I'd know, right? The idea of him touching someone else nauseates me.

Lachlan is naked, standing in front of the vanity. I gasp seeing his right bicep torn up and dripping with blood. My stomach clenches with a much different kind of worry. "Oh my God, what happened?"

"Guy slashed me. It's nothing. It'll stop bleeding after I clean it up."

"Oh." I stand there and wait for him to look at me, but he doesn't.

"I'll wrap it up after I shower." He saunters toward the hot spray, giving me the most amazing view of his naked ass and a back full of rippling muscles.

I shake my eyes away. I can stare at him all day long. Instead, I scoop up his clothes caked in blood. Figuring out the washing machine was ridiculously easy. After using a pre-treatment spray, I add detergent and toss in the shirt and pants.

By the time I come back to the bedroom and look inside the bathroom, my husband is in a towel and brushing his teeth, his arm wrapped in gauze.

I step in cautiously and lean against his warm, wet back. "You smell good."

"I didn't ten minutes ago. That fucker got me worked up." He turns around and hugs me. "Another reason I didn't jump into bed with you. I stink up pretty nasty."

"It wouldn't bother me. You're a man. It's expected." I sink into his arms, his knife wound not limiting how he holds me.

But the smell of copper overwhelms me, and I snap my eyes open. "Lachlan, the wound must be deep. You're bleeding through the wrap."

He lets me go and unravels the blood-soaked gauze. I heave, seeing the deep gash in his bicep close-up. "Aww fuck."

"Lachlan!" I point to the crimson speckled bathroom floor and blood stains all over the shower wall. I press a towel into the wound and cry out, "Lachlan, this won't stop bleeding!"

"It's nothing." He grips the end of another towel and tears it in half. But before he can make a tourniquet, he doubles over and face plants onto the bathroom floor, shaking and out cold.

*

"Thanks for getting here so quickly," I let Griffin into the house, who's soaked from a late July rainstorm that has steam lifting off the ground.

It took him about twenty minutes after I called, scared out of my mind.

A pretty woman with long, dark hair in a raincoat follows Griffin inside. "Katya, this is my sister-in-law, Darcy. The one I told you about. She's a nurse."

"Where is he?" Darcy, who speaks with an Irish accent like the rest of them, pushes Griffin out of the way.

"In our bathroom. He's breathing, but he's not

coherent. His eyes won't focus. He's lost a lot of blood. I tied a towel around his arm. The bleeding has slowed but won't stop."

I bring them into our bedroom and hold the bathroom door open. My heart is pounding, my stomach ready to revolt from all the blood.

"Oh God." Darcy drops to her knees and digs into a knapsack. "Griffin, lay him flat on his back and lift that arm."

I stand back, feeling helpless. He's my husband. I'm supposed to take care of him. "What can I do?"

Darcy's green eyes lift to mine. "Are you familiar with smelling salts?"

"No. Show me." I reach for the tiny white tube in her hand.

"Just snap the top off and hold it under his nose. He'll jerk his head back."

"I'll hold his big noggin." Griffin comes up on the other side of him. "He's a strong son of a bitch."

"Then what?" I sink to the bathroom floor, the tube in my shaking hand.

"I'm going to stitch him up," Darcy says without flinching.

"He *needs* to go to the hospital," I say.

"Lachlan doesn't do hospitals, Katya." Griffin's voice goes dark.

"What if he lost too much blood?"

"I'll know once he wakes up." Darcy nods for me to continue.

Thanks to my sweaty palms, it takes a few tries before I'm able to snap the tube open. Once I shove it under Lachlan's nose, his head jerks up. Like a mechanical bull, he bucks and roars.

"Mate, it's me, Griffin. Relax, you passed out. You lost too much blood, you git. Darcy is here to stitch you up."

"Lachlan, sweetheart, look at me." I hold his head. "You're going to be fine."

"What happened?" he groans.

"That gash on your arm," I remind him. "You lost too much blood and passed out. I called Griffin."

His lips go flat, but they melt into a faint smile. "Good girl."

Griffin slides away. "He sounds fine. I don't think he needs a transfusion or anything."

"Should we move him?" I ask.

"It's cramped in here, but the light is amazing." Darcy crouches down beside the torn-up arm and flicks a giant needle. "Hey, Lachlan. It's Darcy Quinlan. I have to stick you with an anesthetic. I won't lie, it's gonna hurt."

"Do it," Lachlan rasps.

"Keep your eyes on me," I say softly, stroking his forehead.

I catch Darcy raising the needle and brace Lachlan, but he doesn't budge. God, he's tough.

"*How* did this happen?" I ask him. "How did someone get so close to you, you git!"

"Git," he chuckles at me, still looking out of it.

Mumbling in his extra-thick accent, Lachlan explains that he and Priscilla paid a visit to a clean-up team associate. They suspected he might be a spy, collecting evidence to blackmail them. At gunpoint, Lachlan interrogated the guy. "We took his piece and checked him for other weapons. Guy had a knife taped to his hip. I turned around, and he swung at me, tore the sleeve of my shirt. I felt a sting, but thought it was a scrape."

"Scrape," Darcy scoffs. "The areshole just missed the tendons."

Lachlan keeps his eyes focused on me. "You look scared, little wife."

"I saw all six-six of you collapse. That scared me."

His good hand brushes my chin. "It takes more than a scrape to take me out."

"It wasn't a scrape." I run my fingers through his thick, dark mane. "Was it okay that I called Griffin?"

"Aye."

I watch Darcy, and jealousy cramps my stomach. "I need to know how to do that. Darcy, can you show me? I got lucky that Griffin was close and that you were available. You've got two children, isn't that right?"

She smiles at me. "I do. I also have a mother-in-law who loves to babysit."

"I still want to know how to do this."

"Come watch me." She waves me over. "It takes practice."

"I don't want to sound silly, but I know how to sew. I made my own costumes when I was little. Even when Papa offered to buy me whatever I needed for recitals, I still made my own rehearsal and audition gear."

"It's not that different. I've been taking surgical nursing classes, but it took a while to get used to the needle driver." She's got my husband nearly stitched up. "I'll order you a practice kit."

"They make practice kits?"

"Enough." Lachlan stirs and gets to his feet. "This won't happen again. I don't need my wife stitching me up. She's a dancer, not a doctor."

Darcy hides her smile and then winks at me. "Two seconds, Lachlan. Let me finish."

He exhales roughly and sticks his arm back at her. She finishes, then wraps him up in fresh gauze with tape on the ends. Griffin and Darcy leave our bedroom, and I feel their eyes lingering on the sea of blankets we mess up by making love. Every morning and every night.

"This is your gun and your punching arm, Lach," Griffin points out once we're in the living room. "You need to take it easy for a few days. Priscilla and I will handle things."

"A few *days*?" I shriek. "No. My husband is seriously hurt. He passed out! Darcy, when will those stitches come out?"

Darcy looks at Griffin as I challenge her. "The gash is sitting right over the muscle, which isn't easy to keep isolated, even in a sling." Bracing herself, she mutters, "Two weeks really is the best time frame."

"*Two weeks?*" Lachlan roars, and Griffin shoves Darcy behind him. "The stitches in my face came out in five days." He points to the scar across his left cheek.

Darcy pushes Griffin aside. "Lachlan," she says his name in a commanding tone. "Facial wounds are different. So are gashes on the palms and the bottom of the feet. Our skin may look the same everywhere, but trust my medical background, it's not."

"Lachlan, please." I press on his chest. "I don't want you going after people compromised."

Breathing heavily, he stares down at me. I'm trying to cage a lion. I lick my lips and pull him down for a kiss. "Please. It'll go quick. We'll...keep busy."

"Can I not move it at all?" He glares at Darcy above my head.

"Of course you can. You just can't strain it. *Pummeling* people will strain it." She saunters up to him. "Don't forget who my husband is. I know what you do to our enemies."

Her saying *our* hits me. *She's* one of them. She speaks like them. I don't. I've been treated like an outsider since I arrived in Astoria. Right now, I feel that chasm again, and it makes me sick.

The other night at the gala, sitting with Isabella and Priscilla, I felt like I fit in. But maybe I'm fooling myself. My father and Maksim have caused so much trouble.

Maybe people see me as guilty by association.

Lachlan doesn't make me feel that way, though.

"Please," I whisper against his chest, loving how his massive arms come around and hold me.

"Aye," he rasps. "I want you to look at it in a week, though, Darcy."

"I will do that." She nods with a smile.

Griffin and Darcy leave with the rain thrashing against the windows at the front of the house. I glance at Lachlan holding me in a decorative mirror near the door. He's so much bigger than me. I can disappear inside him, lost, and wrapped in his arms. The reflection staring back at me paints a different picture. I feel like we're the same. He's elevated me, made me feel important.

Our...

I am an O'Rourke.

And no matter what, I want to stay one.

CHAPTER TWENTY-FIVE

LACHLAN

Two weeks my arse.

I adore Katya for caring about me, for risking my wrath to make sure I heal properly. The problem being so damn big, not many people can lift me if I'm hurt. Another reason I'm conditioned to stay sharp and on my toes. One eejit with a lucky swing nearly took me down.

But word will get out that I'm hurt and sidelined. That puts my family at risk.

As if my thoughts are on the fucking family Wi-Fi plan, I get a text from the underboss:

Riordan: Heard about your arm. Priscilla and Connor got you covered. I've also been recruiting some fierce talent from Dunbar. Raw, hungry motherfuckers who hate all things Russian.

I squeeze the phone to the point I could break it hearing Dunbar. Pain radiates down my arm, and I drop the cell on the floor.

Katya picks it up. "Let's get you into bed."

I push myself by holding her with both arms, ignoring the throbbing stabbed one. "I can't take two weeks off."

We play chicken—her watching my eyes as I squeeze her arms. It's a race who will tap out first. In the end, I give in.

"Wasn't Riordan in a coma for a month?" She waves her hands. "Did the O'Rourke empire collapse without the underboss?"

"That was different." I won't denigrate my brother's importance compared to mine with further details. "And it was three weeks."

"Darcy agreed to check on you in a week. If you want, I'll call her back in five days."

I lift my left arm and stroke her hair. "Negotiating with me?"

"How do you think I survived in the Bratva?"

I think about that, and consider how people underestimated her. "Five days."

"Consider what we can do for five days?" She pulls me down for a kiss.

I roar with laughter. "Care to make good on that, little wife?"

"Care to stop me?" She shakes off a very thin, see-through nightgown and sinks to her knees.

Feeling feisty and wanting to test my wife, I step back and grip the outline of my hard cock. "If you want my cock in your mouth, baby, *crawl* for it."

Licking her lips and looking sexy-as-fuck naked, she sinks to the plush carpet. Like a panther on all fours, she crawls to me, her back arched in a cat pose. My kitty kat.

If there was a time to take the Lord's name in vain...

I squeeze my eyes shut, muttering, "Jesus fucking Christ," and relax when I don't burst into flames.

If killing a priest didn't incinerate me first...

Reaching me, Katya looks up with those big brown eyes that have me spiraling with need.

"Are you sure you want me to do this right here in the living room?" she mewls.

"Why not? It's just us." The freedom to be stark naked and fuck my wife's mouth in my living room is so damn satisfying. Growing up with seven siblings, I felt smothered and controlled.

Katya unfurls the towel that managed to stay on my waist throughout this ordeal and takes my swollen cock into her hands. "How can anything so dangerous be so beautiful?"

My fucking knees buckle. I had the power to deny myself pleasures of the flesh. It'd been easy when I wanted to be a priest, and easier these two plus years pining for Katya. Now, I question my sanity, because I can't go one damn day without being inside my wife.

"Are you talking about me or my cock?"

Katya licks the tip, and my head falls back. "Both."

My thick, heavy cock breaches her soft, pillowy lips and I forget my name. Man, how weak would I have been, had I experienced this before my decision to become a priest? I'm certain, one taste of this shattering pleasure, and I might have made the decision to give up my dream on my own.

Feeling her warm, wet mouth around my throbbing cock, my ears ring with an evil hiss. I question if the devil is whispering nonsense, so I won't want to keep this woman. He won the first two rounds, made me push Foster to his death, then stripped me of my emotions the night I killed Father Eamon.

Not this time. I'm more dangerous and powerful than ever. Katya is fucking mine.

My cock thumps, and she gags on my hard length. But with a look of sexy determination, she goes right back to work. "Do you feel what you do to me, baby?"

She pulls off and smiles to lick the tip then circles the head with her tongue. "You'll have to hold me down and show me."

When she wraps her lips around my cock again, I brace my legs for the feeling of euphoria that I assume resembles free falling from a plane. I lavish the fact that I'm her first. The idea of another man standing here with my wife on her knees infuriates me.

With my cock sliding further inside Katya's warm, wet, greedy mouth, I'm questioning if I'll let her go to London. Can I live without these carnal moments that yank me out of the darkness?

As every inch slides deeper down her throat, I harden painfully and worry, I'll just grab her head and fuck her face. Hurt her. How can something feel so damn good?

I stare down at my pretty stolen bride with eyes just for *me* and with a cunt only I've ever sank into. I've whored my flesh all over this city, but *this* isn't something I've felt before. It goes beyond the crackle of electricity she brings into the room. It's because she's all mine.

I take a breath, my nostrils flaring at her scent of arousal. "Are you wet, baby?"

She bobs off and licks the underside of my cock while it drips pearly precum from my sensitive tip. "You'll find out."

"Damn right, I will." I want to come down her throat, but that won't stop me from fucking her right away.

The devil gave me a wicked dick and an insatiable appetite. His plan may have been to break me. *Me*. One of the most feared men in Astoria, wealth beyond measure, by giving me a wife I adore.

Fuck, I adore this girl. Is this love? Would it be terrible if I loved her?

Yes, because she doesn't want to stay with me. She wants to dance all over Europe. My heart aches, and I turn brutal, shoving my cock in and out of her mouth.

I twist a snarl of hair, adorably knotted with bed head from a full night's sleep while I was out hurting people. I force her to take me deeper into her mouth. A wicked vision forms of her doing this to someone else. She's tasted sin and will want more of it. Fuck, she initiates sex more than I do.

"You like me fucking your mouth, don't you?" I push harder, deeper. "You like sucking your husband's cock?"

"Mmmm," she groans.

I reach down and grab one hand that's been fisting the base of my shaft. "Massage my balls." Fuck, they're so tight.

Her warm hand gives an enthusiastic little squeeze paired with a throaty moan, and I'm barely holding on. "Deeper, baby. Keep going. Give me what I need and I'll pay you back, I promise."

She squeaks a moan of pleasure while I'm on the brink and hurtling toward a violent orgasm. I unclench my stomach and give in to the wicked waves hovering and let pleasure flood through my veins.

I pull out and push her down until I'm on top of her. "Open, baby."

Straddling her face, I unload into her mouth, hitting her lips with milky ropes of my release. God, this is so fucking filthy. But she laps me up with a smile on her face.

She loves challenging me, and I love making good on my threats. "Now get in our bed. I'm going to fuck that tight pussy for the rest of the day. You wanted me home. You're gonna pay for that with a sore cunt.
"

CHAPTER TWENTY-SIX

KATYA

Lachlan reaches down and lifts me into his arms after a very salacious threat to fuck me until I'm sore. But it's him I'm worried about.

"Your stitches!" I bellow.

"It's fine. I can't feel anything other than my cock pulsing right now." He hikes down the hall carrying me into the bedroom.

I'm reminded of the blood splatter in the bathroom, but push that away. Lachlan's reaction to my going down on him struck a match to my sex. If he's not inside me soon, I'm going to combust.

He lays me down and dives right into my center with a tongue that drives me crazy. "So fucking wet and sweet."

"Just for you."

"Damn right. This is mine." He fingers my slit, and my womb clenches. "That's right, baby, get that one out of the way. I'll give you more. So much more." He continues to lick and suck on me until I can't breathe or see straight.

"Lachlan," I say his name, choking.

"Aye," he groans. "What does my wife want?"

"I want you inside me." A feeling of emptiness attacks me.

"I want you on top." Lachlan squeezes my ass cheeks and rolls onto his back.

The bed is a mess of sheets and blankets. I don't even get a chance to make the bed, we're in it so much.

"We need to change these sheets. We do despicable

things on them." I climb on top of him and sigh in happiness at his heavy cock, stiff once again, and waiting for me.

I lower only one knee and tease him, rubbing my wet center along the crown.

"Fuck…" he groans.

When it's slick enough, I slowly lower onto his shaft. He stretches me so sublimely, the fullness is delicious and devastating.

"Easy, baby. My nine inches will hurt you," he groans as I keep lowering.

"I can handle you."

"Aye, you can. That's why I love…" He can't *love* me. We're just getting to know each other.

I lower my head, shocked at what he'd say. "That's why we fit."

"We fit perfectly." He tugs me down until my chest presses against his.

His cock strains to bend at that angle, the pressure stretching me even more.

"Now. Shut the fuck up and fuck your husband's cock like a good girl."

"Aye." I bless him with the saying he and his brothers throw around. I could answer *Da*, but I don't speak Russian. And *Oui* doesn't feel right. I don't feel French or Russian.

All I feel is Irish. Nine inches worth!

I lean back and pivot my hips. It grinds the coarse coils of his neatly trimmed pubic hair against my clit. I run my hands through my hair and push my tiny boobs out.

"These tits drive me crazy." His fingers capture my taut nipples.

I admit, I don't look at them with disappointment anymore.

One hand grips my waist, grinding me down harder as

the other teases my stomach with feathering touches.

I'm aware I just made him come, and he'll go at me for a while. I want to be all he needs. Mob men cheat on their wives. Heck, my *maman* was Papa's mistress. Guilt fills me that I'm a product of a selfish act. But deep in my gut, I don't think Lachlan would do that to me. Unless I move away and give him permission. My heart hurts, thinking of us separated.

"Katya, you okay?" Lachlan's dark eyes find mine.

"Uh, huh. It's unbelievable."

"You look lost in your head. Time to get you back in the game here." He flips me over until I'm on my hands and knees. "Grab the headboard, little wife. I'm taking over."

CHAPTER TWENTY-SEVEN

LACHLAN

I thought being sidelined would drive me nuts. I never imagined I'd want to spend the day in bed with a woman. One woman. Yet, my wife satisfies me like nothing else.

Without my brothers needing me to troll the streets at night, I hold Katya until dawn, often waking up with her mouth around my cock.

I worry I'm addicted to sex. Or maybe I'm just making up for the two and a half years I gave it up. Or could I be subconsciously getting my fill because she might leave me? Then what? If I stay married to her, I'll never break my vow.

What if she insists on a divorce? Then what do I do?

I push away the covers to join her in the shower and pin her against the wall. I kiss my way down her body. "Open for me."

Her legs part, and I lick her sweet cunt until she cries out my name. With her writhing from an orgasm, I shove my cock inside her. The feeling of her clenching around me has me spiraling in seconds.

I'm in fucking trouble.

*

I drive Katya to school, and without needing to go home and sleep, I say to her, "I'd like to stay and watch you dance today."

"Really?" She goes rigid and twists her ponytail. "It's just rehearsing, and it can be tedious standing around all day."

"I'd like to see your dance routine for the audition."

Just as the words come out of my mouth, a crackle of doom fills the air around us.

She clutches that necklace I hate and stammers for a response. I reach out to stroke her hand gripping her gear bag, noticing her knuckles are white. "Katriane?"

Her eyes lift to me. "You haven't called me that too much."

"I'll call you whatever you want me to call you." Especially if it's *yours*. "Katya, you don't want me to stick around?"

"It's just a grueling day. We start by stretching for close to an hour. Then it's the same routine over and over and over."

"I stake people out, little wife." I brush her hand. "I have incredible patience. And stamina."

She chuckles darkly. "Yes, you do."

I worry she doesn't think she's worth my time to sit around and do nothing but watch her. Support her. "What's wrong, Katya?"

"Papa never once came to see any of my performances, let alone my rehearsals."

Fucking Alexei never showed a personal interest in her dancing. Just paid the tuition bills, to the most expensive performing arts college, no less.

"I think we've established I'm nothing like your father. I'm parking and coming with you." I take control of the situation and find a garage.

On the street, I scoop her hand into mine. She's my wife, and everyone in this world of hers needs to know that.

It occurs to me, with our fingers twisted together, that she doesn't have a ring.

Holy shit, I *never* got her a ring. And she never asked for one. She threw Rahil's ring on top of his dead body. My evil glare at the priest when he robotically got to the ring exchange part of the ceremony had him skipping it.

We get to the main entrance, and I hate seeing only one security guard there. I give him a deep 'hello' and keep walking, whether I'm allowed to be here or not. Katya is my wife, and it's my right to stay with her. I just don't like the idea that he'd let *anyone else* walk in here.

At the end of a long hallway, women who are basically clones of Katya, as far as dress and size, disappear behind a set of double doors.

"I need to change." She tugs me to a corner. "You can't come into the dressing room."

"Says who?"

"Lachlan!" Her eyes slip closed, and I'm getting frustrated that she doesn't want me here.

"Do my looks bother you, little wife?" I've lived with this scar for half my life, but never considered how frail young women might look at me. "And I was kidding about the dressing room."

"Lachlan, you're stupidly gorgeous. That hulking, broody thing you have going on only makes you more attractive. Don't even get me started on the scar."

"I only want you, Katya." I consider maybe she doesn't want me watching other dancers. "I hate surprises, but this spark between us has been a very pleasant one for me."

"I only want you, too." She snuggles against my chest. "My stretch clinic lasts for about an hour. Why don't you get some coffee and come to the auditorium around ten?"

That will give me time to find a jewelry store. "Aye, little wife. I can't wait to see you dance again."

She gives me another squeeze and a soft kiss on my rough cheek. "I'll see you later."

Watching her glide toward those double doors, my brain is aware of other women, but I only have eyes for

Katya. Anger bubbles inside me when I think of men who cheat on their wives. I'm certain my father was a rare exception. Even when my mother was always pregnant.

Then Darragh and Cormac came along and she was done.

It had been great having Darragh and his daughter, Sophie, home for a few days when Riordan was in the hospital. He hinted Cormac was in trouble some way. Darragh, his identical twin, staunchly looks out for his brother. I struggle if I should get involved. To pay Cormac a visit. Darragh assured us he'd reach out if he needed us.

I leave those thoughts behind me and grab a coffee from a street cart. Sipping the vile mess, I call my sister.

"Lachlan?" Shea chirps to me.

"*Me a stór.*" I call her my treasure, and it immediately feels odd, since I have a wife who should have that title. Shea is our only sister and so very precious to us. "I assume you heard I got married."

"I did. You guys are making my head spin. Are they putting something different in the water in Astoria?"

I think about the coincidence of Kieran, Riordan, and me getting married in a matter of a couple of years. Then it hits me, the undercurrent that drove these decisions. The Koslov Bratva falling apart. Which was spurred by one simple action.

Stasia running off. And according to my wife, she suggested it should look like a kidnapping.

"You'd have to ask your BFF Balor, since he knows all about cyber-attacks," I joke to Shea about her love potion in the water. "Anyway, I need a ring for Katya."

"You haven't bought her a ring yet?"

"I've been busy." Consummating the marriage, but I would never say anything inappropriate to my sister.

"Kieran and Riordan were happy with Crest Diamonds."

"That place off Fifth?" I search for a street sign.

"Place? It's a billion-dollar diamond empire." Diamonds are a nasty, cut-throat business run by vicious cartels. "I'll call and make an appointment for you."

"No. I'll call them." I don't care for the red-carpet treatment Kieran and Riordan get. I work the streets and get my hands dirty. I keep it real.

"Okay. Promise me you won't show up with blood on your clothes."

I laugh, but don't know if she's kidding. "I'll see what I can do. Thank you, Shea." I'm about to hang up but ask, "Do I get her an engagement ring if we're already married?"

Shea stays silent briefly, then drawls in the same lilt we all have, "Lachlan?"

"Shea-Lynne?"

"What are you doing?"

"What do you mean?"

"I keep out of your lives there. But I know you... You've never cared about a woman before."

"I'm thirty-eight, Shea."

"Look, I got the whole story. You crashed her wedding, killed the groom because he hurt her, and you married her to keep her safe. Your honor astounds me. But...are you *staying* married to this girl?"

"She's a *woman*," I bark and feel sick that I just spoke harshly to my sister. "I'm sorry."

"You must care about her." Shea sounds shocked, and that bothers me.

"Yeah, so?" My chest squeezes saying that, but it's freeing as fuck.

Yeah, I fucking care about her. I've been living with her for a few weeks. She's under my roof, under my skin.

She's an angel. Sweet. Smart. Not afraid of me, not afraid to challenge me. Likes the same movies as me. Takes care of me. Cares about me.

Funny how the incredible sex we've been having doesn't rise to the top of that list.

The only negative mark in her column is that she might leave me.

"I don't want you to get hurt," Shea says darkly.

"Because she's Russian?" I snap. "Isabella is Italian. No one considered *her* the enemy."

"Lachlan, the Italians were never the same threat. The Russians tried to kill Riordan and what they did to Priscilla when she was seventeen... I'm sorry if I'm skeptical."

"Katya's *not* one of them. She's half French, raised by her mother. Alexei took her in because she's his blood, nothing more. Then he ignored her. It's only because Stasia is missing that he tried to marry her off to a..." I bite my tongue. "A very bad man, Shea. Do you not trust my judgment?"

"Aye, as long as you're happy."

I laugh, knowing what drove my happiness for so long. Violence. Blood. Death. Katya is so opposite that. "I'm happy with her. She's good for me. I deserve a wife, just like everyone else."

"Absolutely. Maybe more, considering what you've been through." Her voice gets low. She was a teenage girl when my life went to hell.

"I'd love to meet her." Shea clears her throat. "I also know you're nursing a serious knife wound. There's a great Airbnb right on the water that came available. The couple got into a massive fight and left after a week. They booked the whole summer. It's stupid expensive, so it's still available. I know the owner, and I'll see if she'll book it for a week."

I remember Katya mentioning wanting to visit Shea in the Hamptons. "That sounds like something my wife would love. I'll let you know."

"Great," she says. "And as far as an engagement ring, if you're like your older brothers, they love giving their women huge diamonds that say fuck you to our enemies."

I roar with laughter. "Noted."

We chat for a few more moments, and I smile when she tells me she loves me. I say it back, and wonder how my voice will sound saying it to Katya.

I stride to the jewelry store Shea recommended, getting there quickly with my long legs. When I open the door, a gasp from a woman behind a counter makes me grin, but a man in a suit quickly appears.

"Mr. O'Rourke?"

"Aye." I fold my arms.

"Archer Crest. Your sister called me."

Of course she did.

"You need rings for your wife?" He glances behind me like I'm hiding her.

"We got married in a rush, and didn't get a chance to buy rings. I'd like to surprise her."

"You came to the right place. Follow me." He leads me to a private viewing room. "Do you know her size by any chance?"

"I don't. She's very petite."

"No problem. I can size it later." He has black velvet trays already laid out. "Tell me about your wife."

"She's a dancer," I say right away, and when Archer's eyes widen, I narrow mine. "Ballet."

"Ah. Graceful?"

"Very."

"Beautiful."

"Crazy, beautiful. And modest about it." I take my

phone out and show him photos I collected of her over the years. Seeing so many of them, it hits me how obsessed I really was with her.

"She goes to East Side Performing Arts?" Archer studies the photos of her coming out of school.

"Aye."

"I'll call over there for her ring size. They take that info from all students for class rings." He taps into his phone.

"What do you recommend?"

"My first choice would be a classic round stone with a double halo setting. The thick diamond band is especially beautiful on slender fingers."

I take it in my hand and imagine it on Katya's finger. I glance at the others, and it's a sea of blinding sparkle. I can't discern one from the other.

Archer Crest. He's the owner, and I trust he knows his business. Knows what a *woman* wants as far as jewelry.

"I like this. What can you offer as far as a wedding band?"

"This matching ring with tiny haloed stones works well." He reaches for me to hand over the engagement ring and slides them onto a black velvet hand.

They do look stunning together.

"Sold."

"A ring for you, or..." He eyes the tats on my hands.

"Yeah?"

"Call me crazy. My brothers do, but I've hired someone to help men such as yourself who do..." He clears his throat. "Dangerous work and don't wear wedding rings. A tattoo with her name on that finger sends a stronger message. Upstairs, we have an amazing artist."

I hadn't gotten a new tat in a while.

"Sure. I'd like to pick out a few more pieces for my wife first. Earrings. Bracelets. Necklaces. She doesn't have any of that." I remember her feeling self-conscious at the gala, only wearing that dull cross around her neck. But she'd told me too late. Not that she needs any of this. She shines all by herself.

I can tell her I love her, but I'd rather show her how much she's worth to me.

"Have a seat Mr. O'Rourke. I'll bring in several sets from our top designer."

After seeing the entire collection, I wave my hand over it. "Sold."

He chuckles. "You don't want to know the price?"

"Don't need to. My wife deserves it. She has to live with me." I joke, shoving my hands in my jeans' front pockets. Dressed in denim and a white T-shirt, my dark hair slicked back, I feel younger. Relaxed.

I return to the private viewing room thirty minutes later with two new tats. *Katya* written in script around the ring finger of my left hand stings, but in a good way. And because the artist was a dude, I took this all one step further and had my wife's name tattooed right above my cock. I thought I would back out when he brought the needle so close to my manhood, but I heard Riordan and Shea's skeptical voices about how I feel about Katya.

"Do it," I muttered to the dude.

Archer shakes my hand when I leave with just the engagement ring in my coat pocket. Because of the insane cost of all the pieces I picked out for Katya, the shop holds the rest until I send someone to pick them up. For safety reasons. If anyone saw me come in here, they could follow me and attack when I'm with Katya. I didn't hold back. I bought a chunky diamond necklace, two bracelets, an anklet, her wedding rings, and three sets of earrings, one diamond, one pearl, and one gold with little hanging triangles. Yeah, I didn't want to be walking around with two hundred thousand dollars' worth of jewelry.

I snicker, wondering if Kieran and Riordan bought this much ice for their women. We don't compete, my brothers and me. We each have our areas of expertise. If anything, it will prove that I'm serious about Katya. I know neither of them tattooed their wives' name on their dicks.

Fuck, I *am* serious about her.

I get back to Katya's school, and that same rotten feeling washes over me being able to just walk in here. Maybe because it's summer...

Pushing my luck, I ask the one guard, "Where's the auditorium? My wife is rehearsing."

He looks me over, his neck craning. "Um."

"Lachlan O'Rourke." I stick my hand out to him. "My wife is Katya *Koslov*." I hate using her father's name since she's mine now. "I assume you were given instructions for her protection. She's *my* wife now."

"Ah, yes, sir." He nods, making me feel a little better. "Let me show you where she is."

"Thank you." I follow him.

"Use this door. It's closer to the stage." He opens it for me.

"Thank you." I step inside to a blast of cool air. The hallways were stuffy because it's almost August.

My throat tightens. *It's almost August.* Her audition is coming up.

My eyes adjust to the shadowed darkness and the empty stage until the lithe figure I've honed in on comes to the center. I step back, not wanting to make Katya feel nervous.

Violins play, the metaphor ironic.

Wearing a dark green leotard with an adorable little see-through skirt, Katya twirls and leaps. She bends in half and with her hands over her head, she leans left, then right. She jumps in a circle and something catches my eye on stage left. A man slowly walks toward Katya, but he's dressed in street clothes, and my hackles rise. I yank my gun out and move forward.

The man reaches Katya, and she leaps into his arms. I relax, realizing the man isn't some slob off the street, but...a dancer, too. Why didn't Katya mention this guy?

She's dancing with a man for her rehearsal?

Anger bubbles in my veins, but I'm not sure who to direct my ire to. She told me so much about her routine, but not that a partner was involved. A male one.

I keep watching. Having no understanding of ballet, I don't know if the way this guy is touching my wife is appropriate. I can only go by her face, which seems soft and easy. She's even smiling. I check my watch. I'm early. She didn't want me to know about this. The routine turns intimate, and I can't breathe, watching a man stroke a face that is mine. Lips I make smile when I'm inside her.

What the fuck is going on? Is she playing me? My sister's voice about Katya being Russian, and how different and ruthless they are, crawls into my brain.

The male dancer lifts Katya, and she slides down his body, his hands clearly touching her breasts. I snap.

"Hey!" I yell, barreling toward the stage. "Let go of my wife if you want to keep those hands."

CHAPTER TWENTY-EIGHT

KATYA

I watch the burgundy scarred floor come up at my face as I free fall out of Adam's arms. A shrill voice yelled from the seats, and he dropped me.

Umph. I fall, my foot twisting just at the right time and angle.

"Sir, you can't go on the stage," someone yells.

I look up, and a shadowed figure in a jacket over a white T-shirt storms up to me. Adam backs off as I spring up, my foot aching. "Lachlan! What are you doing?"

"Why is this guy touching you?"

"It's a dance." I press on his chest, my fingers tightening on his jacket.

His jacket. He's armed, which is why he's wearing it.

"All this time, you've been coming here with a guy touching you?"

"No." I exhale. "Let's go talk."

"Katya, are you ready for your routine?" Fern, the assistant choreographer, cautiously comes up to me.

"What are you talking about? She just danced." Lachlan winds his arm around my waist.

"No. I was standing in for Adam's partner. She's got Covid. He asked me to do the run through with him."

Lachlan breathes heavily, sweat beading on his forehead. "That's why you were dancing early?"

"Yes." My eyes slip closed. "They've been rehearsing for weeks. I watched their routine and knew I could substitute. I didn't want Adam to miss rehearsal time."

Lachlan stares over my head, glaring at Adam, who

looks shaken. "But he's competing against you."

"No, he's not. He and Charli are trying to get into the world competition."

"Oh." Lachlan holds my chin. "Fuck, you fell. He dropped you."

"I'm fine," spills from my lips because I'm programmed to say that, but one step pain shoots up my leg. "Ow!"

"Come with me." Lachlan scoops me up. "Where's your dressing room?"

"There are girls in there, sir." Fern bravely sidles up to us.

"Get them out of there," Lachlan sneers. "I need to make sure my wife is okay."

Fern shakes her head. "Use my office. It has a couch."

"Thank you, Fern." I call out, tucked into Lachlan's arms. "Can I do my routine last?"

"Sure." She nods at me over her shoulder as we follow her.

"Will this hurt you? What I did?" Lachlan lowers me onto the sofa in Fern's utilitarian office.

"No, the instructors are here to help us. Judges from the conservatory only come for the auditions."

He strokes my face. "Are you hurt badly?"

"I'm a little shaken from being dropped from so high up." I rotate my ankle, grateful my foot was just turned the wrong way for a moment.

Lachlan pulls me onto his lap. "I don't like that a man was touching you."

"I can't guarantee I'll never dance with a man again. In fact, I probably will. We're professionals. There's nothing…sexual about it."

"It looked sexual."

"It's a sensuous routine for a reason." I grind into his lap. "You're hard. You must have found it sexy."

"Watching you with another man? No way. I'm hard because you're on my lap." He reaches into his jacket and removes a blue velvet box. "And before I do something about this hard-on...here."

"What is that?" My heart leaps at the sight of the logo: Crest Diamonds.

"It's for you." Lachlan nuzzles my neck, pressing our waists together.

"When did you buy this?"

"After I left here this morning."

I pop the box open and gasp at the stunning, *massive* engagement ring. I understand him wanting me to wear a wedding ring, but a gorgeous diamond ring? Men give women rings like this when they're in love.

"Lachlan." I go breathless. "I can't take this. I don't need it."

"Yes, you do. You deserve it." He kisses my neck, rocking his hips into mine. "I want you, little wife."

"We're in someone's office."

"People here know who you are. And now they know who *I* am and who you belong to. No one will bother us. I should have gotten you a ring sooner."

"What about you?" I touch his hand and gasp, seeing my name carved and encircling his red, swollen ring finger.

"I don't know what to say. You didn't have to do *this*." I'm so overwhelmed because tats are permanent. He branded himself as mine with my name.

"I'm married and I want people to know." He holds my chin. "Unless you don't want to stay married to me."

It leaves me breathless to face the question that has been haunting me for weeks. "I do want to stay married to you." Why shouldn't I? Who else will treat me like this?

"What if you get the spot in London?" His voice turns

dark.

My heart pounds, and my throat tightens. "I don't know."

We stare, neither of us looking ready to hash out long-distance relationship plans and logistics.

"In case you're still not sure." He slides me to my feet and lowers his pants.

"Lachlan!" I screech. "Did that hurt?"

"You bet." He tattooed my name, my full name, first and last, right above his cock.

PROPERTY OF KATRIANE O'ROURKE

"I don't know what to say." I just *know* I want to do the same for him.

"Don't say anything. Just kiss me, little wife."

I crash my mouth down on his, and it's magic and electric. Furiously, I unsnap my leotard, and Lachlan yanks my panties out of the way. With both of us still mostly dressed, he shoves himself inside me hard on Fern's sofa.

"Lachlan, you're not wearing a condom again." I still don't know what's up with my cycle.

He stops for a moment, like he didn't even realize. "You agreed to marry me. You wanted to sleep in my bed. You wanted me to fuck you. I got indelible ink right above my cock for you. And now you *want* to stay my wife. If I get you pregnant, so be it. This… This is what I want. If *you* don't want it, tell me to stop."

My world turned upside down in the last couple of weeks. First, I'm almost married off against my will and then this… Whatever the hell this is with Lachlan. No one can predict where life will take you. I could get hurt at any time and lose my ability to dance. Today was an example of that. A partner dropping me can blow my entire future. My husband will go to the ends of the earth to protect me. Is the chance to hear applause worth the risk of losing that?

Swallowing hard, I say, "Please don't stop."

"Good girl." He pounds me, our skin slapping together, until he comes in powerful waves.

I fly over the edge and come so hard, I see stars. Damn, he's so deliciously warm, and his cum tingles inside me. It's wonderful.

I grip his shoulder, my eye catching the beautiful diamond he put on my finger for all to see. He tattooed his commitment to me. Ink he can never take off. Not without a medical procedure and a bruised ego for getting something so wrong.

Happiness fills my heart, but can what we have last?

CHAPTER TWENTY-NINE

LACHLAN

"How long have you been sitting on these hits?" I ask Griffin in Balor's downtown command center as we go through security footage of two losers who should be six feet under.

I passed my five-day test, even though my stitches sting and itch like crazy. Too bad. I'll tough it out.

Griffin runs a hand through his hair. "With Ewan on the city council now and Connor working for Riordan, we haven't really found someone we trust to take these guys out without it getting back to us."

"We're not the only ones with cameras," Balor says, swiveling in his gamer's chair.

After a moment of quiet, Griffin adds, "Priscilla is only comfortable castrating rapists."

"You're okay with these pricks walking around after stealing from us, G?"

"I didn't say that."

My arm throbs, bloodlust kicking up inside me. "I'll do it."

"Whoa!" Balor jumps from the seat. "Kieran won't like it if you do more damage to your arm."

"I'll deal with him. Griffin, let's go." I check my gun and realize I need to swap it out for a ghost gun from our armory. Balor's been making them, perfecting the technology. "Balor..." I strut up to him and squeeze his shoulder. "Good work."

Without waiting for a response, I push through the double doors and stride down the long dark hallway with Griffin on my six. "Do we know where these guys are now?"

"Now? You want to just find them and fill them with lead during the day?"

I stop and glare at him.

Griffin exhales and gets on his phone. "Pris, I'm sending you two photos and addresses. Get these guys to the black site." He laughs to himself, putting his phone away.

"Something funny?"

"Your sister-in-law is a badass."

Protectiveness howls inside me. "She's pregnant. I suggest you find someone who can replace her for these takedowns. I won't risk my brother's wee one."

She's worked out better than we could have imagined, since most eejits don't suspect a beautiful woman can be as deadly as she is. Will Riordan make her quit after she has his kid? And will they have more?

Griffin blinks in the burning sun when we get on the street. "How's Katya? Plan on having wee ones with her?"

My lips twitch, thinking of how I've been fucking her without a condom. "Not sure."

"Really? She doesn't want kids?"

"We haven't talked about it," I lie, stroking the center of my chest. Changing the subject, I say to Griffin, "What do you think happened to Stasia?" I twist to face him in the car while we wait for Priscilla to call us back.

"That's out of left field."

"Katya got a few postcards from her."

"Really?" He sounds surprised. "From her, not a kidnapper?"

"She wasn't kidnapped," I confess the information weighing on me.

"Lachlan..." Griffin goes breathless. "How long have you known this?"

210

"A few weeks. Katya told me. I wasn't sure what to make of that info. If it's even important after all this time."

"It blows the theory that someone off'd her and buried the body."

That still might be the case, and I hate it. "If nothing else, I want my wife to know where her sister is."

Griffin blows out a breath. "I couldn't imagine not knowing where Siobhan is."

Fuck, I feel the same about Shea. "Your sister and that husband of hers getting along?" It feels like forever when I showed up at her wedding, and talked about Stasia with Ewan. She'd just gone missing. Man, how things have changed around here.

"Aye. She's happy." He sneaks me a look because after Norah died, Ewan told Kieran he could have Siobhan. Then she ran off for three years. Had to be dragged back to New York.

But that billionaire fought for her.

I cup Griffin's shoulder because it all worked out. Kieran found his second chance with Isabella and is completely in love. My heart squeezes, seeing a light on the horizon that I, too, can open my heart like that.

"Let's just drive to the armory," I say, signaling I'm done talking about love and now need to concentrate on pain.

At the armory, I grab the loaded black ghost gun I need and shove it into my jacket.

Griffin's phone buzzes, and he laughs. "Jesus, she's good. Priscilla got them."

"Both of them?"

His eyes move across his phone, reading her text. "Yeah, both of them. And that's not a coincidence."

"What the hell does that mean?"

Griffin throws his SUV in drive and heads toward our

private warehouse. Once he's on a straight road, he tosses me his phone.

My eyes bulge at the photo collage Priscilla sent. I get her on the phone. "Pris, what the fuck?"

"The young guy says he's being trafficked by Zed," she says.

"Zed?"

"The older one."

She and I share in our visceral disdain for sex crimes. Her being a victim, and my first premeditated kill being a child rapist.

"Separate them and work on the younger guy," I tell her. "Keep Zed chained up."

"I kind of stabbed him."

"Kind of?"

"He took a swing at me."

Despite her being on our hit team, I'm shocked and disgusted by any man who will raise his hand to a woman.

We get there and I strut inside. The moment Zed sees me, he kicks his legs, as if that will save him. "No. No, no, no. Not *you*."

"Aye," I rasp and look over my shoulder at Priscilla in the glass interrogation room with the other guy. Fuck, it's a *kid*.

"You've been busy." I take out my gun. "Any others?"

"Others?"

"Young boys you're grooming and raping."

"I told that bitch—" He shuts up when I point the black plastic barrel at his head and twitch my thumb on the hammer.

"That's my sister," I drawl.

Priscilla is an O'Rourke. She's one of us. Just like my wife.

"Fuck. I'm sorry." He struggles against the chains

binding his arms behind his back. "Man, I'm just trying to feed my family."

"Family?" I glance back at the room. "You got a wife?"

"And two kids. I'm doing what I have to do."

I fold my arms, the gun nudged against my stitched-up bicep, everything twitching and burning. "Tell it to someone who cares."

"Man, please. I'll... I'll work for you. I have a whole network I can flip on."

"So, you're a philanderer. You're a rapist. And now a rat? You think that works with me?"

"I'm not raping that kid. He *loves* it." Zed snaps, revealing his true feelings, remorse out the window.

I look over at Priscilla with the kid again. "He's what? Sixteen?"

"Whatever."

Fuck, that means he's younger.

"Guy, listen. It's who I am. It's a sickness, all right? I can't help it."

His words spiral me down a vortex, flashed back in time to Father Eamon's confession...

Staring down my Da's gun, Father Eamon had also cried out:

"I can't help it, Lachlan. It's who I am. God forgives me. I beg every day for that atonement."

I became the man I am today when I filled him with lead from my father's gun.

Now I'm faced with the same evil.

I unload into this guy. Release the clip and reload. Stepping around his dead body, I empty the next clip into his groin. I stop when my armor-piercing bullets practically slice the guy in half, his guts spilling out like worms.

The room goes silent when I stop and hear breathing behind me.

Griffin nods. "Good one."

"Aye." I put the gun in my coat and catch Priscilla staring at me from the glass room. The 'kid' is hunched over in his metal chair.

When I get in there, she says, "Lachlan, they forced him into helping Zed."

My phone buzzes, and I itch to check it because Katya is at school. I can't stop thinking about her. I'm not the same man I was three weeks ago. My breathing doesn't feel right when she's not with me. "Follow me, Pris."

"Stay here," Priscilla says to the kid.

"Yes, ma'am." He's not tied up, but sounds scared as fuck.

"Find out what else he knows about Zed's operation," I say to her, low and controlled. "See if he'll give us names. Tell him we'll protect him."

"Aye." Her lips snarl, looking at Zed. "We can really use a break to bust up that annoying theft corridor upstate. A shitload of our inventory keeps going missing."

"I trust you, Pris." I put my hand on her shoulder.

"Lachlan, you're bleeding." She brushes her hand on my arm.

"What else is new?" I take out my phone and frown, not seeing a text from Katya. What the hell made it vibrate? "Griffin!"

"Yeah, boss?"

"Help Priscilla with this kid. He's not to be hurt."

"Aye."

I go to check in with my wife when I see a message flashing across the top of my lock screen:

You are receiving this message because you are the emergency contact for Katya Koslov.

My heart stops.

Active Shooter at East Side Performing Arts.

CHAPTER THIRTY

KATYA

The sound of gunfire doesn't seem real. Like it's in my head. Something butt-dialing me from my memory back when I lived with my father, and I heard endless rounds going off at all hours of the night.

The first time I heard it, I peed myself. Stasia had found me and held me until I stopped crying.

Now, I'm holding myself, tucked under a makeup table. My watery eyes find a face staring at me from across the dressing room.

I didn't imagine this.

"Where are the announcements?" Della whispers and flinches when more staccato pops go off. "Fuck, that sounds close."

Only, we don't know where it's coming from. The dressing room has one door into a hallway that veers off into the auditorium, a door that's always open. The other door leads to the stage manager's office.

The sound could be coming from either place.

We were taught in drills to turn off our phones. I hold mine tight, wishing I could text Lachlan. I'm so scared, and I want my husband. I've watched this movie too many times on television. Grainy security footage of a crazed gunman stomping up and down the hallways of a school looking for students to kill. It always seemed impossible.

Until now.

I really thought I was safe here. It's a performing arts college, for crying out loud!

A soft ticking draws my eyes back to Della. "Why is

your phone on?" I hiss through clenched teeth.

"I'm saving my ass."

"How?" I wave my arms. "Who are you calling?"

"911!"

I roll my eyes. Surely, they already know someone is running around a major school with a gun. Then again, it's the summer. Does Lachlan know? Is he calling me? Oh God, he'll go ballistic. With my phone off, he can't find me.

But if I put it on, and he calls me, the gunman will find me. What a choice!

"Ugh, 911 is actually busy!" Della gets out from under the makeup counter.

"Where are you going? We were told to shelter in place."

"And be a sitting duck?" She rushes to the door, and I close my eyes, picturing her falling back with two bullet holes between her eyes. "Not me."

Opening my eyes, I see she's gone. I exhale in a moment of relief. If the shooter was right there, she'd be dead. I don't want anyone to die, but I also don't want a bullet in *my head*. It's so horrible how these things turn into every man for themselves. I slide out from under the counter, too.

Tiptoeing to the door, I gather all my senses that I use for dance to figure out what's going on in multiple directions. Including above me. The auditorium is big, and I can duck behind a row of seats. I'm also small enough to crawl underneath.

"Damn," I mutter under my breath, wishing I paid attention to where Della went. Whatever direction that was, no gunfire erupted. She found the safe route out of here. But which one?

We are in the middle of a two-hour break, where many students do extra stretching in the clinic or get lunch.

Does the shooter know this? Does he think the dressing room will be empty?

God, I feel so alone. It hits me like a physical blow, because I started feeling like I belonged, not only to Lachlan, but to his gigantic family. For years, I figured out how to survive my loneliness. And now to be dragged back into this isolated abyss is crippling.

I take a step toward the auditorium because there are multiple exits, but freeze. What happens when I get out of there, though? Beyond the many doors are mazes of hallways. I don't trust the acoustics, especially since all the rehearsal rooms' transoms are open because of the heat. Gunfire can sound like it's coming from anywhere.

Feeling too many options are not in my favor, I opt for the back hallway toward the office with one exit, hoping the shooter doesn't know about it. I turn for that door, and a mass of chaos hits me all at once.

Della is backing up, muttering, "No, please." She bangs into my chest, the back of her head hitting my nose, hard.

Blood trickles down my leotard.

It all feels like a vacuum when my brain catches up, and I see a guy, around twenty-five, with dark greasy hair pointing an AR-15 at Della. "Get back, you bitch."

The unknown has been obliterated. He's right here, which means he's not in the auditorium. If I use all my strength to run, I can make it to the seats for cover and then slide under to reach a door.

Sorry, Della.

I turn to run, but stomping footsteps catch up behind me wickedly fast.

"Hey!" the gunman yells.

Pain explodes in the back of my head, and I lose my balance before everything goes black.

CHAPTER THIRTY-ONE

LACHLAN

Griffin drives his Escalade like a bat out of hell toward the tunnel to reach Manhattan. "Fucking traffic!" He pounds on the steering wheel.

I've got Balor on the car's speaker phone. I'm too wired to hold my phone next to my head. "Break into that campus' cameras. *Right fucking now.*"

All calls to Katya are going to voicemail. Shutting her phone off is the right thing to do, but I'm losing my mind not hearing her voice. Not knowing if she's okay. Plus, without that signal, I won't be able to find her. Now, I know why men put trackers on their women.

"I'm already in." My brother's heavy breathing punctuates the eerie silence of the Escalade's interior.

"She's been rehearsing in the main auditorium." I give him the street I entered from so he can find it on a campus map.

"I got ten security screens up. I don't see anything. But fuck..."

"What?"

"Tons of cops are outside the school already."

"Did they take the guy down?"

"Hang on, let me break into their radios and listen to the traffic."

"Jesus, he's good," Griffin mutters.

"There's a swat team scoping out the classrooms off Fifth," Balor reports a moment later.

"Fifth!" I think of the sprawling campus layout. "That will take forever to get to the auditorium. Do they know how many dancers are rehearsing in there?"

"I can't break into the conversation and tell them!" Balor snaps. "They'll find my signal and cut me off. Where are you?"

"We're about to go into the tunnel. Will I lose you?"

"No, there are transmitters now."

"Fuck!" Griffin slams the brakes as a car two lengths ahead of us skids out of control, veering into on-coming traffic in the opposite lane and then flips over. "We're fucking blocked!" He twists around to back up, but there's a row of cars behind us.

We're boxed in.

"Fuck this. Sorry, Griff." I open the passenger door and hop out to run through the tunnel. Passing the car teetering on its roof, I mutter, "Sorry, man. It's a fucking straight lane."

How do you lose control driving straight going fucking thirty-five? He's not my problem. I hope there weren't any kids involved. That softening sets me back. Kids. I never cared about kids, and that needs to change. Darragh's got a daughter. Kieran and Riordan are both expecting.

Kids will be all over the place. Just like when we grew up.

"Balor!" I yell into my phone. "I'm running in the tunnel." I race at top speed in the citybound lane, since it's completely clear now.

"You? Running?" he sounds shocked.

"I know..." I don't remember the last time I moved this fucking fast. Maybe to save Riordan's ass over the winter, but even then, I don't recall the wind going through my hair like it is now.

I'm racing like this because of Katya...

Headlights swing toward me, and I jump out of the way. "Arsehole!" I yell at the guy who thinks he can race down the citybound lane and avoid this traffic. He'll be stuck facing the wrong way when the traffic is cleared.

"Balor!" I yell into the phone as I run. "Anything on the cameras yet?"

"No."

"When I get there, I'm going inside."

"Considering what you look like, they may shoot you, thinking you're an accomplice."

"Get an NYPD boss on the phone right now!"

"Riordan!" Balor patches in our underboss and gives him an update. "Okay, he's on it."

A pinch of light greets me, and I run as fast as I can toward it. The smell of diesel and exhaust chokes me. Outside, the fresh air is a relief, but the afternoon sun blinds me.

Traffic on the approach is snarled as I weave between cars. Sweat pours into my eyes from the heat and Katya's school is still three agonizing city blocks away. The dark bronze sculpture of ballet shoes outside the main entrance shines off the sun. Like a heat missile, I zone in on it and let it draw me in. Until a horn blares, tires screech, and next, I'm flying into some arsehole's windshield. It breaks, and I think my arm does, too.

I roll off and keep running on pure adrenaline.

Aww fuck. There are *so* many cop cars, men in blue pacing up and down the street in front of the school. They'll have to shoot me, and I hope these fuckers miss. No one sees me until I run right past them. I'm that fast.

"Hey!" one yells, and I hear footsteps chase after me.

One leaps and takes me down to the cement.

"My wife is in there!" I yell, flipping over and throwing punches.

Two cops grab my arms and keep me pinned. If they search me, they'll find my ghost gun which isn't registered, obviously.

I get to my feet, and with a glare that can rattle any

member of the best police department in the world, I say, "I'm going to save my fucking wife. Shoot me, if you want to stop me. But if something happens to her, I'll find out who you are and kill you." I break free and tear toward the main entrance, knowing I can be gunned down in an ambush by this so-called active shooter.

No one follows me. Pity, I can use the backup.

After passing through the main entrance, I gasp, seeing the guard I spoke to a few days ago lying dead on the floor with a bullet in his skull, blood all around his head.

"Damn it." I pull out my gun, and considering how the guard fell, I determine he was shot from the direction of the classrooms. I hate that I really don't care about any other students. I'm not a hero. I just want my wife. I want to find her and get her the hell out of here.

Bloody footprints from this poor guard's head lead right to… The auditorium!

The doors are closed, but all the lights are on. Did everyone scramble out of here? I take my phone out and call Katya again, but calls are still going to voicemail.

She still has it off. That means she's in trouble or is hiding. When I was here a few days ago, there were tons of people milling around. Did those pieces of shite just leave her?

I think about the door I snuck in through near the stage. I glance inside and see nothing. I also hear nothing, which is eerie as hell considering the acoustics in this place.

Figuring there's no way to be quiet, *and* that I'm an excellent shot, I throw the door open, loud enough that I hope the fucker who did this is inside and takes a shot at me. Shows himself so I can pick him off.

Nothing.

Fuck!

I hop onto the stage and head to the back hallway

toward Katya's dressing room. A noise behind me turns me around, and I nearly pull the trigger. Gasps from five cops have me lifting my hands. Sure, they come in behind me. Let me be the human shield.

I signal the direction I'm going, and the lead cop nods.

Stage Right's back entrance is clear, and my memory kicks in from carrying Katya down this corridor. I creep up on the dressing room and stop at the closed door. If students rushed out of here, it would be open.

Why is the door closed?

And where the hell is my Katya? I lean against the door and listen. The sound of unhinged yelling makes my blood run cold. It's the muffled rant of a guy yelling at someone.

I drop to the floor and squint under the door to find this guy's position in the dressing room. I see dirty sneakers facing away. This arsehole has his back to the door. Perfect. I get up and jiggle the handle. Too quickly, and too rough, though, not realizing how loose it is. The metal clanging gets his attention.

Motherfucking rookie mistake.

"Who's out there?" the guy yells at the closed door. "I got two sluts in here."

Sluts?

"I'll put bullets in their dick-sucking mouths."

I eye the pile of cops idling in the hallway. Shaking my head, I wrench the doorknob to open it up and hop back. A flurry of bullets from the open door hits the opposite wall. It's deafening. But I hear screaming over the blistering hail.

The voice I'd know anywhere: Katya.

I wait for the spray to stop when the unmistakable sound of a cartridge jamming sparks my chest.

"Damn you piece of shit!" the guy yells.

I step into the open doorway, lift my ghost gun, and

without saying a word, I prepare to put a beautiful bullet in his head.

Click, click, click.

Fucking fuck, I emptied my clip into the rapist. My gun is out of bullets. I make eye contact with the guy trying to get his AR-15 to work. Roaring, I leap on top of him.

I pummel him with my fists. He brings the gun up and whacks me with it. My bloody nose drips into his face as I laugh at him. He looks terrified, and in that one second break, I get a hold of his shirt and smash his head into the floor. Over and over and over.

"Stop!" a cop at the door yells to me, pointing his gun. "I think he's dead."

With my hands full of blood, my thirst for vengeance not quite clenched, I'm ready to ignore the cop when a girl screams. Different from Katya.

"Mark! No!"

She knew the guy?

I lift off him, seeing this dark-haired dancer crying over the dead guy. My wild eyes search the room until I find my wife crouching, folded into a ball in the corner. I don't remember the steps I take to get to her. Next, she's in my arms.

"I'm here, baby. Your husband is here." I hold her, cradling the back of her head, which is caked with blood. "Aww, fuck. You're bleeding."

"He hit me with the gun handle. I passed out." She squeezes me and squeaks, "I can't believe you're here. Oh God, all that blood on your hands."

"Literally and figurately. Of course, I'm here." I draw her face to me, needing to see her eyes. "You made me your contact. I got an active shooter notification." With her tucked into my chest, I stand up. "Griffin and I got on the road within seconds."

"Take me home, please." Her legs wrap around my

waist, and it's the best I've felt in hours.

I don't bother telling her about my running-through-the-tunnel adventure. I'll get to that when she's calmed down, and I have her in a safe place.

The girl who was crying over the dead guy is now sitting on the floor with two cops talking to her.

"Who is she?" I whisper to Katya.

"Another dancer. The guy was her boyfriend. Ex, really. She broke up with him."

"I can't imagine why."

As I turn to leave the dressing room, a cop steps in front of me. "We need you to make a statement."

"The fuck I do. I'm taking my wife home. Ask around who I am. Then send someone in charge to come take my statement. My wife was in here for an hour and you motherfuckers—"

"Lachlan," Katya whines.

I clear my throat. "You sat outside for an hour."

"We had a team in the other building. He made demands. We were waiting for a negotiator."

"Last I heard, we don't negotiate with terrorists. He got what he deserved. You were all crouched right here." I motion with my head. "You saw what happened, how he shot at me. Write what you want." As I'm saying this, I know it's not that simple, and that Riordan will have to smooth this over.

Especially since we're not in Astoria.

I keep walking and sigh in relief when no one follows me.

"How's your head, my wife? I felt blood."

"It's pounding," she says, sounding drained.

I consider if she needs to go to the hospital. Outside, I walk her to an ambulance. An EMT waves me over.

"Was she shot?"

"No. She was hit in the head with the butt of a semiautomatic."

"Come here, sweetie." An EMT pats a gurney.

"Don't leave me," Katya moans.

"Are you kidding me?" I lay her down and hold her hand.

"Age, height, and weight, sweetie?" she asks my wife and types into a machine. Looking at me after Katya answers, she says, "Did *you* get shot, sir?"

"No. Why?"

"Your hands, your nose, and your arm are full of blood."

Katya pulls at my jacket sleeve. "Lachlan, your stitches!"

"I'll be fine." I fist some gauze to stop my aching nose from bleeding and then clean my hands as best I can with wipes.

The EMT smiles and shakes her head. "Tough guy, huh?"

"You have no idea." Katya grins at me.

"Sweetie, it looks like just a nick that bled. I can take you to the hospital for a CAT scan."

"No," Katya whines. "I want to go home."

I hold her. "Is there any kind of test you can do here?"

"Sweetie, look at me." She holds up a pen light and makes Katya follow the light with her eyes, which are red and watery. "Be honest, on a scale of one to ten, tell me the level of pain?"

I know this is an unfair assessment since she endures a lot of pain, the way she punishes her body. But I keep my mouth shut. Here I stand, full of blood and busted stitches, but I just want my wife in my bed. I have Darcy on speed dial to fix me up and if Katya needs more care.

"Five. Maybe. My ears are ringing, so I think that's making it worse."

"The guy unloaded an assault rifle two feet from her

head," I tell the EMT. "My ears are ringing, too."

"I can't force you to go to the hospital, sweetie. But I think you're fine." The EMT removes the blood pressure cuff. "Your heart rate is a little elevated, but your BP looks normal, given the circumstance. If you feel sick to your stomach, have trouble breathing, or experience any dizziness, please go to a hospital."

"I will."

"Thanks, Miss," I say to her and scoop my wife off the gurney.

"Good luck, both of you."

A horn honks, and I look across the street to see Griffin standing there. He somehow made it out of that tunnel. Then I see the guy standing with him, and I can't keep the smile from my face.

I carry Katya toward them. "Shane Quinlan, son of a bitch. What are you doing here?"

"I heard what happened." He speaks with the same lilt as all of us.

"How did you know it was me?"

"You're not tagged, but I knew it was you." Shane shows me a video on his phone. "Not many six-six dudes with balls to wrestle New York's Finest and then run into a building where bullets are flying."

Anger bubbles in my veins, seeing a fucking video of me being tackled by the police. The audio picked up my screaming: *My wife is in there!* The sound of my voice is guttural, primal. I sound unhinged and... Wildly in love.

I guess I am.

"I need Balor to delete that," I mumble to Griffin, who nods and gets on his phone.

"When I saw it was you, I rushed over here to check if you needed any help." Shane rubs his chin, looking at Katya. "When did you get married?"

I figure Shane and his brothers don't talk too much

since he left the Quinlan firm to work with Siobhan at her husband's hotel, The Sterling.

"A few weeks ago," I answer. "Katya, this is Shane, Griffin's brother." I introduce them. "He works here in the city."

"Nice to meet you." She squirms, and I set her down. I don't want to make her look weak.

"Same here." Shane smirks at me.

"Getting bored at that fancy hotel, mate?" God, I can use Shane. I've known him forever, and I trust him. "Want some real action?"

"Maybe. My boss is a pain-in-the-arse control freak."

I laugh, and whisper to my wife, "His twin sister is his boss."

"Oh."

"Good to see you, Shane. I need to get Katya home." I steer my little wife to Griffin's car and put her in the backseat. My phone buzzes, and I answer, "Balor, I got Katya. She's safe."

"I heard. Good. You need to look at the video I just sent you."

Assuming it's the same one of me barreling toward the school being taken down by cops, I say, "I saw it. Delete it."

"It's going viral. Kieran's bird will be at the Harbor Helipad in an hour. You're instructed to get on it and go straight to Michigan. He wants you to lie low."

Ironic, since I wanted to take that bird to Michigan on my wedding day, but it was pulled from me. Katya and I are both hurt. I don't want a long whiny trip across three states.

"I'll take the bird. But I'm going to the Hamptons. Shea's got plenty protection." I hired them. "I spoke to her, and she's got a place for me to stay." I know when to follow orders and when to bitterly argue that no one tells me what to do.

It's not about me anymore. My wife is shaking and needs a place to relax, heal, and feel safe. That ocean sound wave machine lets both of us sleep well. Real waves will do wonders.

I kiss Katya gently on the cheek. "Want to go convalesce in East Hampton with me?"

CHAPTER THIRTY-TWO

KATYA

Ears ringing, and my mind a whirl, I give in to being herded around by my husband.

He killed yet one more person for me. Like nothing happened, he struts through his house, shirtless, with his arm bandage soaked in blood like it doesn't bother him. All while I'm falling apart.

I'm not built for this world.

I stand in the middle of the bedroom where I've kept my clothes, because Lachlan doesn't have bureau space for two people. For a Neanderthal, he's also a clothes horse.

The Hamptons... He's taking me to East Hampton where I'll meet his sister.

"Little wife, are you all right?" His voice sounds out from the doorway.

I glance at the stand-up cheval mirror and realize I haven't moved. I'm not changed, I'm not packed. And I'm certainly not all right.

Warm hands press down on my shoulders. "Let's get you out of these rehearsal clothes. They're full of blood."

Fingers deftly tug down the tiny cap sleeves of the leotard. It's stretchy enough to loosen around my arms. Lachlan rolls the bodice down my body, ignoring my bare breasts. He cares for me like I'm a child, and I don't like that. I don't want him to see me weak like this.

Pressing on his hands, I say, "I got it. I'll meet you in the living room."

The shakiness of my voice straightens him to his full height, and for a moment, I'm frightened of him. He says nothing, though.

"What?" I snap, feeling ready to collapse.

He draws a hand toward my face, and I muster every ounce of strength not to flinch. My brain assures me he's not going to hit me. My heart knows he'll *never* hit me. A finger lands on my cheek, and he swipes across a line that imitates his scar.

The pad of his finger drips with my tears. "Does that answer your question? Katya, you're crying, and you don't even know it. You're traumatized. Your mind and your body aren't in sync."

I gently touch the scar on his left cheek. "Trauma. Were you traumatized when this happened?" I say softly, standing in the middle of the room with just a pair of thin panties, one side wedged in my ass. I don't have the energy to pull it out. I should change them. I'm pretty sure I peed myself once. Or twice. I'm sure I stink, but Lachlan seems completely unaffected by my disheveled appearance.

He sits on the bed I never slept in, because from the very first night, I wanted to sleep with him. We're eye level when he talks. "Aye. It was my very first kill, and it wrecked me. I wasn't always like this. I wasn't always this cold and ruthless."

"Do you want to talk about it? That day?" I need to think about something else or I'll completely collapse.

"Do you want to hear about it?"

Glancing out the window, I notice the sun lowers at a rapid pace, and a helicopter is waiting for us. "I want you to share with me whatever you're comfortable telling me."

He tugs me so I'm standing between his open legs, ignoring my half-naked body.

That scar on Lachlan's cheek is the gateway to his deeper secrets.

"Tell me *that* story, please."

CHAPTER THIRTY-THREE

LACHLAN - AGE 18

I follow Father Eamon off the church altar, his steps hurried to get to the sacristy — our preparatory room in the back. His service ran long thanks to another passionate homily. I consider telling him to cut them back. I watched the crowd in the pews getting restless. Some older folks even dozed off. Some left. It was the early mass where some parishioners stop for what they think will be a 7:30 a.m. quickie before work.

Classes for me don't start until nine a.m. Not that I care if I'm late. I have enough credits to graduate high school, and even if I didn't, if the school tried to fail me out, my da would make sure I got a diploma. Delivered by the principal herself to our house.

I doubt Mrs. Horse Face would try that. Hofstadter, whatever. No one in my family has tested her because my brothers before me, Kieran and Riordan, were angels. Okay, they weren't, but they were *smarter* than me about getting caught.

Me, I don't give a shit.

Sorry, Jesus, I repent inwardly, looking up at the wood and brass coffered ceiling.

"Fidgeting crowd today, Lachlan." Father Eamon noticed, apparently.

"Maybe too much coffee," I offer instead of telling him he's long-winded.

Personally, I drink in his sermons. Younger than the other priests here at St. Agatha's, Father Eamon is a personal inspiration to me. Young, energetic, charming, and dare I say, handsome. He showed up here, just at the right time. I expected my da to laugh at me when I told him I wanted to be a priest, since most of our pastors were older men, ordained later in life.

It made sense for some wrinkled old dude to give up sex and other vices after a lifetime of getting some. Someone young, like Father Eamon? That's the real sacrifice. He's my assurance that I'm not crazy for wanting to dedicate my life to the church.

Give up what my older brothers brag about. Sex.

I have no interest in girls. I'm not into dudes either. I wondered for a while if I was, but nope. Even all the dick I saw in gym locker rooms did nothing for me. My blood gets moving here in the church with the smell of sweet candles, incense, and lacquer to keep the pews shiny. The history and tradition are so rich and fulfilling.

A ringing sounds, and Father Eamon pulls a cell phone from his pocket. He winks, answering it. "Good morning, Mrs. O'Rourke." He speaks with the same brogue we all do. "I'll drive Lachlan to school myself. I apologize, my service ran longer today." He pauses, his eyes still on me with a widening smile. "I see. That's fantastic news. Do you want to talk to him?"

My heart races as I step to take his phone. I don't have one. Turned it down when my da offered one to me. No reason for it. I'm either at school, home, or church. My da works all the time, and Ma is home with my younger brothers and sister. We live on the other side of town near the water. Da built us the biggest house. He's sort of the king around here. Even the mayor bows to him.

"Ma?" I say into the phone and detect the smell of something familiar on the plastic screen. Whiskey. "Is everything all right?"

"Aye, Lachlan. I couldn't wait for you to get home. The postman brought our mail early. It came, Lachlan. Your acceptance to Fordham."

It's hardly a surprise. Kieran is on track to graduate salutatorian. And Da gives plenty of money to the school. I act grateful anyway. "That's great news, Ma."

Fordham has the Theology program I need to get into seminary when I graduate. With plenty of sons to work for my da, Ma convinced him to support my decision to be a priest.

Who doesn't want a priest in the family? It's like a ticket straight to the front of the line. Da's money and power won't do him any good in the afterlife. In fact, considering how many people he's killed, he needs me living a life of celibacy and sobriety to balance out his evil.

The sound of yelling and a shattering crash spin me around. I race back to the sacristy and my brain struggles to process what I'm seeing.

"Ma, I gotta go." I end the call and shock rushes through me when I find a man yelling at Father Eamon, swinging a knife at him.

"How dare you touch my boy, you sick pervert!"

"Charles, you're mistaken." Father Eamon blocks his face, but his robe sleeves are blood-soaked.

"Hey!" I yell and charge the man I recognize as the father of Michael Foster, an altar boy my age.

Mr. Foster turns toward me, and his eyes widen, taking me in. I'm six-six, and I guess he wasn't expecting me. Most people don't. He swings the knife, and my left cheek explodes with a crazy, stinging pain.

"Son of a bitch." I hold my face and gag at all the blood I see in my hand.

"Get out of here, Lachlan!" Father Eamon is on his knees, cornered next to the fireplace. It's roaring with perfumed smoke, but mixed with copper in the air from all the blood. This is a smell that will haunt me forever.

Mr. Foster will certainly kill Father Eamon. I'm not

going anywhere.

"Give me that." I grab the knife, the blade slicing into my palm, but I get it away from him.

Michael's da puts his hands up in a defensive position and has nowhere to run, since I'm blocking the door to the sacristy.

I grab the man by the throat and put the knife to his face. "Don't like it, do you?"

"Lachlan, don't," Father Eamon whines. "We don't hurt people. Let him go. All of this is a misunderstanding."

Charles narrows his eyes on me. "Oh God, *you're* Lachlan O'Rourke? The lunatic son of Fergus O'Rourke." The look of terror in his eyes that he just dug a knife into O'Rourke flesh kicks up my adrenaline and delicious satisfaction. "Figures, you're a criminal just like your corrupt old man." Him bad-mouthing my da flips an evil switch I didn't know I had.

"Aye, that's me." I squeeze harder, watching him turn blue.

"Stop. Please." Mr. Foster struggles and manages to kick me in the shin.

"Fuck!" I push him, and he stumbles, falling backward.

His head smacks into the stone hearth with a sickening thud. Fueled with rage, I lift the knife, ready to plunge it into his heart, when a bloody hand grabs my wrist.

"No, Lachlan. We don't strike others who want to do us harm. The Lord judges and punishes. *We* don't." He knows I want to serve God and be a priest like him. "We're here to guide souls."

Perhaps I'm not cut out to be a priest because I don't have the same grace in my heart to forgive. I'm shaken to my core, but I push it away. Like my father, I'll make my own rules when I'm a priest in my own church. Hopefully, far away from here. Back home in Waterford,

Ireland maybe.

I look down, ready to cast my first sin. Show God what I'm willing to do to protect and avenge a good man of faith, like Eamon. But blood seeps onto the hearth's stone and down the side from the man's head. All that's left are his cold, lifeless eyes staring at the ceiling.

Bollocks. He's already dead.

From me. I pushed him. I did this. I wait for remorse to swamp me. But it doesn't.

"Shite." I throw the knife down, worried my prints are on it. But Mr. Foster doesn't have stab wounds. Father Eamon does.

"We'll say he fell. Look at us. We're both cut up. Good heavens, Lachlan, your face." He reaches out to touch me, but instincts make me back away.

My left cheek throbs. "Why did Mr. Foster say you hurt Michael?"

Father Eamon takes off his blood-soaked robe and covers the man. "I don't know."

"Did Michael do something wrong?"

"I don't know what Charles was talking about."

It hits me what Michael's da must have meant by *hurt.* I'm not naïve to the scandals that have been rocking the Catholic church. I just haven't met a priest who did any of that.

Father Eamon approaches me. "We have to get you to a hospital, Lachlan. You need stitches." He picks up the phone I dropped. "This is Father Eamon Gallagher from St. Agatha's in Astoria. A man with a knife attacked me and my altar boy. We're hurt badly. Please send an ambulance."

"What do I tell them about Mr. Foster?" It strikes me now that Michael doesn't have a father. Because of me.

"You'll say nothing. You did nothing. You protected me. You grabbed him and he cut you. Then he fell on his own. *That's* how it went down, Lachlan."

Except, that's not what happened. I'm surprised he's asking me to lie. Even if he's protecting me. I don't need his protection. This *was* self-defense. In a way. The man stabbed me. The man was attacking my priest. My mentor. My hero.

You hurt my boy...

I can't get those words out of my head. They sounded so guttural. So real.

Three police cars, two ambulances, and my da show up within minutes. His underboss has lieutenants with scanners and Ma told them I was here.

Father Eamon gives his statement, his eyes glued to mine.

"Was that what happened, Lachlan?" the cop asks, my father watching me over his shoulder.

"Aye, he fell." I keep my answer short. He *fell* because I pushed him.

The cop turns, and after a look from my da that has him stepping back, he folds his report pad up. "Looks like an accident to me."

A medical examiner takes Mr. Foster's body away, and I never make it to school. Instead, I go to the hospital to get fifty-six stitches on my face. The cut came dangerously close to my eye. Ma shows up crying. Kieran and Riordan show up, too. They're not crying. They look worried.

"Rior, take Ma to get some coffee," Kieran tells him. When Riordan steers Ma from the room they gave me, my oldest brother speaks low and in my face. "What happened?"

"I told the cops. I told Da."

"Now tell me what really happened."

I laugh. He's already acting like he's in charge.

"Mr. Foster stabbed Father Eamon, then he stabbed

me."

"I see that. How did Foster end up with a busted head?" He's concerned because they found me standing over a dead body.

"He fell."

"On his own?"

I glare at my brother, trust issues swamping me. "Not...not exactly."

"You pushed him, didn't you? Because you wouldn't let someone hurt a priest."

Put that way, I feel proud. "Damn right."

"There's only one problem with what you did, Lachlan." Kieran drags a chair next to my gurney. "I didn't want to tell you this."

My heart spikes. "Tell me what?"

"Rumors are spreading like wildfire all over the city about Father Eamon. Da ordered an investigation weeks ago. Norah's brother, Ewan, has been working on it. That man who died..." Kieran narrows his eyes at me.

"Mr. Foster. Michael Foster's da."

"Aye. It's rumored he went to the Russians to put a hit on Eamon."

"You're lying."

"I'm not. Father Eamon's been...hurting boys."

"Don't say that!" All I ever saw was the good in my hero. "It can't be true. He's a good man!"

"The dead guy was the good guy, Lachlan." My brother eyes my huge bandage. "Except for scarring you for life, of course."

"I didn't kill him for what he did to me. I'll bleed for the church. I killed him because he would have killed Father Eamon."

"You shut up," Kieran hisses. "You never admit that to anyone again, do you hear me?"

"You're not *anyone*," I bark, my stitches stretched and

painful. "You're my brother."

"Aye. And I'll never tell a soul, Lachlan. I'll be in charge one day, and I'll always protect you." He cups the back of my neck. "Ma said you got your acceptance to Fordham. I'm proud of you."

"Proud." I push him away. "Da bought my acceptance. My grades are shite."

He cocks his head. "I don't want you to go back to that church until we figure out a way to get rid of Eamon. You're starting Fordham this summer, not the fall. And living on campus."

"No!" I feel the walls closing in on me. "I'm going on the summer retreat with Father Eamon."

"Over my dead body, Lachlan. You're not to be alone with that man ever again. It's either Fordham this summer or Ireland with me and Norah."

I certainly don't want to be a third wheel with Kieran and his new girlfriend. "You can't tell me what to do."

A shadow approaches, and my da comes into view. "Maybe he can't. But I can."

When I'm not on my back, I'm a few inches taller than him, but he still scares me. He's powerful. Even Kieran shirks back. Da loves us, but there're eight of us. He rules with an iron fist because he can't risk any of us saying or doing something that will bring heat to our doorstep.

"Lachlan..." He goes breathless, seeing the bandage on my face. "You heard your brother. You're getting out of Astoria and away from Eamon. There's a terrible scandal brewing. I can't have you walking around with that hideous scar on your cheek, advertising you were there when Foster was killed. I got your name stricken from the record as being a witness."

My da's power in Astoria was nearly unmatched back then. I felt high and mighty bearing his name, but after

that day, I realized I had a lot to learn.
About everything and everyone.

CHAPTER THIRTY-FOUR

KATYA

"Only, the lessons that really stuck all these years were how to kill, and how to do it without emotion." Lachlan returns to the present. "All I needed to do was turn off my heart completely." He stares at me, making this personal between him and me. "For years, I refused to let down my guard and expose my heart to someone."

I close my mouth when it dries up because it's been hanging open for several minutes. "Have I hurt that ability?"

He kisses my hand. "No. You make me stronger." Glancing at his phone, he says, "Katya, we should get going. We have plenty of time to talk more this weekend."

It occurs to me it's a Thursday. I suspect the school will be closed tomorrow and my rehearsals canceled. "I'd like that."

He brushes his mouth over mine and whispers hoarsely, "I was so worried about you." The intensity in his voice draws more tears from me, and next, I'm sobbing in his lap.

"I'm sorry, Lachlan."

"For what, little wife?"

Sniffing, I finally tell him, "I *don't* like that. Calling me little wife. Not anymore. Like I'm insignificant."

He scoffs. "It speaks to your size and how delicate and precious you are to me."

"Exactly. I'm not precious or made of glass. You caught me at a bad time. My world was shredded when

Papa forced that marriage on me. And now this."

"This... As in our marriage?" He grins.

"What's so funny?"

"The fighter in you is coming through. That sharp spunky girl I talked to that day at the gazebo and in the church parking lot." He gently gets me to my feet. "I like it. But I don't believe in coincidences, Katriane."

I amble to one of my bureaus and take out a pair of clean underwear. Slipping them on, I say, "Do you mean us meeting up in the church?"

He goes into my closet and takes out my weekender bag. "Aye. Besides teaching us how to use weapons and how to stalk prey, another side of my training was mental. Philosophical. And metaphysical."

With a bundle of shorts and T-shirts from the drawers in my hand, I drop them into the open bag. "Metaphysical?"

"The idea of ethereal forces. That something greater is out there guiding us. Directing us."

I step inside my closet to snag a few sundresses. I'm still the Irish Enforcer's wife and want to look polished next to him. "How did that line up with your spirituality?"

He stokes my hair. "You're smart. That's the exact connection I meant. It did, and it didn't line up. You either believe in one almighty power or give in to another version where souls never die, where the earth absorbs the dead and releases energy to counterbalance other energy."

"That's so deep, Lachlan." I hold my chest.

He smiles at me. "You're still topless, Katriane. I want to do something about it. But a helicopter has our name on it."

The humor in his voice tugs a grin on my lips, and I feel the cloud lifting around me. "I just feel so comfortable with you."

"Good. I feel the same way." He leans into my ear. "But seriously, put something on because my resistance is wearing thin."

Smiling, I take an orange T-shirt dress and slide it over my body. With a pair of white tennis shoes, I say, "Let me get my things from the bathroom."

He takes my hand and brings me in there. I see a saddle brown duffle bag sitting on his bed. Our bed. After I toss a few basics into a makeup bag, I catch my face in the mirror. I'm pale, and I have circles under my eyes.

Lachlan drops a kiss on my shoulder. "Ready?" He didn't call me little wife, and I suspect he won't again since I objected. It came naturally to him, and I feel bad balking about it.

"I'm sorry I snapped at you calling me little wife. If that's how you see me... Your little wife..."

He kisses my neck. "The important word is wife. You're mine."

What he did today proves that. Proves how much he cares about me. Risked his life for me. Mark had an assault rifle!

It hits me that even if I get the spot in the conservatory, I don't think I want to take it.

*

We arrive in East Hampton in the glow of twilight. We sat in the helicopter's soundproof cabin. The route was mostly over water, so there was nothing special to see. I kept my head in Lachlan's chest, crying on and off from the built-up stress.

After we land, Shea O'Rourke, the one-and-only daughter and sister to seven brothers, steps out of a white Escalade. A man in a navy blue suit follows her.

Her guard is tall with a square jaw, but his eyes are

hidden behind dark shades. He looks serious, with no hint of the same humor that lingers on the tip of Lachlan's tongue.

I've grown up with guards and can pick up on ones who have a thing for their client. But I say nothing, as I suspect Lachlan might lose his shit.

Dressed in a white suit and a satin, lavender blouse underneath, Shea's long, dark hair contrasts against the pearly fabric. She's stunningly gorgeous with curves and a sexy gait.

Lachlan tugs me to his side. "Alo, Shea. This is Katriane, my wife."

She holds out a hand, several glittering bracelets clinking together on her wrist. "It's so wonderful to meet you, Katriane."

"Same here." I shake her hand. "Please call me Katya. God, you're so pretty."

"Me? Look at you. You're the picture of beauty and grace. Fitting for this beast." She punches Lachlan in the arm not bandaged. Something she neither asks nor frets about.

I twist my braid draped over my shoulder. "I don't feel very beautiful today."

"You've been through a terrible ordeal." She strokes my arm but yelps when she zeroes in on my left hand. "Lachlan, this ring!"

"I have good taste," he quips, holding me closer. "But Archer pulled great options for me."

Her body stiffens. "*Archer* helped you himself?" She clears her throat. "Archer Crest, the owner?"

"Aye." Lachlan eyes her bodyguard, whose jaw tightens.

It's innuendo overload.

"I have a party I need to show my face at, or I would have dinner for you. But I called Everleigh's on Pantigo, and they are holding a table for you."

It strikes me how all the O'Rourke women work. Shea owns a premier party planning business. Kieran's wife runs a foundation, and Priscilla works for Griffin Quinlan. It fills me with hope that I can dance for a living, and my husband won't mind.

If he stays my husband.

Lachlan's words of no coincidences and ethereal forces driving elements in the universe intrigue me. How fate brought us together.

I feel sick... If Lachlan hadn't gone to a strip club the night before my wedding, I'd be in Russia with a man who beats me. And not here, in one of the most beautiful places in the world, with a husband who considers me precious and only hurts me when he makes love to me with a little too much enthusiasm.

Lachlan helps me into Shea's SUV, closes my door, and gets in next to me from the other side. "You hungry?"

"Yes," I say, my stomach waking up.

"Lachlan, I rented you a car," Shea announces from the front seat. "It's at the house. Do you want one of my interns to park it at Everleigh's?"

"Aye, thank you."

A small traffic jam on Pantigo has us creeping along. My fingers are sweaty in Lachlan's hand, but he doesn't let go. I think about Rahil, who hissed, touching me. Lachlan squeezes me tighter. Panic settles into my throat as the closed space of the car and that helicopter ride are catching up to me after being trapped under the makeup counter for an hour waiting to die.

My breathing goes ragged, and a humming noise settles deep in my throat. "Air. I need air."

Lachlan notices and barks, "Pull over!"

The driver swings the SUV in front of parked cars.

"What's wrong?" Shea turns around with worry in her

pretty eyes.

"My wife needs air. We'll get out here and walk."

"It's just at the end of this block." Shea reaches into her purse. "Here are the keys to the house. It's going to be a beautiful night. There's an amazing back patio with an ocean view. Take a few hours to look at the stars."

"That sounds like what we both need." Lachlan takes the keys and kisses Shea's hand. "I'll text you when we're there."

"Thank you so much, Shea," I say to her, still feeling wrecked.

"You're very welcome." She smiles warmly at me, and for a second, I remember what it's like to have a sister, and how much I miss Stasia. It's crushing, but I push it away.

Lachlan opens the car door and glances over his shoulder, his stern expression reminding me to wait for him to open my door. I feel silly waiting, though, so I reach into my purse to give my hands something to do. I don't want to seem like a princess when Shea is clearly an independent woman.

My door opens, and Lachlan reinforces the princess status I don't want by lifting me out of the car. In fairness, the running board is nearly a foot off the ground. With his hand in mine, we get to the sidewalk bristling with people. It's lean bodies dressed in summer pale colors as far as the eye can see, and I'm walking around with the dark knight. Lachlan draws cautious stares from everyone we pass. He ignores it and keeps his head held high. It's proof how powerful his family is. He was not only *not arrested* after beating Mark to death, but the cops just let him go.

We weave around people, and a stand-up banner in the middle of the sidewalk stops me in my tracks.

Miss Theresa's Hampton Dance Oasis.

Miss Theresa? Dance Oasis?

Lachlan sees it, too, and looks down at me. "Is that?"

"I don't know." I squeeze his hand. "Can we check?"

"Of course."

We stroll faster as I watch the plate glass window get larger and larger. My breath hitches, seeing my old dance teacher. "It's her!"

I must be gawking with my jaw dropped and possibly licking the glass when Miss Theresa notices us outside. Her face lights up. Then she signals to an assistant to take over the row of little girls dressed like swans.

"Katya?" she greets me. "What are you doing here?"

"I saw the studio on Mayfair was closed a few weeks ago." I fight to keep the hurt out of my voice.

She willingly made a video recommendation for me a few months ago, then closed without warning.

Miss Theresa stares up at Lachlan, her eyes blinking like she knows who he is. Most business owners know the O'Rourkes as well as my family. "Hello."

"Oh, I'm sorry." I lean into his wide forearm. "This is my husband, Lachlan."

"Nice to meet you, Lachlan." She stares in shock that an O'Rourke married a Koslov.

"Same here." He nods to her. "My wife told me a lot about you."

"She was one of my best students." Gasping, she turns her eyes back on me. "Oh goodness. The shooting at East Side. I heard about it, but the girls have a dress rehearsal. I had to focus." She studies the full breadth of Lachlan. "You're the man in black who rushed inside to get her out of there!"

"Aye. That was me." He shows no sign of uneasiness over that video going viral.

"Another dancer's ex-boyfriend was the, um...shooter," I add, feeling embarrassed for Della.

"Goodness. Is she all right? The girl?"

"Yeah." I clear my throat. "My husband saved us. Both of us."

"Thank goodness." Miss Theresa clutches her throat.

"Why did the Astoria studio close?" I change the subject.

My teacher blushes. "I opened this new studio a few years ago. The traveling back and forth got to be too much, and I couldn't manage both any more. It pained me to close the Astoria studio and sell our house there. I invested so much in Astoria. It's not just the business. I own the entire building. Which might make it harder to sell. Or..."

"Or?"

"Someone might buy the building and turn the studio into something else." Her classes were always packed. Surely, it's a loss for the city.

"I hope not."

She gives me a once over and then Lachlan. I squeeze his hand with both of mine. Showing her I'm willingly and happily his. She lived in Astoria for a long time and might have heard about the St. Agatha's wedding massacre. I don't want her to think Lachlan stole me against my will.

I'm *happy* being his wife.

"Theresa, we're ready for the final run through." Her assistant peeks out the glass door.

"Yes, yes. I'm sorry to cut this short. Dress rehearsal. The recital is at the high school tomorrow night. We're sold out, but if you want to stop by, just flag me down, and I'll get you in." She winks.

"I would love that." I look up at Lachlan. "Can we?"

"Of course." He lays a peck on my forehead. "I want to feed my wife now. She's had a long, hard day."

"I'm so glad you're all right." Miss Theresa hugs me.

Her sweet perfume shoots memories at me of how happy I was every time I set foot in that studio.

That. I want to give that feeling to someone else.

Miss Theresa goes inside, and we continue to the restaurant, where, sure enough, the owner greets us himself. He brings us to a table, and even takes our orders.

Dinner is pleasant. We eat but don't talk. We don't need to. We're that comfortable with each other. Lachlan's phone goes off several times, and he sneers at it. Fallout from what he did today, for sure.

What he did for me.

And how he put everything at risk for me.

Again.

I can't imagine his family will continue to allow him to get away with being so reckless.

For a *Russian* wife.

CHAPTER THIRTY-FIVE

LACHLAN

I deal with death nearly every day. It doesn't blip my radar, but I worry I've ignored how the shooting, and Katya watching me kill yet another man affected her.

We get to the beach house rental, and she perks up seeing the ocean. I open a bottle of red wine, even though she's a few months shy of twenty-one and I prefer whiskey. I murder people. Giving alcohol to my wife, who is technically underage, won't affect my sentence if I one day face justice. If they come for me, I'm in for life.

With two glasses in my hands, I steer her to the patio, where we sit and listen to the crashing waves. Fuck, this is peaceful. My house overlooks a stagnant harbor. A tributary of river water, but there's no sound and very little movement other than the natural ebb and tide of the river flow. The roar of the ocean is invigorating.

Katya finishes the wine in silence. She's in shock. I pull her onto my lap and stroke her back, hackles raised, knowing she's still so stressed over what happened.

"Christ, you're shaking."

"It hits me on and off. I still can't hear well."

Guilt swamps me, and I feel like a heartless jerk. My tactic to make that dosser empty his magazine didn't take into account my precious angel was a few feet away. I should always think of her. Can I do this? Can I be what she needs?

"The ringing will stop. I promise," I assure her. "If

it's still bothering you, I'll find a doctor in the city to **check** your hearing." I stroke her cheek, and it heats under my skin.

I kiss her tentatively, wanting to take her mind off what happened, but not take advantage of her vulnerability.

"Lachlan…" Her soft voice stills me.

"Aye?"

"Do you love me?"

The question hits my chest like a physical blow. I live on panoramic mode to see everything coming at me from all angles. I wasn't expecting this. Choking, I mutter, "I…uh…"

How do I answer this?

Say yes, arsehole.

"Never mind." She struggles to get off my lap.

"No." I squeeze her waist.

"You don't?" The pain in her voice guts me.

"I meant, no, don't move. Katya, I don't know what love is. I never expected to have a wife or to share this kind of intimacy with someone." I gently tug her chin toward me, my throat tightening as I turn the tables on her. "Do you love me?"

She shrugs. "I get this feeling when you look at me. I get excited when I see you. You make me feel incredibly safe and cherished. And… You're so gorgeous, my body comes alive when you touch me."

Nodding, I consider the weight of her explanation, the depth. "I feel the same way. I like having you around. I never imagined someone living in my house with me. But it wouldn't feel the same without you."

"We're married, but we've just gotten together. It's silly to think we can have those kinds of feelings, I guess." She clears her throat. "Maybe in time?"

I'm not the kind of man who likes to wait.

DEAL WITH THE DEVIL

Maybe this is love, but shouldn't it hit me upside the head? Then again, I have a pretty thick skull, and it's hard to get my heart rate up. But damn, this woman charges me up like I'm plugged into an electrical socket.

"Katya, you've been rehearsing for weeks to audition for that school in London," I remind her of the cloud hanging over us whenever I look at her.

She's leaving me.

"There's no guarantee I'll get it."

"I can make sure you get it," I rasp, knowing I can control that outcome even though the idea of her leaving me gives me hives.

"Don't do that. It wouldn't feel right," she sharply rebukes me.

"I want to give you whatever you want."

"What if I...want to stay with you?" She nervously tugs on the hem of her dress. "I can finish my senior year at East Side, then audition for local theaters. Or...something. I don't expect to be taken care of while I do nothing."

I'm a rough guy. A princess who sits around and expects to be pampered isn't my type. Unless she has my child. Visceral possessiveness cuts through me. My brothers are having wee ones, and I see that primal gleam in their eyes looking at their pregnant wives.

It hits me. I'm *hooked* on this woman. I don't want her to leave me.

"I *want* you to stay with me. And I want you to do whatever it is you want to do when you graduate." With the proper protection, of course.

"That means this is a real marriage now." She strokes my left hand full of tats, poking the finger with her name on it.

"I guess it is."

Stress lines form above her nose. "Your family thinks

this is temporary."

"Probably not anymore after seeing the way I ran toward a man with an assault rifle for you."

"But—"

"Shhhh." I gently kiss her lips. "You're still wound up, angel. Don't worry about my family."

"I like that. Angel." She blushes.

"And remember, that doesn't mean sweet and weak. There are some pretty badass archangels out there. I watched how you dance. You're fierce, my angel." I kiss her again, and she opens to me with vigor and passion. "So, tell me… How can I make *you* feel better?"

She licks her lips, the top one swollen again from bumping into Della. "I think you know."

My body tenses as my cock hardens to a thick brick in my pants. "Fucking you until you're mindless?"

She exhales. "God, yes."

"Come on." I lift her up and bring her into the bedroom.

We make love for what feels like hours, and I make her come three times. Only when Katya's phone buzzes for the third time does she take her eyes off me.

"Who is that?" I ask after pumping my second round of seed into her.

Having sex without condoms goes unspoken. I forgot to grab them when I packed, or my brain subliminally didn't remind me.

Katya gets up and walks to her phone. "I'm in a group chat at school."

She's naked, her body glistening with sweat from the workout I gave her. The way her ass shifts teases me to no end.

"Oh…" Katya holds her throat, reading a text.

I leap off the bed. "What?"

"My audition…" She tosses the phone and sits down to

rock on the edge of the bed.

"What?" I eye the phone, ready to look for myself.

"They moved it up to Monday."

CHAPTER THIRTY-SIX

LACHLAN

I watch Katya nap on the sofa after we spent the morning on the beach. The sun knocked her out. I want her to rest up and be strong for her audition. I also want to kidnap her and lock her in my house so she can never leave me.

Those ideas vividly playing out in my mind make me nervous that I'm not thinking rationally. Heck, with Kieran angry with me for busting into Katya's school locked and loaded, I'm tempted to rig this audition and then go live in London with her.

Someone there can use a hitman.

Hitman...

My brain twitches and next, I'm dialing a number for the one man who understands me best.

"Aye, mate. Good to hear from you." Ewan Quinlan picks up on the first ring. "How is that new wife of yours?"

Ewan may very well have been my father's enforcer had I gone to seminary. Priscilla's father, Craig Nolan, served my dad loyally before he died. Ewan was his top hitman and investigator.

I was fresh from the camp with the taste of blood in my mouth from what they put me through. Ewan and his brothers, Griffin, Connor, *and* Shane, worked for me for years, doing investigations, interrogations, surveillance, and hits.

I'm closer to Griffin, who's my lieutenant, but the guy fucks around with women. He can't help me.

"She's experiencing some temporary hearing loss. I drew fire from the shooter, figuring he'd empty the

magazine on his assault rifle and give me the kill shot."
A shot I couldn't take.

"Do you want Darcy to look her over?"

"I'll see how she feels tomorrow." I don't mention the audition on Monday. "I'm actually calling to ask you something *about* Darcy."

"Yeah?" His voice turns low and dangerous. "Something wrong?"

"Not at all. How... How did you know?" I rub my eyes. "How did you know you loved her?"

Raucous laughter erupts on the phone. "If you have to ask someone how they knew, then you're in love, mate."

Heat crawls up my neck. "Can I have one clue?" I'm grasping because he's right. If I'm even thinking about this, then I must be in love.

The 'Zero to Sixty' is throwing me off. How she went from a distant obsession I didn't think I'd ever touch, to a woman in my bed every night who thinks she loves me, too.

"A clue? When you're ready to throw everything away to be with her. When you can't think of anything except the next time you'll smell her hair. Aye, I'm talking about you, love." He muffles something away from the phone, suggesting Darcy is right there.

"It's probably not good for an enforcer to be so reckless, aye?"

Ewan laughs. "When you have something to lose, the stakes are even higher. Then you're ruthless, not reckless."

"I feel like I can't do both," I admit, quietly. "I can't love her and be this heartless murderer."

"Sure, you can. You love your ma and your sister. Everything you do is to protect them."

I think about that, freaked out that it's so simple.

"Do you miss it?" I'm curious how he's dealing with

being a city councilman instead of a hitman.

"Sure, I do. But I get home, and my daughter runs into my arms. Next, her mum and my other wee one sink into them, too. That feels better than any kill." He clears this throat. "Except for the beating I gave the fucker who hurt my Darcy years ago."

I recall Griffin mentioning that when Ewan was in Waterford, where he hooked up with Darcy again after five years, he damn near killed the scumbag who'd hurt her.

"I ran right past those cops yesterday, not caring if they shot me. The drive to get to Katya, to protect her… It ate me alive."

"I think you got a case of true love, Lachlan. I'm happy for you if it's mutual. Do you think she loves you?"

"She's young," I say in response. "She's got one more year of college."

"That gives you both time to grow into your relationship."

I think about Kieran and Isabella. I watched him grow to love her even though he was hell bent on not feeling anything. Ewan's sister, Norah, and Kieran were so in love. When she died, my brother wanted to die with her. He had more emotional baggage against him falling in love than me.

The guy is head over heels now.

"Aye," I say and want to get off the phone to keep watching Katya sleep. "Thank you for the talk."

"Any time. Oh, hey, Griffin told me Shane showed up at Katya's school. Thinks he may be itching to get back into the action with us. He was my best cyber guy. Can Balor take him on?"

"Does he want to sit in front of a computer or be on the streets?" I don't think Balor needs help, and Shane looks like he's had enough of sitting behind a desk.

"I'll talk to him. He's coming for dinner tomorrow."

I laugh inwardly at the interrogation the poor guy will get. "Thanks for the talk. I'll be in touch."

I end the call and take a shower. After watching my wife while listening to the sound of the waves, she opens her beautiful brown eyes. I smile and drop my towel.

Wiping the sleep from her eyes, she coos, "Someone is excited I'm awake."

I stroke my cock. "Aye. Can you take me again, angel? Are you sore?"

"Good sore." She reaches into her panties, and her eyes flutter as she touches herself.

I strip her down to nothing but her sweet-smelling skin and whisper, "Get on your knees and turn around. Hold the back of the sofa. I'm very worked up." I rub her pussy from behind, feeling her get wetter and wetter with each rough stroke.

"I want you inside me," she mewls with her head down.

Kissing the back of her neck, I push the head of my cock into her cunt. "Fuck..."

"My God." She wiggles that delightful ass at me. She's petite everywhere but with a juicy ass.

I groan, sliding deeper into her wet heat. When I'm all the way inside, I grip her hips so tight she yelps. My hard, thick length penetrates her, her tiny cunt choking my dick. I slam into her again and again. I'm being too rough, I know, but I don't know how to be anything else right now. Every inch of me is buried inside her, and my nerves rattle with the high that sex with my wife gives me.

I'm goddamn addicted.

Katya cries out with every powerful thrust of my cock. Her cunt is scorching and fucking soaked. My orgasm, that feeling of falling, hits me sooner than I expect it. I clench my stomach to stave it off, sending euphoria through me even more.

It's hard to breathe, each ragged gulp of air burning my lungs. Lust kicks up my drives into Katya, my fingers digging into her ass cheeks. I pray she's bruised and marked. I also hate myself for wanting that at the same time.

Katya lets go of a guttural moan as her tiny cunt convulses around my cock. Her core strangles me, but it's so fucking slick from how wet she is.

Her fingers with white knuckles dig into the back of the sofa, and her hips push against my cock, forcing me to go even deeper.

I empty my load inside her, and she groans, taking me so good.

I pull out and kiss her. "Thank you, angel."

"Mmmm." She giggles. "I *really* like that."

"It's how I saw you that first night. Angelic." I climb onto the couch and wedge her between me and the cushions.

She sinks next to me, her body warm and soft against mine. "You're more connected to the metaphysical. Angels are around us. I believe that."

"I was just inside one. So yeah, they're real."

We lay still for a few minutes when Katya lifts her head and says, "Tell me what happened when you killed that priest."

My body hardens, and I'm flooded with dread. "Why do you want to hear that? Right now?"

"I think there's something locked inside you. Some kind of guilt. Have you told anyone what happened?"

My throat tightens. Fuck, I never gave out any details. To anyone. "No. Never."

"You killed Rahil and Mark for me. You killed that boy's father to protect the priest. You kill other people for your family. But I get the feeling you killed the priest for you. I want to hear how it felt to kill someone for you. Because it was personal to you."

Is what I did to Eamon behind the rage of every kill? If I unlock that, and let it go, will it soften me? Or will it allow me to be more open with Katya, so there's nothing between us?

Before I can stop myself, I close my eyes and sort through that night, not sure where to start. The primal part that drove me to find Eamon kicks at my gut, and next, the other half of my damaged past with Father Eamon is dripping from my tongue. Clear as if it's happening in front of my eyes right now.

*

I stalk Father Eamon, who moved out of Astoria when he got assigned to another church. My stomach flutters at how easily I figured out his schedule and how regimented he is. How easy it is to get to him. What arrogance? To do what he did and think retribution isn't coming for him.

I watch him get out of his car, an old clunker, and stumble into a beat-up rental house. It strikes me as odd that his new parish did not invite him to live in the rectory. That tells me the pastor of his new church knows about him. And no one wants to be near him. What a farce.

What am I signing up for? Will I one day have to share papal duties with a man like Eamon? Or...Eamon himself. He's young enough.

Fuck no.

The conversation with Michael Foster rings in my ears. He doesn't know I pushed his father, but he knows I was there. I found him in his car overlooking Astoria Harbor a few months ago. I worried the guy might off himself. He was piss drunk, and one look at me after not seeing

261

me for a year since I'd been at Fordham, broke him. He admitted what Father Eamon had done to him. The guilt ate at me. My poor friend was already going through something terrible, and I went and took away his dad.

It made me sick. Kieran had been right. My *hero* had been abusing boys.

It broke my heart to watch Michael cry that he didn't fight Eamon off. He'd been afraid because Eamon was a man of the cloth. We all respected Father Eamon. We all *loved* him.

My faith challenged, I decided no one had the right to hurt my friend and get away with it.

Then I meticulously planned this night...

With my gun tucked into my waistband, I leave my car, a Mustang Da bought me as a reward for getting into Fordham. I groan inwardly, knowing it was really payment for my obedience. But no one tells me what to do.

It's late, and Eamon's been at the pub drinking. He stumbles from his car and wanders into his house, a dull boxy thing with tan siding.

Moving like stealth, I slip into the driveway to enter the house from the back. I staked it out beforehand and know the layout. Lights flick on as this monster walks through the rooms on the lower floor. He lingers in the kitchen, something that gives me pause, because I worry he'll grab a knife.

After finishing several more shots of whiskey, he shuts the lights and climbs his way upstairs. With the bottom floor dark, his neighbors won't spot me. I wait until a light in one bedroom blazes on.

Aye, how rewarding it will be to kill him in his bed. Especially since Michael had said Eamon lured him to his bedroom at the rectory. Disgusting.

I slip on a glove and easily break the backdoor's rusted

nob to get inside. I wander to the staircase and consider my weight, staring at the wooden steps. Damn, I wish they were carpeted.

Maybe he's too drunk to hear me. Even if he comes to the top of the stairs, I'll just shoot him. I don't give a fuck if he knows it's me. He's not seeing another sunrise.

I want to surprise him in his bed, though.

Climbing as quietly as I can, I smell cigarette smoke. He smokes, too? His hacking cough covers the creaking of the stairs, so I get to the top quickly. Amber lamp light spills out of his bedroom door and into the narrow hallway.

Slowly, I get there and leer inside.

Fuck, he's praying!

That slows my roll.

Forgiveness.

It's the foundation of the Lord's teaching. Does Eamon have a sickness? It stalls me for a second, and I wonder if it's my place to judge a man, when that is clearly God's job.

I take a step back, but the floor whines under my weight. Father Eamon jumps up, and our eyes lock.

"Lachlan?" he calls out to me, shirtless, with dark pants, the top button undone. Catching my stare, he looks down at himself. "Shite, boy... Are you here for the reason I think you are?" He strokes himself over his dirty trousers. "The reason I hope you are."

A shockwave of epic proportions runs through my system. The guy is coming on to me. I don't personally hold the same feelings of homosexuality as the church does, as far as eternal damnation. Between consenting *adults*, I don't give a fuck.

"Come here, Lachlan. On your knees." He unzips his pants fully. "Worship me, and I'll give you what we both need."

Need? What does he know about my needs? His sick needs took everything I *wanted* away from me. But I say nothing. I think of Michael, who also said nothing. I get it now, because I'm at a complete and utter loss for fucking words.

"Lachlan, I know you're confused. It's okay. So was I." He keeps stroking, his bulge growing by the second. "I'm still a man of God. He created us in his image. That means somewhere inside him, he's like this, too."

I don't move. I'm shocked. I expected he'd see me and know I was here to hurt him, to cry out, beg for his life. Instead, he's trying to seduce me.

"I can't help it, Lachlan. It's who I am. God forgives me. I beg every day for atonement."

I glare at him.

"Come here." Eamon takes out his fat cock. "I'll be gentle with you."

"No," I finally mutter.

He smirks, and licking his lips, he says, "Good boy. I like a fight."

That makes me grin, and I hope the light catches my scar. "Me, too," I drawl, taking out my gun.

"Whoa." He stumbles back. "What are you doing? I'm not armed."

"I didn't say it would be a fair fight." With a suppressor on the end of my Ruger, I empty the clip into Eamon's chest.

He falls back onto the bed, and in a matter of seconds, blood soaks the sheets. I stare at his cock and consider if I should zip him up. Then I'd have to touch him.

No... I leave it hanging out. Let him suffer the indignity when the cops show up and take photos.

Leave no doubt of the sad pervert he is.

*

Tears stream down Katya's face when I open my eyes

to look at her for the first time since I started speaking. "I'm so sorry, Lachlan. You had no choice. You did the right thing."

Fuck, no one's ever said that to me. Just made me feel like the devil for killing a man of the cloth. It never left me how, with the weight of my gun on him, Eamon couldn't break from his wanton lust.

"I want to make something clear..." I say, just to get the thought out there. "I didn't fault him as a man wanting another man. I don't consider that a mortal sin. I can even overlook a priest who couldn't control his celibacy and perhaps sneaks off to get satisfaction. But to fuck a helpless kid? Boy or girl?" My teeth clench. "Ones who trusted him the way I did? Looked up to him the way I did? That's the fucking disgusting part. *That's* the unforgivable part. Sure, I took a life without judge and jury, but he admitted his sins to me. I had to end him."

I just never expected it would rip the spine out of my life plans.

I refused to feel sorry for myself, being denied the life I had wanted serving God. I took my new life in stride. Made the best of it.

This life has given me a wife who brings me to my knees, and I say silent prayers, thanking God that she's mine. I want to tell her I love her. I want to hide her away from the world so she can never leave me. But my choices were taken away from me. I won't deny hers. She's going to her audition, and I have to roll the dice to see where it leads.

CHAPTER THIRTY-SEVEN

KATYA

I breathe heavily, staring at the opposite side of the stage. My finale is a spirited run and a double twist high in the air, landing on one foot. My ears are still ringing, and I'm so dizzy my heart is pounding.

I swallow, considering just ending the routine here. I glance at the judges' faces, hungry for me to finish. No doubt they were briefed on the routine, so they know how to score. The man and two women write notes, their faces even. I wonder if that's on purpose, or rather that I haven't impressed them so far.

After the shooting, a few girls dropped out. That leaves me and two others to compete for the one open spot. They went first and were flawless. All while I'm a shaking mess. I doubt I'll get any bonus points considering what I went through.

Fairness is a distant dream, a ring so high I never reached for it. Living this past month with Lachlan has made me realize my worth. Made me fight for it. He will appreciate that I didn't give up. And that I'm professional and flexible. Ironic term for a ballerina when that's all we are... Flexible.

Not that I care how this goes. I'm not going to London. I'm only here because I worked for this and want to see it through. I can't send the message that doing what Mark, the shooter, did will silence my ambition.

My stomach twists as anger tightens every muscle, and I shake out my limbs to loosen up. I still want to dance for a living and to be *offered* the London spot will work in my favor someday.

My husband sits a few rows behind the judges. He's the only other person in the auditorium. Even if every seat was filled, he'd stand out. He's so broad, dressed in black, with tattooed hands — my name on one of them — he keeps close to his face.

Lachlan used his muscle to get in here when security measures kept the other family members out. No one tells Lachlan O'Rourke no. The fact that he killed the gunman made the school bend the rules.

He holds up those tattooed, murderous hands and air claps for me. It's confusing, his support. If I get this, he expects me to go.

I recall diving into his arms at Miss Theresa's studio, and I'd give anything for him to be on stage now so he can hold me.

Shaking my head, I prepare for my leap. The part of my brain that remembered this routine takes over, and it's as if I'm not in control of my body. With every stomp, a wash of white blinds me. Every tap feels slippery, or maybe my nerves are shot. My stomach clenches as I try to adjust, but it's no use. With my balance on the skids, I trip and tumble across the stage.

The pain makes me cry out, my nose still sore from last week. Through watery eyes, I see my husband climbing over the seats and jumping onto the stage.

"Katya!" Lachlan is there to lift me up.

The audition is blown, but I don't care.

The music stops, and Fern rushes over. "What happened?"

Holding me against his chest, Lachlan sneers, "She wasn't ready. That's what happened. You let a madman with a machine gun in here —"

"Lachlan, don't. It's not her fault," I choke up.

"Don't make excuses for them."

My body sizzles with heat, but I realize he's right. I'm taking the blame, even though it's not my fault. "I wasn't ready because five days ago, another dancer's ex hit me in the head with the butt of a machine gun. It threw me off." I clear my throat. "When will the judges render their decision?"

Fern rolls her eyes like I'm stupid. With competition for the conservatory so tight, messing up like this disqualifies me. Nodding, I limp off stage with Lachlan holding my hand.

"Get your stuff. We're going home," he says, anger humming from him.

Home...

I don't make eye contact with anyone, just change out of my audition clothes. Lachlan waits for me in the hallway and says nothing until we get into his Wagoneer.

As I'm putting my seatbelt on, he says, "If you want that spot, I'll get it for you."

"I don't want something I haven't earned."

"One slip up doesn't mean you don't deserve it."

I close my eyes. "Fine. If you want to get rid of me so bad, then do it. Get me in."

"What?" He threads his fingers with mine. "You think I want to be rid of you?"

"I'm Russian. I understand."

"Katriane, look at me."

I turn my head, embarrassed to be crying from the stress. "What? Why do you want me? You don't even know me."

"Have you not figured out how I've grown to love you?"

My heart jolts. "You have?"

"How can I not? You're perfect. Perfect for me. I'm no picnic. I come home covered in blood, rage pouring out of me, and you don't even blink an eye."

"I know you won't hurt me," I shrug.

"And that's because you got to know me as much as I got to know you. The energy between us. I... I like it." He shakes his head. "No, I love it. I love you." He twists his bulky body toward me. "Katya, my world is filled with so much hate, it's a miracle to have the chance to love you."

"I love you, Lachlan. I really do. I only went through with this audition because I want to be a dancer. I didn't want to give up."

"I know, angel. I know. I'm so proud of you. Now I have to prove that I love you." Lachlan tears out of the parking garage and weaves through traffic. Despite the cell phone laws, he cradles it against his shoulder. "Hi, it's me. I'm stopping by. With Katya."

My throat goes tight... God, he's facing my father. Making me face him. "Lachlan, no."

"It's about time," he says to me.

Holding my hand the whole way, he confuses me when he doesn't make the turn to my father's estate. "Wait, where are we going?"

"My parents' condo. They'll be leaving for Arizona in a couple of weeks. It's better for my mother's health."

"Lachlan, please no. Don't force me on them."

"They don't know you. And that's my fault." He kisses my hand. "They'll see when we're together how right you are for me."

We drive across the border to a beautiful high rise that overlooks the East River. I've heard about this exclusive building filled with CEOs and celebrities. Gangsters, too.

Holding my hand, Lachlan walks us into the lobby and to the security desk. "My da's expecting me."

The guard at the desk hands him a keycard, and hits a button to open steel gates. We step into an elevator, and

Lachlan puts the keycard into a slot marked PH.

Penthouse.

The elevator opens, and two guards in suits with assault rifles block the door. I gasp, and shrink back, the sight of a gun like that triggering me.

"It's okay, Katya." Lachlan holds me against his chest. "They're always here. Kieran insists on this level of protection for them."

Lachlan surprises me by speaking in another language to one of the guards. I'm guessing it's Gaelic. It sounds so pleasant compared to Russian. But what is he saying, and why can't I know? This makes me uneasy, especially since his face goes grim after several exchanges back and forth.

Squeezing my hand, Lachlan says to me, "Brace yourself, angel."

My heart jumps into my throat thinking I'm walking into a war zone and am about to face an onslaught of hate.

From people with the same name as me.

CHAPTER THIRTY-EIGHT

LACHLAN

Katya needs to know. Needs to understand. I want this marriage to last. There's usually one surefire way to make a woman know how important she is to you...

But as soon as the condo door opens, the smell hits me. Antiseptic. The sound finds me next, the whir of machines.

Da ambles into the foyer, dressed in a pair of black trousers and a dress shirt with no tie. "I told you on the phone not to come. It's not a good time."

"Did you just meet me? I don't follow orders too well." I tuck Katya's hand in the crook of my elbow as I fold my arms.

"You follow your brother's orders."

"He didn't send me to that awful training camp."

"I guess you would have preferred prison. Because that's where you would have been if I didn't intervene."

I don't argue and I've buried this tension between us because I understand my da has seven other kids, one being his only daughter. Then Ma got sick. Forced him to retire and hand everything over to Kieran.

"And never did I get a thank you," he adds.

I think about that, and he's right. To an extent. "It's hard to say thank you for being sent to a place where I was barely treated like a human. I'm guessing I wouldn't have starved or been beaten in prison."

Da scoffs. "Maybe not a lad your size."

"I know you've had your hands full." I clear my throat. "I want Ma to meet my wife."

Da studies Katya, surely remembering how I punched a hole in the wall when he told me I couldn't go to seminary. Then I swore I'd never get married to spite him, knowing he wanted another generation of O'Rourkes. Now here I am, parading a wife around. Happily. Willingly.

When Da's eyes turn down, wisely choosing not to argue further, I step forward. "How is Ma?"

"Not good."

I lean into Katya and whisper in her ear. "This is why you haven't met my mother."

She blushes. "I'm sorry. I had no idea. What can I do?"

I kiss her hand, amazed at how giving she is. "Nothing, angel. Just...love me. Let my ma see that I'm loved." I assume she cares about that.

"I do love him." Katya speaks up, hugging me. "And I'm so sorry for Mrs. O'Rourke."

The way she holds me must put a look on my face Da's never seen. My father's expression changes immediately. Like what we feel is so obvious, it's undeniable.

"You call her Clara or Ma," Da demands.

"Thank you." Katya lowers her eyes. "I'd like that."

"Can we see her?" I ask.

"The nurse is cleaning her up," Da says, running a hand through his graying hair.

God, he looks like shit.

After a few minutes, we walk through the living room and down a hallway into the master bedroom. I hide my gasp seeing Ma look so frail.

"We think the stress of Riordan being in that coma triggered a stroke," Da whispers.

I remember those days, how she struggled with her cane and eventually used a wheelchair. MS is a slow killer.

"Lachlan," Ma calls out to me in a weak voice, reaching

for my hand.

"I'm sorry I haven't been here. I've been busy." I step toward her, judging how comfortable Katya is being close to someone who looks that sick. There's not an ounce of resistance. She's right there with me. "Ma, this is my wife, Katriane. I'm sorry you haven't had a chance to meet her yet."

Ma's lips form a smile. "Hello, Katriane, I'm sorry I can't offer you a cup of tea, or make you a nice meal like a good mother-in-law."

"I'm only sorry we haven't met sooner." Katya immediately studies Ma's body.

"We met before," Ma says. "Briefly. You were at the swim club with your sister."

"Right." Katya turns to the nurse. "Have her muscles atrophied?"

"We're trying to prevent that, Mrs.," the nurse responds.

"I hate that physical therapist," Ma mumbles.

"I can help." Katya smiles at me. "I have another month off until school starts again. I understand muscles and tricks to keeping them strong."

Shite, she's positive she won't get the conservatory spot. But she doesn't sound upset. She loves me and wants to stay with me. Now wants to help my ma.

"Can I massage your legs?" she asks my mother.

"Sure." Ma sits up.

Katya and the nurse hover over my mother, and my father pulls me out of the room.

"Come with me," he says, ambling toward his office. "Close the door."

"I'm in love with her, Da." I think I'm about to be pressured to divorce her.

"That's obvious, since you're not exactly a lap dog who loves everyone."

"No. I'm a fucking junkyard pit bull you trained to kill."

"You got a way with words there, Lachlan," he snickers. "I'll give you that. And she's in love with you, your filthy mouth, all your scars, and your temper?"

"Aye." I fold my arms. "She calms me. I said I'd never marry. But here I am, happily married to a woman I love."

"I worry more that you'll stay alive. Love is a bonus." He sits down. "Your mother isn't doing well. She wants to live out her final days home. In Ireland."

My heart jumps. "It's *that* bad?"

"Aye." He breaks down.

I try to comfort him, but the tough guy waves me off. "Did you tell Kieran?"

"Not yet." He rubs his knuckles. "She's holding on to hug your brother's wee ones." He eyes me with a grin. "Riordan and you will have to bring yours over there."

I barely catch the reference to myself. "*My* wee one?"

He scoffs and takes out two cigars from a humidor behind him. "I have eight kids. You think I don't know when a woman is pregnant?"

I take the cigar and lower into the chair in front of him. Fuck... I got Katya pregnant. "We haven't been using protection. And I, um..." I wouldn't have hesitated to show off my virility to my father when talking about sex with someone else, but my wife deserves respect.

"Fucking like an O'Rourke and making kids." He just smiles, and his eyes soften at me. "We needed to get those words out, didn't we?"

"Aye." I nod and chew on the end of the cigar. "I'm guessing if I didn't marry Katya, I never would have had a reason to."

"I like her even more now."

"Even though she's Bratva?"

"Half." He holds a lighter up to me. "Alexei is no different from me. Just toils with a different kind of poison." He takes a few puffs and then waltzes to his safe. From inside, he takes out a large white envelope.

"What's this?"

"Open it."

I do, and I have to sit when I realize what I'm looking at.

Katya doesn't believe she's a Russian princess, but according to these papers, she's a French one.

"The lineage looks a little muddy, but through her grandfather, she's royalty, isn't she?" I glance up at Da, who nods. "How long have you know this?" I slap the papers down in my lap.

"Since she showed up here as a twelve-year-old. It's my job to know everything about the enemy."

"And when were you going to tell me?"

"When you told me you were in love, and the marriage was real."

Anger bubbles in my veins at what else he knows. "Where's her mother?"

Da turns grim and shakes his head. "Alexei had her killed."

This information shouldn't bother me. I kill so many people. Just when I try to have a modicum of respect for Alexei simply for being Katya's father, the man who took her in, and didn't turn her away, I find out he killed her fucking mother.

"For years, it meant nothing to me that he killed a woman, who was basically his—" Da stops when I stand to my full height.

"Say what you want about her father, but do *not* use that word about my wife's mother."

Da nods and sits. "Her grandfather's money has been in a blind trust for years. It's only a few million. But it belongs to her. There's a yearly pension too, commensurate with her grandfather's title. Which will pass to that wee one if it's a boy. Have your brother Eoghan look it all over and make the necessary calls for her to collect her money. Unless you think she won't want you if she's a rich, royal French princess."

I crack up. "She doesn't care about money like that." But my wife will appreciate she has independent wealth. I'm strong enough to share this with her, because I believe she loves me.

"Do you know where her mother's body is?" I want to give the woman a proper burial.

"No."

It hits me. "That's why you told Katya to call Ma, Ma."

"Aye."

"She's the only mother Katya has now, so I want to make the most of it while she can."

Da chokes up. "I don't know how I'll live without her."

I know exactly how he feels. I dodged so many bullets to keep Katya all mine.

Da and I finish our cigars, leaving the past behind us.

When I see Ma again, she already looks like she has more color in her cheeks from Katya massaging her muscles.

"I'll come back tomorrow if you want," my wife says eagerly.

"I'd love that." Ma sounds happy, and that warms my heart.

Fuck... Katya could have ended up in London.

We go back to my house and it feels wrong to live so hidden like this, especially if I have a wife who will want to come and go as she pleases. "Do you want to shop for a new house?"

She turns to me. "Lachlan, I don't want to make you move."

I pull into the garage and turn to her. "I want you to have a house you choose to live in. That you picked out. This is just another place you were forced to live in. No more. I love you and want to give you everything *you* want."

Her eyes turn watery and she sniffles, saying, "I love you, too. So much."

"Then it's settled." I get out of the car, and at her door, I sink to one knee. "Katya, will you *stay* married to me forever?"

She laughs and straddles my bent leg. "Lachlan, I'd *love* to stay your wife. *For*ever." She kisses me on my scar. "And ever."

I consider when I should tell her that her mother is dead, even though I think she suspects it. I know she has no idea she's a millionaire French princess.

We have so much time now. I'll tell her gently and I'll be there for her. I'll be everything she needs. She means everything to me.

"Come with me, my angel." I lift her and bring her into the house I can't wait to sell. "Let's start our forever right now."

CHAPTER THIRTY-NINE

KATYA- *THREE MONTHS LATER*

"The monster is back!" Addie shrieks and bolts toward the door of the dance studio.

"Oh, no! It's *my* turn to kill the monster." Nicole rips the plastic sword from the props box and pushes Addie out of the way.

"Ahhhh! The munchkins I love to eat. *Glom, glom, glom.*" Lachlan pretends to eat the little girls who are brave enough to climb all over him. "Mmmm, tasty. Yum!"

He rises to his full height with two kids hanging on his biceps and swings them around. Two others have latched onto his legs as he drags one behind. Giggles fill the studio, and it's what makes me smile the most these days.

That and a few other things my husband does when we're alone.

Lachlan reaches me with four kids all over him. "Alo, Miss Katya."

"Hello, my wonderful husband." I kiss Lachlan's cheek and peel the gleeful four-year-olds from him.

Their moms amble inside from the street a few minutes later, leaving me to suspect they stalk the studio to get a glimpse of the 'monster.' The most handsome *and* scariest man in Astoria.

"I finished early and wanted to see how your arm feels." Lachlan rubs the bump on my inner elbow, swelling from the tracker I agreed to get implanted.

"It's a bit itchy." I don't mind it and it's for my protection. I have nothing to hide from my husband.

"Not as much as this?" My neck still stings a little from Lachlan's name tattooed across my jugular.

PROPERTY OF LACHLAN O'ROURKE

My neck because, if I fall into the wrong hands, anyone who would dare to slit my throat would think twice about ending Lachlan O'Rourke's wife

"I got an itch, too, if you know what I mean?" He kisses me, and I turn my head to see a group of moms standing there.

"Give me a minute." I shuffle toward the four mothers who were brave enough to trust me with their little girls when I had zero teaching experience. They probably just need a break for a couple of hours a few days each week. So long as *I'm* not a murderer, the moms drop off their little girls and go have a coffee, or just luxuriate with an afternoon nap. Also, I'm also not charging them. I don't plan to charge anyone for a year. I want to prove myself.

Lachlan telling me *my mother* is dead was a blow. I knew she loved me and wouldn't have stayed away from me all this time on purpose. Finding out for sure that she's gone gives me closure. Learning my father had her killed infuriated me. *And* Lachlan, who begged Kieran to exact revenge. His request is being considered. For now, I'm never speaking to my father again.

Of course, finding out Grandpapa had ties to the French throne when he died a few years ago was surprising. Even though it's technically a defunct monarchy, it came with a pension of a few hundred thousand a year. And a title! His estate was worth several million dollars in American money. Eoghan took care of all the legal paperwork for me and invested my money.

I bought Miss Theresa's business and the building with

my first pension check.

I didn't see any reason to finish at East Side to give me a degree and a professional license to dance all over the world when I have the exact job and life I want right here in Astoria.

Greeting the moms, I say, "I'm thinking of a little Christmas pageant next month. A very trimmed down version of The Nutcracker." I glance over my shoulder. "I've already cast the Nutcracker Prince." Leaning in, I whisper, "He doesn't know it yet."

"I doubt he'll say no to you," one mom whispers back.

"Not the way he looks at you," another says, lifting her sleepy daughter into her arms.

"I promise he'll be gentle with the kids." I cross my fingers behind my back, because he does get rough with them. But they're tough little girls, who nearly pass out from laughing at his antics.

"Oh, I spoke to Lola at the gymnastics center," Nicole's mom says, smiling. "She said she'd love to do a cross promo event for their gymnasts who also do dance." She texts me often to meet for coffee and I consider her a friend.

I clutch my new cross. "Thank you." The necklace Papa gave me now sits in a box. Lachlan replaced it with a gorgeous, braided gold chain and vintage pendant from his mother's collection rumored to be blessed by the pope himself.

Nicole's mom leans in for a hug and whispers, "Is the morning sickness still an issue?"

"It finally passed." I swipe at my three-month pregnant belly, which isn't showing yet.

But it will be, considering the size of my husband. I just don't know how massive I'll get carrying six-foot-six Lachlan O'Rourke's baby. Wee ones, his family calls them. It's adorable, especially since Lachlan's child will be anything but 'wee.'

He's so thrilled to be a dad. He loves holding and feeding his nephews, Kieran's twins, who have finally arrived. I know my husband secretly hopes we have a boy, too. Then I see how he smiles at the tiny dancers here at the studio, and I know he's picturing a little girl. We're married and in love, so there's no stopping us from having as many kids as we want.

When the studio is empty, Lachlan winds his arm around me and kisses my shoulder. "Ready to go, princess?"

"Yes!" My heart beats quicker, excited to spend the weekend in East Hampton with Shea, who's hosting a fall gala Saturday night at a fancy winery.

"Yes, what?" He pinches his chin. "You never came up with a nickname for me."

"I'll just call you what your baby will. Daddy."

He calls his father Da. I called my father Papa. We wanted something different for us.

Lachlan looks ready to pass out at being called Daddy. Daddy Lachlan. "We need to leave right now."

Laughing, I say, "Let me grab my bag."

The bells over the door jangle, and two hulking men stand in the vestibule, their faces shadowed. My heart scrambles into my throat as I dig my nails into Lachlan.

He goes still as a statue, his face unreadable. Until the two men come into the light. I sigh in relief, but Lachlan looks alarmed as his brothers, Eoghan and Balor, amble toward us. Their grim faces fill me with worry as spots cloud my vision, fearing they are here to give me bad news.

Stasia...

Lachlan knows his brothers like the back of his hand. He pulls me toward him, cradling my head. "What are you doing here? Both of you?"

"We're here for Katya," Eoghan says, his voice stoic and absent of any emotion. His sharp, dark gray suit is the epitome of dressed to kill.

"No," I whimper and cry into my husband's broad chest.

When I cleaned out my mailbox at school, I handed over Stasia's strange postcards. Without a sample of her handwriting, and with her social media accounts dark, there was no way to authenticate if she had indeed sent them.

Or if she's even alive.

Eoghan and Balor don't say the obvious. Since no others showed up in the past two years, she's probably dead.

"Is it Stasia?" Lachlan asks, bracing me for the most terrible news a sister can get.

"Aye," Balor answers.

"How bad?" Lachlan holds me tighter.

"Pretty bad." Eoghan shoves meaty hands into his pockets. "For us."

"Us?" Lachlan sneaks a look at me.

"What's happened?" I stare at each of my new brothers-in-law with desperate, questioning eyes. "Talk to me."

"We know where she is," Eoghan says.

My breath hitches, and I wiggle out of Lachlan's tight hold. "Is she alive?"

"Very." Balor pushes his signature thick horn-rimmed glasses up his long roman nose.

"Oh my God." Relief washes over me, and the air is breathable again. "Talk to me. Where is she?"

The brothers look at Lachlan, who says, "You didn't answer me. Why is her being found bad for *us*?"

"Considering where she is and who's she's with," Balor says.

"I'm going to smash both your heads together," Lachlan barks at his brothers. "You're scaring my wife. My *pregnant* wife. Now, fucking talk!"

The way they stare at me, it dawns on me... They don't trust me. "I'll remind you both, my name is O'Rourke. A name I took willingly. I am part of this family, and my husband comes first. And by extension you. I kissed Kieran's ring. *Now tell me where my sister is!*"

"She's in Seattle," Eoghan finally answers.

"Seattle? Why—" Lachlan's jaw drops. "Wait..."

"Aye." Eoghan ambles forward. "Katya, your sister is alive and well. In fact, she's pregnant, too."

"No," Lachlan grinds out. "You're kidding. Who..."

My brain catches up. Lachlan's youngest brothers live in Seattle. The identical twin doctors.

"There's more to the story." Eoghan's face turns grim. "It's pretty ugly. You should both sit down."

More? Ugly? My sister is...pregnant. But from which twin brother?

It doesn't matter. If my father finds out Stasia has been with either of Lachlan's brothers all this time, *and* she's pregnant, he's going to kill every single O'Rourke.

Including me...

You can read the dramatic next installment to the Astoria Royals Series in Ring of Truth, which is EXCLUSIVELY featured in the Merciless Desires Anthology.

Find out once and for all what really happened to Anastasia Koslov and which O'Rourke brother is responsible.

HERE'S DEBORAH!

Deborah Garland is a four-time Award-Winning Author!

In addition to a great book, she loves pugs and chocolate and eats her bacon cheeseburgers with a Grey Goose Cosmopolitan.

After years of doing the whole corporate thing, it was finally Deborah's turn to make the dream come true of being a published author. Her 2017 debut novel, Wait for Me, was a Golden Leaf finalist for Best Contemporary Romance. She writes strong and witty heroines and the heroes fall hard for them.

Deborah's novels have received words of praise from RT Book Reviews, Kirkus Reviews, InD'tale Magazine, Library Journal, and Uncaged Magazine.

Give her your heart and fall in love with her flirty dirty romance novels.

STAY IN TOUCH WITH ME...

My newsletter followers get not only a good laugh each month, but also updates on new releases, sales and giveaways.

Sign up at my website:

www.deborahgarlandauthor.com/blog

Don't forget to follow me on any of these platforms:

Amazon * TikTok * Goodreads

BookBub * Twitter * Facebook

Instagram

I love to hear from readers. Contact me at:

www.deborahgarlandauthor.com/blog/contact

Made in United States
Troutdale, OR
04/02/2024

18877505R00181